Praise for Lewis Libby's *The Apprentice*

"*The Apprentice* is an exhilarating, astonishing flight of invention—more real and more vivid than the world you're living in now. It has the propulsive drive of a thriller and the metaphorical power of a genuinely literary work."

—John Podhoretz, *The New York Post*

"An extraordinarily visual book. Mr. Libby makes the reader experience every scene with an intense vividness . . . lend[ing] a curiously dreamlike quality in which everything seems real, yet somehow magically strange, and one is never sure what may happen next. *The Apprentice* proves to be a singular and satisfying novel."

—Cynthia Grenier, *The Washington Times*

"With its subtle clarity, haunting locutions, erotic tensions, *The Apprentice* is a timeless tale of love, greed, and violence reminiscent of a Kurosawa film. A striking—utterly unusual—elegant novel."

—Howard Norman, author of *The Bird Artist*

"Libby [is] a writer of strikingly original talent. *The Apprentice* strikes a masterful, and beautiful, balance between high suspense and great stillness. And Libby's style has a double-edged power, the prose and imagery unerringly clear and at the same time disorientingly strange. There's a complete confidence about the vision, and the rare voice in *The Apprentice* that is remarkable to find in a first novel—in any novel."

—Ann Hulbert, author of *The Interior Castle*

"Reminiscent of Rembrandt . . . Suspended in the storm's blurred whiteness, with starkly graphic, disconnected, and startling images, *The Apprentice* combines the purity of a Japanese woodblock print with the chilling timing of a *roman policier*."
—Leslie English, *Advocate Weekly's Literary Supplement*

"An extraordinarily literate first novel . . . Lewis Libby is a writer who can soar."
—Joseph Bottom, *The Weekly Standard*

"A devilish puzzle of murder and intrigue . . . The dozens of enigmatic characters, many of them nameless, move about the ghostly landscape with a purpose that proves both unpredictable and inevitable. Like most of what precedes it, Libby's ending dazzles."
—*Minneapolis/St. Paul Magazine*

"Tightly dreamlike . . . Libby maintains a sense of mystery and claustrophobia."
—*Publishers Weekly*

"Skillful . . . exotic and extreme"
—*Library Journal*

The Apprentice

by Lewis Libby

Thomas Dunne Books / St. Martin's Griffin   New York

THOMAS DUNNE BOOKS.
An imprint of St. Martin's Press.

www.stmartins.com

ISBN 0-312-28453-5

First St. Martin's Griffin Edition: February 2002

10 9 8 7 6 5 4 3 2 1

Acknowledgments

The author would like to thank the many who leant their time, wisdom, and patience to the improvement of this book. Foremost among these is my wife, who served as editor of first and last resort. Without her support, this book might never have been written; without her insight, it would not be the same. That it should, in addition, have been published, is due to the faith Amanda Urban showed. I was blessed to have the enormous talents and generous good nature of my friend, Ann Hulbert, on which to rely. For the title, and the final push to let the manuscript go after so many years, I am indebted to Walter and Tova Reich. Terry and Brandon Fortune, Leonard and Suzanne Garment, Steve Sestanovich, Frank Fukuyama, Richard Ravitch, and Phil and Ellie Merrill were among the first to read the early drafts, and their advice informed changes for months to come. At Graywolf, I wish to thank Fiona McCrae, Lisa Bullard, Ian Morgan, and my gentle, graceful editor, Anne Czarniecki. From earlier times, William Maxwell and Emily Hahn lent their belief in the work; and I can hear the voice of Dudley Fitts still. My brother, Hank Libby, supported this effort from its Colorado origins. Finally, I thank, as well, my parents, in this as in all things.

For my family

The Apprentice

Snow Country

Northern Honshu, Japan

Late Winter, 1903

1

On the edge of a ridge removed from the sea lay a small wooden inn half-buried in snow. Four hooded figures, grunting against the storm, struggled unbidden into its darkened entry. Snow swirled in around them, and the clouds of their breath were torn away.

The tallest of the four bore upon his back a wicker trunk, and this he lowered awkwardly until his upper body collapsed upon it. A hunched, dwarf-like figure dropped with a cry to the earthen floor beside the trunk and huddled shivering and bobbing its head. A short girl-child stumbled over the dwarf and sat heavily against a platform at the edge of the entry. The last of the four pulled jerkily at the wood slat door to shut out the storm.

A pale light approached from the recesses of the inn, and a broken female voice, deadened by the wind and the wooden walls, called out to the entry. Soon a middle-aged maid appeared, holding an oil lamp before her. She shuffled hurriedly to the very edge of the wooden platform and, although barely an arm's length away, thrust the light out into the air.

Shouting above the storm, the woman asked the four wayfarers if they had passed through a village with the pox. She bent her body forward and peered from face to face to read their answers. The lamp, shaking in her hand, cast a yellow globe of light that caught the snow settling in the air and lit the near side of the wayfarers. Their shadows moved against the walls.

The tall man slumped over the trunk said they had been to no place with the pox, nor was there disease among them. Then he straightened and called upon the woman to vouch the same and breathed upon his hands as if to warm them.

Raising the lamp to the side to see better, the middle-aged woman named several villages in particular, and the tall man shook his head at each and swore they had avoided them all and others farther south where the pox was found. With the movement of the light, the shadows rushed across his face so that his features, like liquid, seemed for an instant to rise and fall.

To the side of the entryway stood a steep, unlit set of stairs. Crouching in the dark at the top, a youthful apprentice to the inn looked down at the wayfarers and tried to judge their answers true or false. He looked at the man and the huddled dwarf and at the tiny girl-child slumped on the platform, and in the moment that he looked at the last of the four, the outer door closed against the storm and a girl turned back into the room.

The girl wore a matted fur cloak the color of a yellow dog. She tilted back her head and shook off the snow-covered hood, and the lamplight caught the bottom of her nose and parts of her eyes and the bridge of her forehead. She put the backs of her hands to her cheeks.

It occurred to the youth in the dark at the top of the staircase that none of them knew he was there.

The wayfarers turned their heads suddenly and looked toward the outer door, and the youth saw that it shook violently from a gust of the storm. Snow blew in through cracks in the wall and around the edges of the door and snow on the floor whipped up around the wayfarers' legs. They looked toward their shadows on the door and far wall long after the gust had passed.

The middle-aged maid had set the lamp down on the steps, and the girl who wore the cloak of yellow fur now moved closely over it. She wiped at her nose and held her hands near the flame, and the lamp lit the front of her body.

Then the girl reached into her mountain trousers and tugged at her clothing. The young apprentice could see the movements of her hand inside her pants.

Creeping silently to the very edge of the stairs, the youth crouched slowly down to get a better look. His mouth, inches from the floor, hung slightly open.

❋

The apprentice entered the main room of the inn. Across from him a dozen wayfarers sat close upon one another, pressed around a firepit sunken into the floor. Not a word was passed among them. They hunched their shoulders and held their arms around themselves and bore all manner of clothing. They wore odd patches and patterns all but blackened, and some wore tattered leggings and some frayed mufflers or strips of wadded cotton wrapped around their heads, and one wore backward a European hat. The small fire before them filled the room with an acrid smell and cast a yellow-orange light on those huddled closest to it and on the faces of a few just beyond. Occasionally the light would catch the clouds of their breath in the cold.

The far corners of the room were in darkness except for one lamp and the glow of a few smokers' pipes. From one side came the indistinct sounds of men talking in low voices. Despite the cold, there was the smell of sweat and wet clothing.

As the apprentice drew closer to the firepit, he had difficulty stepping around those who lay in the shadows or sat huddled and rocking for warmth. He could see the tops of some faces and even the wetness of some men's eyes as they caught wisps of firelight. Struggling with his balance, he had to look down repeatedly into the darkness at his feet, and the obscure movements there gave him the sense that the floor itself was shifting.

The apprentice could not see if the girl who had worn the cloak of yellow fur was in the room. He glanced about quickly, for he knew those on the far side of the fire could see his eyes.

"You," an old man's voice said from the darkness near the apprentice's knee.

The apprentice could not make out the face of the man who had spoken only inches away. He tried to lean to the side so that the dim fireglow might catch the man's face; but each time he moved, the man, who seemed to misunderstand, moved with him.

"He wants to know when the snow will stop," a female voice to the side said, and then with a biting tone to the old man, "He doesn't know."

A narrow-faced man by the firepit had taken up a piece of wood and sat beating the end impatiently against the coals. He called to the apprentice, "How long before a new path is beaten north?"

"If the snow falls all night?" The youth tilted his head to the side. "Nearly a day to dig out," he said. "Probably another before there's a new path north."

There was a silence as the wayfarers listened to the storm strike against the sides of the inn. Some looked up into the darkness of the rafters. In scattered places the white of hoarfrost could be faintly seen clinging to the beams.

A spasm of coughing seized a form curled up on the floor beneath a thin blanket. Around this form like an island lay the only patch of empty floor. The cougher's head was turned downward into a wad of cloth to stifle the sound. A tattered blanket shifted as the cougher's legs convulsed.

At a sound the youth turned toward the blackness of the entryway. He hoped to see there the girl who had worn the cloak of yellow fur, but it was only the middle-aged maid Matsuko with her thick hips. She entered the room with a pile of worn cushions.

The youth looked into the emptiness after her, where the light of the fire did not reach. He did so, although he knew in truth there was no reason for the girl to be coming from the entry.

Even so, he liked the sudden feeling that came upon him at the thought that he might see her.

Some of the wayfarers began to grab at the cushions. The extra cushions would be from the storage room, the youth realized. He should have thought of getting them.

In the darkness beyond the firepit sat men who were headed north to tap the spring sap from lacquer trees. One with thick forearms had said that he knew the way north and that they would be leaving before a new path was broken. He said that anyone who wanted could come along. The narrow-faced man nodded as he turned part way toward them and examined the group more closely. Two of the tappers of lac were so deep in shadow they could barely be seen. The features of another, half-caught in slanted firelight, seemed distorted. The narrow-faced man hesitated, and then dipped his head and made an indecipherable sound. He turned back to the fire.

The tapper of lac with thick forearms snorted and whispered something to those just around him.

The woman Matsuko, on the verge of leaving the room, said that some travelers had been lost heading north the previous winter. She said that their bodies had not been found until spring, and that it would be safer to wait for the villagers to beat a new path. She nodded her head for emphasis.

It could be true, the youth knew. Yet he knew, too, that the woman would not want to lose an extra night with lodgers.

The tapper of lac had started to talk about bodies found in the snow. He said that he had once been fishing beside an avalanche site in spring, and that as the snow melted he had found a boot in the middle of camp. "We dug it out, and there was a man in it. Frozen. And bloated. He was upside down in the snow."

The tapper of lac leaned his head forward near the ear of the narrow-faced man and opened his eyes wide so they shone yellow in the firelight. "This is the strange part," he said, "as the snow melted, more bodies appeared. Each afternoon there'd be another one, sometimes two. Just popping out. Very spring-like."

"What did they have with them?" a man's voice said from the darkness, laughing.

The tapper ignored him. "When the bodies had been out a day or so they started to stink and we had to worry about wolves. So we dragged the bodies out onto the river."

"Did you get a reward when you turned their valuables in?" the voice from the darkness insisted, and laughed again. Peering there, the youth saw two hunters whom he had registered that morning. One, pox-faced, sat forward with his neck craned into the air.

This time the tapper laughed too. "The vultures had to struggle, because the insides were still frozen. At night some wolves began dragging the bodies all over the ice. Then the ice finally broke," he said, "and the fish got 'em." He paused and showed his yellow teeth. "They all ate better than we did."

The storyteller pushed himself back and the tappers of lac all laughed. Some of the guests by the fire peered more closely into the shadows, but the faces of the laughing tappers could not be clearly seen as they rocked back and forth and slapped one another on the arms.

The apprentice lowered his head. He had heard it said that in the famine years men would camp near avalanche sites in the spring to rob the dead. He avoided looking at the tappers of lac.

In the blackness beyond the fire lay the corridor that led toward the bath. It was there, the youth guessed, that the girl who had worn the cloak of yellow fur would likely be. He thought about her rising from the water.

The wayfarers gathered about the edge of the sunken firepit had begun to poke at the embers and press closer above the failing flame. In the growing darkness, even the faces of those just beyond had grown indistinct. The youth knew he would soon have to make a show of adding more wood.

❉

"Performers," the woman Matsuko said again.

The youth, standing in the kitchen by the sink, regarded the thick, middle-aged cheeks of the maid with distaste.

"The new guests are performers," the woman had said as soon as he entered the kitchen.

The youth had regarded as a curiosity this unexpected bit of information, and he tried to bring together his image of performers with his image of the girl in the cloak of yellow fur.

In his mind's eye, he saw her vividly as he had first seen her, tilting back her head and putting the backs of her hands to her cheeks. He could still feel his confusion at the thought that she might look up to the top of the staircase and see him watching there.

Even moments later, he had not been sure why he had hidden at the top of the stairs. There was the girl, of course, but he had seen good-looking, even beautiful girls before and he had not acted so shamefully.

He knew that there were those who enjoyed merely staring at young girls, but he had no reason to believe that he was one of them. Such people, he thought, enjoy the idea of being caught and embarrassing the woman, while he had been greatly afraid. Besides, he had watched the tall man and Matsuko and the others as well, and he remembered the way the snow on the earthen floor had swept up and around their ankles from the last gust as the door had closed.

"They'll want to perform," the woman Matsuko said. She was splitting bits of pickled vegetables. Her cheeks shook with each cut. She stood over the warmth of the cooking stove, and clouds of steam rose around her.

The apprentice set down sharply some bowls to wash. He knew as well as Matsuko that he would have to make arrangements with the performers to share their earnings with the inn. It was one of his duties. She was reproving him for not having done it already.

"In the old days," she said after a moment, "we wouldn't have taken performers."

She was reproving him, too, for being new.

The apprentice, who came from a village farther north, had arrived only that fall, before the deep winter snows had buried the inn halfway to its eaves.

The youth listened to another gust hit the side of the inn. The storm was getting worse. He knew he would lose a day digging the inn out of it.

But it was the storm that had closed the coastal road and brought so many guests to the inn. It was the storm that had brought him the girl in the yellow cloak.

Turning from the sink, the youth saw the woman Matsuko just leaving the kitchen with a tray of sake for the guests in the main room. As she closed the door behind her, he caught a glimpse of the dim glow from the firepit.

The youth stood alone in the kitchen. He had bowls to wash. He looked around.

Off the entryway, just down the corridor, was a small room that was used as an office. In that room, not long before, Matsuko had registered the performers.

The youth stared at the door to the main room without seeing it and brought his fingers to his lips. The woman Matsuko might just set the tray down and return. But if she were detained by the guests, he would have time to check the register for the name of the girl who had worn the cloak of yellow fur.

He knew it was foolish to want to know the girl's name, and more foolish still to worry about Matsuko, but he would not normally take the time to go to the register with so much to be done, and he was afraid Matsuko might guess of his interest in the girl.

Still he hesitated. Even if she were delayed by the guests, he could not be sure that he would have time to get back to the kitchen before she returned.

But he wished to know the girl's name.

He heard the voice of a guest call out to Matsuko.

The youth opened the door to the corridor and crossed quickly to the office. The door at the other end slid open easily.

He turned the register toward him and read hurriedly up the page. The performers were the last to arrive and their names should have been easy to find. Yet their names were not there. He shook his head to clear it and, using his finger as a guide, read once again, more slowly, starting from the end. He checked the page before and the page behind and cursed and started to turn away when he saw a name out of place. Matsuko had written in the margin to save paper.

He read a man's name, Jiro Ueda, who might be the performer, but it read simply, "and three." They had paid for one night.

The youth replaced the register and hurried back toward the kitchen, closing the office door behind him, crossing the short corridor, trying to keep his footsteps quiet on the wood. The walls rushed by his eyes. He opened the door to the kitchen and stepped in.

Matsuko was squatting at the base of a cupboard, holding an old tray toward the light. The apprentice almost fell over her.

"The lacquer has cracked," she said. The crack and its shadow ran along the edge of the tray.

The apprentice bent to show his concern, but his breath still came too fast. He stepped instead to the other trays at the far end of the counter.

"Are any of the others?" he said.

"They are such nice trays. We've had them a long time."

The youth rubbed his palms on the sides of his legs. "I checked the register. For a moment I thought maybe we were wrong about the number for dinner."

The woman Matsuko nodded, still examining the tray. She picked at the crack with a thick fingernail.

"I forgot that old man and his wife."

Matsuko nodded again and, replacing the tray, put her hands on her thighs to push herself up.

"You must have a lot on your mind," the woman said, looking up at the youth.

The apprentice thought she looked at him oddly, but he said nothing. He turned to go to the main room to see to the guests.

Then he turned back. "I didn't see that dwarf in the register."

"It's there. And it better not foul the entryway. I charged them full rate for it."

"Do we feed it, too?"

"Oh no, I told them we wouldn't. The performer has two girls. He said they'd take care of it." The woman looked at the youth, "They're pretty girls. One was quite striking in the bath."

The youth felt uneasy hearing such things from Matsuko.

"What do I care what she looked like in the bath?" he said. His voice sounded high to him.

"I just thought you might like to know that she is pretty," Matsuko said, "in case you couldn't tell from the top of the staircase."

❀

Coming around the corner of the entryway, the apprentice nearly walked into the performers. He stopped suddenly, just keeping his balance.

The man Ueda was sitting at the bottom of the staircase with the tiny girl-child on the step just above him. The older girl who had worn the cloak of yellow fur was squatting near his feet at the edge of the earthen passageway that ran through the inn. She was stroking the oversized head of the dwarf and speaking to it in a low voice. The girls were flushed and clean from the bath. Their collars stood open from their necks and the skin showing there looked pale in the dim lamplight.

The apprentice was so startled that he stared openly at the two girls in turn, ignoring the performer who sat before him.

"Well, well, the spirits led us to you," the man Ueda said. His eyes bulged oddly so that the whites could be seen all around. His fingers were long and thin with reddened knuckles and when he spoke they moved like grass in a wind. "We pushed too far in this storm, but we wanted to reach the village before the theatricals began. It could have been trouble for us."

At the edge of his vision, the youth had the sense that the tiny girl-child was staring at him.

"It's not easy for performers, you know," Ueda said, "and to find a hot spring, too." The tiny girl-child behind the man suddenly giggled, and the apprentice was not sure if she was laughing at him, or if she was embarrassed at the way the man spoke on. The youth could not help glancing at her, but when he did she looked quickly away. He was immediately distracted by Ueda, who had leaned forward and was tugging at the youth's sleeve.

"You're the innkeeper, then," Ueda said.

The youth suspected he was being mocked. He knew he looked too young to be the master of an inn. "I'm only an apprentice," he said, "the master is away. Traveling."

The two girls now giggled and exchanged a look into each other's eyes that at once became serious and fixed.

"With all these poor travelers," the man said. "Fate has an eye on us. And you an apprentice, too. My name's Ueda." The man dipped and raised his head and the whites of his eyes swam up out of the dark.

In the midst of this speech the older girl, squatting by the floor, had begun to speak into the hunchback's ear in a voice so low that the youth could not follow what she said. She spoke only while the man spoke, and stopped speaking almost as soon as he finished. The dwarf stared intently up at her with its chin just inches from her chest. Upon the creature hung a rough garment of twisted grass and unfinished cloth too small for its limbs and frame. At the gaps protruded clumps of shiny hair and hair hung thick about its face and grew low upon its forehead. It was altogether unlike any being the youth had ever seen.

"I am Setsuo," the youth said. He was annoyed that the man was still pulling at his sleeve.

"And upstairs? Are there truly more wandering souls?" the man Ueda was asking. He released the youth's sleeve and began to scratch at his chest. As the youth looked back toward the man, he saw the tiny girl-child had shrunk down on the step so that only her eyes were visible above his shoulder. The girl's eyes were dark and wide. The youth decided he should look directly at her, and he started to smile, but her eyes drew wider still and he was afraid he might have startled her.

"Lots of guests upstairs, I suppose," the man Ueda said again, scratching now at his stomach. "They've probably been a burden to you since before the snow."

The apprentice thought the man might be about to bargain for a part of a room upstairs. Or perhaps he was gauging the money to be made from the guests. The youth wondered when the man would ask permission. His master, the innkeeper, would expect a share of the fees.

"The innkeeper must have faith in you," the man said, as if following the drift of the youth's thoughts, "to allow you to handle an inn so filled upstairs and down for days on end. But I can see you handle it well."

Now the tiny girl-child sat up and as the apprentice followed her look he was startled to see the older girl staring intently at him with her lips together. She held the hunchback's head pressed sideways against her chest and its flattened face glowed in the lamplight. The youth wondered if the girl would speak, but she merely stared at him in an open, almost challenging way.

The dwarf's face looked pained and it tried to move its head, but the girl pressed it more firmly against her chest. Slowly at first, and then with greater force, the dwarf began to squirm beneath her, kicking at the earthen floor between her legs. The oddity of this movement gave the apprentice the chance to free his eyes from the girl's stare, and he glanced downward across her neck and shoulders and the vague outline of her leg where her trousers were pulled up tight around her crotch and the inside of her knee.

"In winter most take the coastal road. There usually aren't this many guests," the youth said, looking quickly back to Ueda. As he spoke, he half-saw from the corner of his eye that the girl who had worn the cloak of yellow fur had turned her face away and resumed her odd incantation to the hunchback, who had settled back on the floor looking up at her. "But the storm closed the road, and with the spring theatricals in the village—"

"—So these travelers have barely settled in and we're keeping you from your duties," Ueda said, interrupting and standing with startling speed. He walked right past the apprentice. "Maybe we can keep them distracted for you," he said as he turned out of the entryway. The two girls hurried along behind. The apprentice stood suddenly alone, still facing the stairs.

In a moment the hunchback had huddled completely over itself in the frozen mud of the entry, playing with its feet.

❀

The woman Matsuko called the guest "the old samurai," but the apprentice saw no reason for it. The man sat stooped with his feet splayed and the socks upon them were cheap and well-worn. His eyes were moist and many-veined, almost dreamy, and his lower lip drooped. The old man's clothes were loosened at the waist. He smelled of sulfur from the bath.

The woman had said he brought with him to the inn weapons wrapped in straw, but none could be seen just then in the tiny room.

The apprentice set down the tray he had carried upstairs and took up from it a vial of sake. Only then did a light seem to come into the old man's face.

"I'll need plenty of this to sleep tonight," the old samurai said. He raised his cup to indicate the sake and tilted his head back toward the wall to indicate the storm. Listening, the youth realized that the storm was much louder there on the second floor, where the snow had not yet buried the inn.

"By tonight the storm will bury the second story," the apprentice said, "it will be quieter then."

The old samurai's eyes wandered as he seemed to consider this, tilting his head once again. Dim patches of frost clung in places to the crevices in the walls, and a dust of snow lay along the edge of the floor. Standing still for a moment, the youth for the first time heard the sound of the wind whistling through the cracks in the wooden walls and felt the drafts. He was ashamed the wall had never been fixed. He realized that the old man's comment about sleeping had been a complaint.

"The snow will stop the drafts," the youth said.

The old samurai waved his hand at the youth's words. "The foreigners bury their dead in boxes," the old samurai said.

The apprentice had said that the storm would bury the second story, and the old man's thoughts had turned to death.

The youth wondered if he could just leave the sake and go. Matsuko would be looking for him, and he was hoping to see again the girl who had worn the cloak of yellow fur. He felt a wave of impatience, for the old man seemed on the verge of a talkative mood from which it would be difficult for the youth to free himself, but before he could act the man had pushed his cup forward for the apprentice to refill.

"I've heard they use the body parts later," the old man said more emphatically. He leaned his head slowly to the side and opened his lips. "In poultices, I think."

The youth bent forward to fill the old samurai's cup with sake. To the youth's surprise, the man used his free hand to hold back the sleeve of his outstretched arm in a courtly and old-fashioned way. The youth wondered if it were such actions that had led Matsuko to give him the name.

"You know," the old samurai said, "some years back the government forbade cremation to please the foreigners. Corpses stacked up, but no one would bury them. The streets stank. And then you know what?" The old man smiled so naturally the youth had to smile with him. "They ordered the corpses burned again, just like the first order had never been issued at all."

The apprentice opened his mouth to speak, but the old man had not finished. "For two weeks the sky was black. Black. Ten thousand corpses, they said. Every day we could just walk outside and watch the old generation burn away."

The old man opened his fingers toward the ceiling as if he would conjure in his palm the funeral pyres of ten thousand souls. He pushed his lower lip out farther. The lip glistened in the candlelight.

The apprentice made an appropriate noise in his throat and started to rise. He looked for an opening to speak. He was afraid Matsuko would be critical if he spent so long with the old samurai without raising the subject he had come for, but the old man seemed to take no notice that the apprentice was lingering with something to say.

"I need my bedding," the old man said.

The apprentice nodded and reached to the closet to remove the bedding. He drew a deep breath, "It's very crowded downstairs."

"Oh?" the old samurai said while the apprentice pulled the bedding from the cabinet. "Of course."

The old man dropped two coins on the mats between them.

"This room is too tight for others," he said.

The apprentice glanced at the coins. They came to less than Matsuko had said, but he was amazed things had gone so easily. He stepped forward quickly into the room to pretend to protest, but as he turned he felt the bedding tug and heard a tearing sound.

The bedding had ripped on the edge of a nail with a decorative head in the form of a crane. The nail, embedded in the post at the edge of the closet, had worked loose and flipped over so that the crane hung upside down as if in death. The tip of its metal wing poked cleanly through the sheet.

The apprentice apologized and bent quickly to free it. If he gathered the sheets in the morning, Matsuko might not learn about the tear.

The old samurai waved at the air once again to dismiss the apology and sucked noisily at the sake. "Maybe I'll take another bath," he said aloud, as if to himself.

The apprentice tucked the tear underneath the bedding, where it could not be seen. Bending over with the blood in his face, he thought about the girl who had worn the cloak of yellow fur. He saw in his mind the pale skin of her neck where her collar had stood open from the bath.

The youth suddenly realized that the old man might have been talking to him. He grunted and said the waters of the hot spring were medicinal.

"Sometimes it's better to be at a hot spring without a woman," the old samurai said. He was looking at the apprentice. "You can remember the one you want. You can make her young again. You can forget the things you wish you'd never known."

To the youth, who had never had a woman, the old samurai's comment was a cause for sudden sadness.

As the apprentice was leaving, the old samurai called after him to see if any geisha had made it to the inn before the storm.

Alone in the unlit corridor, the youth could feel the storm. He could hear it strike against the outer walls. At least, he thought, there would be no more guests.

For the storm had reached the point beyond the strength of men.

2

When the apprentice reentered the main room, the wayfarers glanced to see if he was carrying food, and then turned away. Those around the firepit tilted their heads inward with their hands outstretched before them. Their shadow hands fell across their bodies, as if to mark themselves for some dark end that all but they could see.

Among the wayfarers there were some who discussed the latest rumors from the south. There was word of fighting in the capital.

Looking around, the apprentice saw that the girl who had worn the yellow fur was in a small group near the oil lamp to the side. He glanced in her direction and then around the room in case she had seen.

The girl had been sitting on her feet with her head angled back and her eyes narrowed. The tiny girl-child stood behind her, pulling a comb through the girl's hair. The hair hung almost to the floor, catching in places the gleam of the lamp.

Without meaning to, the youth looked back again. The girl rocked forward slightly as the comb was dragged through her hair. Her eyes narrowed further. The youth made himself look away, not really seeing, but sweeping the room as if he were looking for someone. He felt his own chest rising within him.

In a moment the apprentice found himself staring down at a small man writing by the light of a candle. The man's haunches rested on his feet, which were tucked beneath him, and he bent so far over the paper that his head threw most of his own effort in shadow. He held in his hand a cloth that he used to wipe at a diseased and watery eye. As he wrote, his head followed the characters and he formed with his lips the words he wrote or wrote the words he formed.

Not knowing what else to do, the youth crouched down by the candle and stared intently at the point of the brushstrokes. It was as though some concern about the man's writing had first drawn the youth into the room.

As the youth watched, the man's eye dripped onto the paper, and he blotted at it suddenly with the cloth. When the man took away the cloth, the youth saw that the ink had bled and what had just been written could no longer be read. Looking closer he saw that the paper was mottled everywhere and puckered and the words smeared, and most of what lay there lay without meaning, never to be read again, perhaps never to have been read at all.

A voice beyond the fire was repeating a rumor heard the previous night at an inn down the coast. It seemed that troops had been seen several days earlier moving south toward the capital. There was word of an attack on a foreign delegation. The substance of these reports was confirmed by others, although several maintained that the troops were headed north.

A man with large ears insisted that he had met a man who had himself witnessed troops moving north. The apprentice recognized the man with large ears as a carpenter named Oka whom he had registered. Oka cited movement north as support for news he had heard but two days before of an attempt to assassinate a minister. "Some of the conspirators," Oka repeated, "were being chased north," but another contested this, and swore that the fighting involved farmers who had rioted near the coast.

A sake brewer rose to his knees and shook his head vigorously. He had been drinking steadily and his voice was loud and even in the cold of the inn he sweated. He said that there had been rumors, in villages to the south, of groups of men hanging about in the forests. A man's voice in the shadows between the apprentice and the firepit spoke of these same reports.

A merchant leaned forward over the fire and said that he, too, had heard that a minister had been killed, and that the group behind the plot was said to favor war with the Russe, and that all this was to save what had been won before, at the end of the last war.

Looking toward the merchant, the apprentice could see from the corner of his eye that the two girls had put down the comb and were listening to the argument. The girl who had worn the cloak of yellow fur sat with her head tilted slightly down. He liked the angle of her eyebrows. Her hair had been pulled back behind her ears in the mountain style and tied with twine. The line of her jaw was taut and the skin there shined. To the youth, she seemed clean.

With a loud pop, the fire spat sparks into the room. Guests by the firepit beat at the cinders in their clothing. From where the youth stood, the cinders could not be seen, and it looked instead as if these guests beat at themselves, beat at the sins within them.

By the side of the fire sat a tall man in a top hat turned backward and a long, black coat of the European style that he wore over Japanese mountain trousers. He wore white gloves, and from time to time the youth had seen him remove these gloves to powder his hands. He had removed one of the gloves now, and was using his powdered hand to pick lice in slow, measured movements from inside his pants.

"Evil," said one of the guests blandly, his chin on his chest still checking for cinders. "When the fire sparks like that, it means the wood witnessed something evil."

A pale, middle-aged woman by the fire folded her arms around the sack in her lap and shivered. "It's the rafters," the woman said, looking up where the wind whistled through the cracks in the walls and the rafters groaned and shifted with the pressure of the storm. The woman's teeth were blackened in the fashion of older days, and when she looked up with her mouth open, only the moisture on her tongue caught the light. Blue veins showed at her temples.

"Eerie, isn't it?" the rope maker Kato said, looking up into the rafters and then leaning intently forward. "It should sound eerie. It's on nights like these that eerie things abound. Do you know the stories about the shrine above this ridge?"

"Kato," Oka said, "you're crazy. Leave her alone." To the woman he said, "Ignore him."

The rope maker Kato, who had rocked forward on the sides of his feet, rocked back, gripping his knees and laughing. His face was bright red from the sake. He was a lean man with glasses and a shrill voice that he raised until others were quiet.

The woman held a smoker's pipe and put this to her blackened teeth and sucked noisily at the stem. "You're just saying that anyway. How would you know stories from here? I wouldn't believe a word of it."

"Oh, but you should, they're true. Ask the innkeeper," the rope maker Kato said, turning on the apprentice. "They're true, aren't they true?"

The youth, who had been watching Kato's face in the firelight, was startled when it turned on him. For a moment, he could not associate any meaning with the words, only the shadows on Kato's teeth as he opened and closed his lips, rocking back and forth behind a tray.

The youth was worried about Kato, who had been drinking since his bath. The man had a strong neck with stringy muscles that stuck out when he yelled, and he had yelled twice already at the fat sake brewer.

So suddenly confronted by the man, the youth felt his stomach tighten.

"Let him be," the sake brewer said.

"I don't know," the youth said. "I didn't know anything about a shrine."

"What? I'm lying? Are you saying I'm lying?" The rope maker Kato had pushed the tray aside and, lurching forward onto his thick hands, thrust his chin out toward the youth. "Lying?" he shouted, his eyebrows hooded and his teeth clenched.

"No," the youth said, "I just don't know."

"Who do you think you are?" The rope maker's knuckles on the mats were yellow.

The man next to Kato, startled by the shouting, looked up for the first time, his head tilted oddly to the side. "I—"

"You! You what?" Kato said, but then he whirled back toward the middle-aged woman with blackened teeth, falling forward dog-like onto his hands. "You think I'm fooling you, but it's him you can't believe. Do you really think he runs this inn and doesn't know the tales of the shrine? Ha!" He turned back toward the youth. "He is fooling you, not I! Do you understand? Not I!"

"I—"

"And," the woman said loudly to Kato, speaking over the youth, "why aren't you scared then?"

Kato sat back, "Not I," he said again, "Not I!" Then he seemed to realize where he was and pushed himself on his hands and knees back behind the tray, drawing it once more into place.

"Innkeeper," Oka said, "it is strange you wouldn't know the tale of a shrine not far from here."

"I've not been here long. I'm an apprentice. No one's told me any tales." He looked around the ring of guests, but he could not read their faces. He stopped at the performer Ueda, who was sitting to the side. The man's eyes were fixed on Kato.

"Still, it is odd," said Oka, his head twisted so that his large ears caught the light.

"In any case," the woman by the fire said, "I wish the storm would stop."

"Perhaps," Oka said, pointing toward the kitchen with his chin, "the maid would know. Why don't we call her?"

Kato snorted. "Perhaps all of us aren't in such a hurry to find out."

"Nonsense," the woman folded her hands, "I am perfectly willing. Call her if you wish, innkeeper. Call her."

The youth hesitated.

Oka cleared his throat and called out. The guests by the fire sat in silence. Oka waited, then called out again, sitting up as he yelled as if this would make his voice carry farther. The youth noted that Kato now sat forward over the fire intently, so that the shadows of the man's cheeks hid his eyes. Then he heard Matsuko entering. She carried more sake, and picked her way through the guests well into the room before she lowered herself slowly to her knees.

"What do you know of a tale about the shrine near here?"

"I don't know any tales about the shrine."

"But at least you know there's a shrine."

"There's an old shrine, but it's not so near. It's up the mountain."

"I mean special tales of evil, sinister tales."

"It is not a good night to be talking of such things," Matsuko said. There was a brief silence.

"Besides," she added, "all these shrines have some stories. I don't know of any special ones here."

"Is . . ."

"You don't know any tales?" Kato said, jumping in.

She shook her head.

"Ha! She just won't tell," Kato said. "You just won't tell, will you? Neither of you will tell. Well, I know." He threw back his head and drank the last of the sake from his cup, sucking at it noisily so that when he took the cup away his lips were wet and with the back of his hand he wiped at the corner of his mouth. His throat heaved, and he gasped as he swallowed. Drawing his eyebrows together, he glared across at Matsuko and tipped the empty cup toward her.

"More," he said.

Matsuko picked up a fresh vial and knelt beside him with her weight back over her heels. Kato held his cup low where she would have to strain to reach it and twisted his body toward her until his face was almost touching hers. One of his hands gripped inward on his thigh and the elbow jutted out to the fire. He peered into the side of her face. His breath could be heard above the storm. When Matsuko finished pouring, she did not look up.

"Matsuko," the apprentice said. "More for Ueda."

The girl who had worn the cloak of yellow fur, sitting to the side of Ueda, looked up at the youth. It was a quiet look, with dark, still eyes, that he could not read. He smiled at her uncertainly and she looked quickly away, and as he rose he felt foolish for having smiled.

Suddenly he stopped. Everyone had stopped. Kato in the first movement of rising with his hand on his knee. Oka with his leg tucked underneath him. Ueda holding out his cup. Matsuko about to pour the sake.

There was a loud pounding on the door of the inn.

❈

In the instants between the blows, the roar of the storm, long ig-nored during the conversation, was heard again striking the sides and whistling through the walls and rafters of the inn. The guests looked at one another without moving, as if, unanswered, the pounding might go away.

Still, in a moment, the apprentice had risen and crossed to the entryway. The heads of guests turned to follow as he passed.

Near the hollow of the entry, the storm and the pounding grew louder.

The youth called out, but no voice responded.

When the youth opened the door, a man staggered in amidst a swirl of wind and snow and collapsed to his hands and knees in the entry. The body hunched limply forward encrusted in snow and sheets of snow blew in around it. The storm had worsened, and as the youth struggled to shut the sliding door, snow blew thickly up around him and stung his eyes. Tears blurred his vision, and his fingers felt the cold.

The man began to topple, and the youth threw himself forward to catch his head before it hit the stairs. Layers of snow on the man's hood and cloak had cracked where he bent, and he drew breath audibly. The youth shook the man's shoulder and asked repeatedly if he could stand.

The woman Matsuko had appeared on the steps and twisted her head low to the floor to see the man's face. She asked if he had been to a village with the pox. The man did not respond, and she began to yell the question at him.

The youth spoke to the man and grabbed him at the armpit to pull him up, but he was too heavy. His face hung level with the ground. The youth leaned forward to look into it.

He started.

The man's face had frozen white and waxy and bore no expression upon it. His eyes stared emptily from darkened sockets and his eyebrows and lashes were thick with snow, and his cheeks pale with frostbite. The man had a beard embedded with ice and frozen spit. Ice filled, too, the nostrils and the hair around his mouth and lips, and his muffler had frozen rigid.

The man's pupils jerked a bit and turned up into the apprentice's face. For a moment they fixed there dully, and the youth watched chunks of ice in the man's nostrils shift with the plume of his breath. Then the man turned his eyes away and began to struggle to rise.

A number of guests had crowded at the head of the entryway and they jostled one another and speculated on the sanity of a man out in such a storm as if he were not among them. One demanded of the youth some certainty that the man had not been to a village with the pox, and others soon took up this call. They said the man should not be admitted to the inn until he had answered clearly, and some said he looked ill, and some held out their hands to point as if there were doubt about whom they spoke.

The bearded man had managed to get one knee up and his foot under him. With the apprentice pulling on his arm, he started to shift himself up onto the platform where the guests stood and, in the act of transferring his weight, he looked up into the legs of the guests at the head of the entry and stopped. The man's head came up and his snow-shrouded face looked at the wayfarers above with narrowed eyes. He jerked his free arm up to his chest as if to clutch his heart through the snow and cloak.

Suddenly, the man broke his arm free of the apprentice and shoved him aside so that the youth slipped and fell back against the wooden wall. Lunging to the door, the man yanked it open and staggered back out into the storm, lurching awkwardly from side to side against the thick snow and the wind and looking back over his shoulder with his mouth and eyes screwed up. In a moment he was scrambling up the snow wall beyond, his legs half-hidden by the swirl of snow.

From among the guests on the platform there now appeared the pox-faced hunter, who shoved his way through to the front and jumped into the earthen entryway and rushed out through the open door into the storm with a cry. Gusts of wind and snow blew in so that the hunter, scrambling in socks and bare hands up the snow wall after the bearded man, could barely be seen. At a commotion the youth turned his head back to the platform where he saw the second hunter, who traveled with the pox-faced man, pushing through the wayfarers as well. This time the guests protested and pushed back at him and some slipped and fell against each other, but the hunter passed through them and jumped down into the entry and grabbed a pair of boots. He bent to tie on a pair of round-bowed snowshoes. He said the bearded man would die in the storm and that he must be crazed and someone would have to get him. Some guests still yelled at him and some said he would fail, and indeed a moment later the pox-faced man collapsed back in through the doorway covered in snow, his hands frozen into claws and shoved under his arms for warmth. But now the second hunter stood and pulled on a cloak that hung by the entrance to dry. He grabbed some gloves and a muffler and a hat and rushed out himself into the storm.

The youth looked up at the guests at the head of the entryway and at the pox-faced hunter cradling his hands, and he looked at a man who had stepped to the door and was trying to close it. Frozen snow swirled in around them and stung their eyes. There was a general din. The storm tore into the entryway and the guests had taken to shouting various views, and the hunchbacked dwarf, tethered at the edge of the entry, shrieked above them all in an alien tongue or no tongue at all and threw itself against the sides of the wooden risers. A hand pulled at the youth's arm from behind, and when he turned Ueda stood in front of him and was yelling into his face.

"What did you do to him?" Ueda said, grabbing the youth by the shoulders, and speaking as if he were repeating himself.

"Let go."

"What?"

"I didn't do anything."

"He just ran back out?"

"Let him be," a transport agent said, approaching.

"Let him be?" the pox-faced hunter now yelled, shoving his balled hands in between them. "They'll die out there."

"What did you do?" Ueda repeated, pushing a hand back at the pox-faced hunter and still shaking the youth with the other.

"They'll die," the pox-faced hunter said loudly.

"Your friend will find him," another guest said.

"In that storm? If he doesn't catch him right away he'll be lucky to find his own way back."

There was a silence.

"Let's yell," one of the merchants said. "Let's yell so they'll know where the inn is," and he stepped to the doorway and yanked it partway open again and yelled into the storm. Other guests joined him, and while the snow raced in around them and they shut their eyes against the wind, they yelled as loudly as they could into the graying light. "We're here," some yelled and "Come back" others yelled and "Over here" one yelled, so that the whole became a mixture as each tried to adapt to the calls of the others and the wind drove down on them and drowned them out.

The youth stood uncertainly for a moment, and then picked up his straw boots and headed into the kitchen. He passed the screaming dwarf, which had wrapped its arms over its head and ears and rocked and stared at him all the while he passed with white-rimmed eyes and its face wetted from terror.

In the kitchen, the youth wrapped three rice balls in oiled paper and then in a cloth and tied the cloth across his chest. Then he wrapped two layers of oiled paper around his socks and scattered dried red peppers in his boots, to fight the cold in the mountain style, and pulled on the boots carefully over the oiled paper and socks. After just a moment he had returned to the entryway, and there he grabbed a wadded headcloth and a muffler, which he wrapped tightly around himself. He felt a pair of gloves to see if they had dried and then took them, too.

The guests were retreating before the cold. The pox-faced hunter stood to the side with his hands tucked once again into his armpits. Only a few of the wayfarers still made their stand in the swirling snow at the entrance, yelling hoarsely into the storm, even while another man was trying to drag the door shut. The apprentice pulled on a coat and a straw cloak. He tied on the long, oval snowshoes that he liked and grabbed a sedge hat. With one backward glance, he stepped past the pox-faced hunter and the wayfarers and out into the storm.

But in that one backward glance, heading out into the storm, the youth had seen the girl who had worn the cloak of yellow fur. She was looking straight at him, her mouth slightly open.

3

The apprentice rushed out into the gloom that filled the hollow beyond the entry. A wall of snow eight feet high hugged the inn along its eaves and blocked the dim daylight from above. At the top was a crescent of gray light from the trail of the bearded man and the hunter.

The youth began his rush to the surface. Soft snow at the edge of the wall slid down beneath each step and his arms found little grip. Voices called to him from behind and a hand reached out to grab his cloak. He scrambled upward with greater efforts and snow filled his clothing and his sleeves grew heavy with drift. Snow sliding down from above chilled his neck and chin and filled his mouth as he panted and his eyes as he tried to see, and when at last his arms cleared the surface, the roar of the storm came down upon his head.

Frozen snow, driven across the surface, stung his face and narrowed his eyes and tears blurred his vision. He pulled himself forward on his belly and crawled from the precipice several yards. Then he rose, head down, and walked blind into the storm until he was certain he would not be blown back into the hollow.

There he stood, bent forward into the wind, and waited for his heart to still. He tried to catch the end of his muffler that the wind had torn loose and whipped above his head.

He heard faintly above the storm a voice calling from behind. When he turned, the upper reaches of the inn loomed before him once again. Its surface was dark and indistinct, except for the line where the eaves were edged with snow. Then the wind blew up a spray of snow that hid the inn from sight.

The calling ceased, and he stood alone. He listened to the wind and the snow beating against his back. The only light seemed to come from the snow that filled the air and swept along the ground around him.

The youth thought about the girl who had worn the cloak of yellow fur and wondered if she was thinking of him out in the storm, or if he was already far from her thoughts, an apprentice innkeeper who could just as easily be in the kitchen. He thought of her ridicule if he should stumble back in too quickly.

The youth lowered his head to his waist and turned back to face the storm and follow the tracks of the hunter and the bearded man. At once the wind and snow forced his eyes nearly shut, and he waded forward blindly with his hands before him. He huddled his face into his chest and breathed into the cloth of his muffler for warmth, but his breath was snatched away, and his cloak, one instant pressed against him by the wind, was pulled away the next. He leaned into each gust like a drunkard.

The trail of the men weaved with the wind, and in places it

seemed one of the men had fallen. The trees that he passed were buried to their middle branches, and small drifts lay against the trunks or clung in the hollows of the bark.

The youth stopped and looked down at his straw cloak. Even as he stood and watched, snow began to cover him.

Soon the trail of the men turned north and dropped down into a ravine where the wind blew waves of snow above the youth. At the bottom he sank to his chest in drift and had to pull with his arms like paddles and use the branches of a fir to lift himself out at the other side.

He had entered into parts where he had never been, and he grew fearful of losing his way. He worried, too, that his trail back to the inn was already filling with snow. The gloom of the storm had deepened and the wind raged from all sides so that he could not tell if he was moving uphill or down. At times drifts whirled up around him so that he bent close to the surface to see the tracks and breathed in snow, and at times he could not see at all, and at times the trees would loom up oddly with a shift of wind and then disappear altogether. Half-deafened by the storm, he called out into his muffler with each step and yet he could not hear himself. His jaw ached.

Rushing from the inn, he had not stopped to wonder much about the men or to think that there might be dangers. Now such thoughts weighed heavily upon him. In his home village, he had been one of the strongest of all he knew on snowshoes, and in leaving the inn he had not believed that he would have difficulty overtaking the two men in a storm. Now he could not catch even the bearded man who had been so near exhaustion, and the man's unexpected strength made him doubt his own. He realized his pride was based on his skill against mountain boys, and these men now seemed to have the strength of warriors.

The youth walked blind into the limb of an evergreen clothed in snow and, stepping to the side, he began to fall.

He knew he was falling along the edge of a drift and he felt his speed increasing, but his face was filled with snow and he was rolling over and over and he had no idea how far away the bottom might be. He tried to keep his arms or feet below him in case he should hit an outcropping of rock or a tree but he was spinning too fast and his arms flailed about.

He landed hard. His mouth and eyes were filled with snow. His arms, splayed out, were stuck in snow, and his snowshoes felt like they were anchored down. He inhaled snow and began to choke and so began to panic. In his panic he convulsed until his arms worked partway free and he thrashed toward what he thought might be the surface. He wanted to scream but he had no air. When his head finally broke free, he tilted his chin back just above the snow and sputtered for air like a drowning man.

The youth waited for his chest to quiet, afraid to move lest he fall again. He looked carefully about.

He was in a snowdrift at the outer edge of the limbs of a pine tree, halfway down an escarpment too steep to reclimb.

He brushed at the snow on his head and in his collar and under his cloak and considered how he might work his way up to regain the rim.

In time the youth eased himself down to the base of the escarpment. He traced his way ahead until he found a fold from which he could make his ascent. He crawled and pulled, and he pushed himself upward like some dark creature from ages past. In time he reached the top. Pausing there, nearly buried in a drift, he craned his neck to watch the snow fall endlessly into the forest around him.

And he saw the bearded man.

❋

The youth sank down into the drift. His heart raced. He had not yet been seen, and he did not know what to do. He watched the bearded man with amazement, as if it were incomprehensible that the man should now appear before him.

The bearded man bent like a supplicant at the foot of a pine with two trunks, one twisted about the other. He fell forward onto his knees and plunged his hands into the drift at the base of the tree as if to draw forth life. The limbs of the tree above shook in protest.

The storm descended on the escarpment once again. A burst of frozen snow swirled up around the youth and forced him to turn his head away. He saw snow race past him and vanish into the void, and he saw the snow that followed on, and the snow that followed after that. Several times he tried to look back to the pine tree, but each time the wind blinded him and each time forced him to turn away.

When at last the youth raised his eyes, the bearded man could be seen once more leaning far forward at the base of the pine, his head down by his knees, his arms pulling at the snow like a man hauling a rope. A spray of snow had arisen beyond the twisted pine so that it stood out against a grayish haze and seemed a singular altar. In a moment the bearded man rocked back on his heels and began to open the clothing above his heart. He moved slowly with his chin sunk down upon his chest, as if he saw there something private and shameful that others should not see. Presently the man pulled from his clothing a package covered in straw. He turned it once in his hands to inspect the closings and then he thrust it down into the snow hole he had prepared beneath the pine. He shoveled snow quickly over the hole and began to look about.

The youth lowered himself beneath the snow drift and began to back away. He had come to help the bearded man, not to spy upon him, and he had no wish to know the secret of this hiding place. He edged back down into the fold beneath the rim of the escarpment and moved quickly away with many backward glances.

The youth realized he had not seen the hunter, and he looked quickly about; but clouds of snow had once more swirled up from the rim and down from the sky and off the branches of the trees, and nothing could be seen.

The fold now darkened, and the snow dropped more heavily than before. As the youth worked his way ahead, the light and the depth of the drifts grew more deceptive. He stumbled several times and grew uncertain of each step. He bent forward at the waist so his forehead was huddled near the snow and, from this angle, barren limbs he had not seen scraped suddenly across his back.

He circled ahead once again and then once again regained the rim. He moved some distance inland to a fallen tree trunk and hid behind it. In its shelter he waited and listened to the snow strike into the drift that lay against the trunk, and he felt so tired his legs shook. He reached below his cloak and removed the sack of rice balls that he had wrapped in cloth and oiled paper. Even near the heat of his body, the rice balls had nearly frozen. He ate one hurriedly.

After a time he saw the bearded man once more. The man's pace was slow through the deep snow. His head hung down upon his chest, and at times he slowed almost to a stop and his body seemed to sway over his knees. When the bearded man drew nearer, the youth stepped out from behind the tree with the two remaining rice balls held before him.

The man held his head down, his eyes nearly closed against the wind, and plodded forward still unaware of the youth. The wind was loud about them and a gust of wind swirled snow up off the ground and dashed it against the man, who lowered his head farther still. A second gust swirled up from the side and the man seemed to fade away until he was all but hidden in a field of white and when he emerged the frozen snow was still beating off him and he was much closer than before. The youth saw now that the man was burly, much broader than he had once seemed.

The youth was afraid to startle the man. He waved his hands forward to catch the man's eye and spoke loudly into the storm, but his words were torn away. At last the man jerked his head up wide-eyed and looked about. When he saw the youth, the man charged the few feet between them. He broke past the outstretched offering and knocked the youth back into the tree. Air burst from the youth's lungs, and his blinded eyes receded and his mouth fell slack. His legs limp and useless, he was sinking and, had the bearded man's body not pinned him to the tree, he would have slid into the snow. He saw as if from a distance the man looking down into the snow and then the man's hand reaching up and tearing the muffler from the youth's face. The man stared at him and then the beard and teeth moved close to the youth's eyes and the man was shouting but the youth was too shocked to understand the words. He tried to nod but his head went white with pain and his vision jumbled once more.

Then the youth felt himself falling free and he slid into the snow. Snow pressed up around his face and when he suddenly could gasp for air he drew powdered snow into his lungs. He tried to rise but his legs would not work and he reached out his hands. His lungs went empty within him. He felt himself jerked back up into the air.

He found himself coughing in the snow with his back against the tree. There was snow in his eyes and face and his chin hurt from the cold, but his lungs were drawing air. Above him stood the bearded man, pushing a rice ball up against his face. He watched the youth. In one hand the bearded man held the oiled paper packet and a knife. To the youth in the snow, the knife looked close and large. The man had the first rice ball entirely in his mouth, sucking grains from his glove even as he chewed, and started to gnaw at the second.

The youth feared he would pass out. His mouth worked pointlessly. He tried to move and at last he managed to twist and hug the fallen tree and then he pulled himself slowly up. Thigh-deep in snow, he pressed his face against the bark to steady himself.

When he turned his head back, he saw the bearded man had raised the knife point. He stuffed the last of the rice ball in his bulging cheeks and stepped forward with the knife.

"I came to help you," the youth tried to shout, but he was not sure if the man had heard and, in truth, he was not sure how loud he had yelled. The movement hurt his head so that he had to lean against the tree and close his eyes.

The youth felt himself grabbed by the cloak and when he opened his eyes he was staring into the bearded man's thick eyebrows and broad nose, but the youth had no strength left in him. He watched the man shouting, but the wind tore his words away.

The youth, sensing some answer was expected, had no idea what to do. He nodded his head.

The man swayed momentarily. Then he seemed to gather force. He screamed again and shook the youth by the collar, and the youth's vision blurred in pain. When he swallowed, he thought he tasted blood.

The youth nodded carefully once more as if he understood, and the man nodded too. Then the man leaned back and shifted his grip on the knife and carefully lowered himself to the level of the youth's groin. The youth stiffened and he saw the knife cut down and across the webbing of his snowshoe. The bearded man struggled for a moment until the strands were cut, and then pushed the youth away.

The youth tumbled backward and fell in the fresh snow. He stared first at his ruined snowshoe and then at the man kneeling above him. The man regained his footing awkwardly, one outstretched arm against the tree, and turning his back on the youth began to walk off into the forest. He did not look back at the youth. He faded into the storm.

The youth drew back and pushed himself up and at once fell over the useless snowshoe. Floundering in the deep snow, he threw his hands before him. He stared quickly around in all directions. He began to shiver. In the midst of the storm he felt the sudden presence of hooded men with daggers.

Then he fled. He rose on his good snowshoe and his hands and scrambled forward, dragging or falling over his useless leg, lunging from tree to tree, tearing at bark with his gloves, and crawling arm by arm to reach the inn.

❀

The youth swayed forward into the growing darkness where he had wandered and in wandering lost his way. The wind swirled snow from the sky and snow from the tree limbs and snow from the drifts surrounding him. Snow choked him and blinded him and bent him in half. Part of his muffler pressed frozen against his mouth and cheek, but the far end whipped free and he groped for it sightlessly in the air above him like a man batting at a ghost. Even this movement hurt his head, and in this trial he grunted and panted into the storm.

The leg with the torn snowshoe was buried to the hip. Snow had slipped inside the boot and packed against his calf, chilling him. He looked down into the hollow about his leg and debated yet again whether he would profit by removing the torn remnants altogether, but by now his fingers were in any case too cold to work the knots.

For the hundredth time he lifted the leg halfway up, feeling the drag of the useless webbing, careful not to lose the straw boot to the suction of the snow. He made a practiced motion with his arms that ached, and swung his boot forward through the top layer of the snow until he sank again to the hip, his legs splayed and locked in weight and weariness.

He rested once more, head leveled against the sting of driven snow, a deaf and timid supplicant to the wind. He was labored even in his breathing. He resisted the peace within the snow.

For some time the youth had been absorbed with the need to urinate, but his frozen fingers had not been able to loosen his trousers, and even if he could, he feared he could not close them up again, and then his legs would freeze. If he wet himself, then, too, his legs would freeze. His mind shifted between the pain from the cold and the pain in his head and his legs and his bladder, and he was afraid to be found in his own urine.

He took another step. And then another.

When at last he raised his head with slitted eyes, he saw just before him a man sitting in the snow.

Startled, the youth started to step back and almost lost his footing. He struggled in a panic to right himself and stared uncertainly at the figure, still immobile, before him.

The sitting man's back rested against a tree. His head and shoulders were topped with snow. Snow drift half-covered his legs and buried his hands to the forearms. In the dim light, the man's face was lost in shadow.

The apprentice tried to yell above the roar of the storm to the man sitting against the tree, but there was no response. He yelled louder.

The youth dropped his head to protect his eyes, and then looked up again. The man had not moved. He still wore his covering of snow. His open arms lay motionless by his sides.

The apprentice lurched closer and stood, unbalanced, over the bad snowshoe. He breathed heavily. He saw snow thick on the man's head, and below the man's brow snow clung to his cheeks and there was a vague whiteness in the hollows of his eyes.

The youth waded forward again until he stood closely over the man and shook him by the shoulder. The head shifted side to side and settled back in the middle. Snow, piled on the man's head and shoulders, ran off down his body in small streams. His arms remained by his sides.

The youth bent lower and stared as best he could into the man's face. He thought the man was dead.

Straightening up, the youth tried to look around into the forest, but he could see little in that dim light. When he realized he had taken his eyes from the dead man, he shuddered and looked back quickly, but the man sat still as he was.

Even standing so closely over him, the apprentice could not be certain if the dead man was the hunter from the inn, and this struck him as a curiosity. He looked into the darkness at the snow-clenched face. He tried to measure the man's height from the length of his arm. With the edge of his glove, the youth scooped at the frozen snow in the hollows of the man's eyes.

The youth touched the man's chin and tilted it back. The head lifted easily and then fell off the dead man's shoulders and hung by only a part of the neck at an improbable angle to the side. The youth's stomach rose and he retched dryly into his mouth. Snow began to land on the darkened wound at the stub of the neck.

When the youth looked again at the toppled head, he wondered if this was indeed the hunter, and if the bearded man had done this, and, if so, why he had spared the youth.

At a thought, the apprentice felt hurriedly along the dead man's legs to his feet. He fell upon them.

Sitting in the snow and wind and gloom, the youth tried to remove the dead man's right snowshoe, but his fingers were thick with cold. The youth pulled the foot up across his own legs and bent over it and worked at the frozen knot with his teeth. The snow-caked straw of the dead man's boot was cold against his cheek and the rope of the snowshoe had a bitter taste. His back hurt, and the youth had to set the leg down and rest. Then he bent over the foot again, his knees and face in the snow, his mouth at the knot like a dog.

When the knot started to loosen, he paused and blew into his gloves for a while. Then he worked the snowshoe free and paused again, his hands too cold to continue. He looked at the remnants of his own snowshoe still bound to his boot, and he looked longingly at the snowshoe he held useless in his hand.

The youth crawled back up the dead man's legs and crouched upon the body, his haunches in the dead man's lap, the slackened legs stretched behind. He worked the dead man's clothing open, blood-slicked and freezing, and rubbed his hands against the fading warmth of the skin within. The lifeless head fell against his knee and came to rest. Drifting snow began to fill the upturned mouth. The end of the dead man's muffler beat fitfully against the youth's side.

When pain and feeling returned to his fingertips, the youth drew his hands from the dead man's breast and felt about inside the clothing. He felt a pipe and some tobacco, a cloth, and a dagger there. Deep inside the sash, he found a wallet, heavy with coin, too much for any hunter. For the first time he came to question his host, hidden in the dark, unknown beneath him. He clutched this clue to its identity and looked into the silhouetted limbs of the tree above him. They stretched black against the deepening dusk. He picked one where he might later tie the man's muffler to mark his find, one last advertisement for the dead.

The chest of the corpse grew colder. He pushed his fingers deep into the armpits to suck the final passage of its warmth.

Pressed upon the body, crouched there like some ancient and folded vertebrate, they looked as one, red-eyed creature and carrion, hunched together, coupled, obscene, bestial in the growing dark.

✹

The youth lay on his side in the snow. A strong gust had toppled him.

The gloom had deepened. Night could not be far away. Something dark, probably his blood or the blood of the hunter, spread across the back of the glove by his face. Snow fell upon it as he watched. His mouth was dry. His head hurt greatly, but less than when he walked. He was afraid to move.

The youth had grown thirsty, and he looked with greed at the snow just inches away. He knew that to eat snow would chill him further and he looked away time and again while his tongue swelled in his mouth and his jaw ached. His head had begun to throb and his thoughts were jumbled. His chin in the snow was numb.

The youth sat slowly up, his legs stretched out before him and his back bent forward. The movement hurt his head. He found himself sitting in a glade before a barren tree. He could see just above the surface of the snow the tip of his snowshoe and that of the dead hunter. One was round, one oval. They seemed to belong to the legs of different men.

He scooped a light handful of snow into his mouth. It formed quickly into ice, and he had to suck at it for moisture. He delayed. He thought it could do no harm if he warmed it in his mouth before he swallowed.

Around him the snow fell endlessly.

He could hear it landing.

Snow began to seep through to the youth's skin, chilling him. He found himself shivering. He could no longer feel his legs.

The snow hissed as it fell.

He looked up slowly. Sitting in the snow, the tree before him seemed tall and it seemed to lean toward him. Still, he could not be sure.

In his mind he asked questions of the tree.

He listened to the hiss of the falling snow.

A veil of snow blocked from his view the trees that spread back into the forest. At times this veil lifted in places and in places, for an instant, he could see black forms recede against the drifts before the veil slipped softly down again and closed them all once more from view. The youth imagined that among these forms were villagers come to rescue him, but none came. In the end he saw only the looming trees.

At length he realized the wind had abated. He knew he would have to get up soon.

He imagined himself standing up and walking off toward the inn, and he imagined himself getting tired and falling and lying once more as he was now in the snow, and he imagined having to get up all over again. How much better, he thought, to be carried there.

Then he shuddered, the image was so vivid.

In his mind's eye he saw a white face with white lips breathe upon him. It was a girl's face.

He called up the image again. The pale breath formed a cloud around his face.

He saw her this time bent forward, the sleeves of her kimono dragging in the snow, her shoulders and neck bare and white. Not just pale. White. She was dragging something off.

The memory came to him.

She was dragging a man by the heels off into the snow forever. It was a story from his childhood. Two porters caught in a winter storm took to a cave for protection, but they had no wood for a fire and the night was cold. In the small hours a girl with long thin arms the color of the snow came for them. She blew into the face of one, and he died. He turned white like the snow, and she carried him off. But when she returned for the other and knelt by his side, he awoke. So beautiful did she find him that she spared his life, revealing herself to be the daughter of the snow.

It was a legend the youth had heard somewhere years ago. He knew there was more, but he could not remember.

Now that he had remembered the snow girl though, he lost his fear of her, and he gave her the image of the girl from the inn.

But, he remembered, she had blown on him.

Above the roar of the storm something faint now caught his ear. He stopped breathing and strained to hear and his heart raced within him. The wind plucked at the sound and pulled it away, but he knew it. He had heard the call of a wolf.

He heard it again. He could not be sure if it was just one wolf. It seemed to have moved beyond the trees to his left, but it could just be the wind that had moved. The wind blew strongly from that direction, and he doubted his scent would carry.

It occurred to him slowly that he might die in this storm. When he left the inn, he had not imagined that death might be waiting. The day had not seemed momentous enough. As if thinking of some other, he thought it somehow unfair.

He realized he was shivering again. He ducked his chin and breathed once more into his collar. The breath gave him an instant's warmth.

A hand fell on the youth's shoulder and he started.

It was not a hand, but a clump of snow that had fallen from the tree limb above him. A small clump of it balanced upon him.

The youth brushed the snow off quickly into the snow around him. He breathed deeply.

Slowly he raised himself up and struggled forward through the snow. He tried not to jar his head. Often he glanced in the direction from which he had heard the wolf. Often he stopped to listen. He grew convinced that something stalked behind him.

Soon he fell again.

4

The youth pushed the door of the inn partway open and crawled into the earthen entry. Snow fell in around him and snow blew in from behind. His face rested in the frozen mud. A fit of shivering seized him, and he curled up with his hands clasped together and thrust between his legs.

Vaguely he heard a call, and then another, and soon he felt the presence of others. He felt hands on his body, pulling at his clothing. When he opened his eyes, feet and knees crowded around his face. He felt people pulling at his legs, and he was lifted into a sitting position. His eyes closed again. A voice called out loudly that there was blood on his head, and he felt people leaning across him to see. His cloak was removed. He was cold then and he tried to protest, but he was too tired. Someone said there was blood on the cloak as well. Soon others had crowded around him, and the youth was hazily aware of being lifted up and carried. The feeling was uncomfortable, his body was held at different heights and at places a hand or shoulder pushed roughly into him. He did not wish to be moved.

He groaned and closed his eyes more tightly. In the darkness of his vision he could see snow falling, falling in sheets, all falling at the same speed but at slightly different angles, layer upon layer upon layer as if it would fall forever, and in truth he did not know if his eyes were closed or if the snow was falling still.

He felt himself dropped awkwardly to his side. Hands trapped under him were snatched away. He was rolled onto his back. His feet had begun to ache. He felt the warmth of a fire on one side of his face.

The youth heard the hissing of the falling snow. He tried to raise himself up, but he felt heavy, held down.

Opening his eyes, the youth saw a ring of faces. Almost immediately a narrow face with bulbous eyes and hollow darkened cheeks thrust itself down only inches from his nose. The movement was so sudden that the youth thought he was going to be bitten. His arms, weighed down, seemed too heavy to lift in time to ward off the teeth, but at length he recognized the face as the performer Ueda.

"How do you feel?" A wave of warm, sticky breath spread across the youth's face.

The youth exhaled through his nose and nodded slightly to show he was all right. Surrounded by so many faces, he felt the need for air.

"There's blood all over his hands," someone said.

He was in the main room. The firepit was near his face. The light from the flames shone orange and yellow on the guests.

The youth closed his eyes again. Something under him was hurting his back. He rolled a little to ease the pain and turned toward the fire. He felt the warmth on both cheeks now. He opened his eyes again.

The face of the girl who had worn the cloak of yellow fur floated up before him, suspended in the blackened air. Her eyes were narrowed and yellowed in the firelight. Her eyebrows were dark, dark, and the edges of her hair glistened.

The youth shut his eyes. He was puzzled at her face, suspended. When he opened his eyes again he saw the girl once more. There was a glint of moisture in her long, thin eyes.

He lowered his head and searched in the shadows for the rest of her. He saw she was sitting on her haunches with her shoulders thrown in shadow, but her face, twisted down toward him, had caught the firelight.

Still, he liked to hold the illusion of her hovering before him.

He looked at the girl again, and suddenly she surged with light. Someone had suggested that a straw fire was best for frostbite, and he felt a wave of heat and light and, turning his head slightly, he saw the woman Matsuko dropping strips of straw into the firepit. The straw caught the light of the flames as it fell like lines from her red hands. She plucked hurriedly at some straw that had caught on her clothes.

The wayfarers were shouting questions at him, one over the other. They wanted to know what had happened, if he had found the bearded man. The name "Itoh" was repeated several times, but he could think of no one by that name.

As the wayfarers spoke they edged closer to him and placed their hands on his body to draw his attention. He watched one whose head bobbed up and down as he spoke.

The youth screwed up his eyes against the questions. He swallowed and moaned from the top of his throat and, lowering his head back down to the floor, he heard a man say that they should let him rest. When he looked out again through squinted eyes he saw that they had taken places around the firepit, and they were engaged in a debate that seemed to have been only slightly interrupted by his entrance. The girl, he realized, was still near him. With his eyes half-closed he could just see her arm and her hand on the mat.

"That poor boy," a voice was saying, "running out into such a storm after those men."

It was the opinion of the carpenter Oka that the men were more deserving of pity, since they were still out in the snow. But others argued that only a criminal would have behaved as the bearded man did.

"Oh come on!" the merchant Kurimoto said, giving each word slightly more emphasis than the one before it. "Does a normal man travel on a night like this, reach an inn on the point of collapse, and then turn right around and run back out?"

Kurimoto glanced around the room. There being no immediate challenge to his argument, he continued with a tone of greater assurance, stopping briefly after each sentence to allow his words time to be considered to their full weight.

"He was a thief. He came in because he was so cold he couldn't stand it. Maybe still carrying, mind you, some valuables he had just stolen. When he saw so many people, he became afraid and he ran away."

"Yes, yes, I think we've already heard that," a thin man said. "But it doesn't explain a thing. Wouldn't he expect to find people at an inn? And why be afraid of us? None of us knew him, and we wouldn't be inspecting whatever he carried."

For a moment the thin man's argument held sway. Others agreed that even the most dim-witted of thieves would not enter an inn expecting it to be empty. Still, they agreed that the man had been afraid of something.

Lying on his back and listening to the guests, the youth glanced up at the girl again. She was watching the wayfarers. On her dirty blue-and-white-striped clothing lay shadows of her breasts. In a moment she glanced down at him without expression. He looked quickly away, but then he met her eyes. In them he saw, glistening in miniature, reflections of the fire.

The transport agent Wakabayashi groaned and shook his round face vigorously from side to side. "I don't get it. I just don't get it," he said. Like the others he had been drinking, and long after he finished talking his head continued to shake back and forth. The youth watched him, afraid to look back at the girl.

"Oh what a fool I am!" The rope maker Kato, who had been sitting with his chin on his palm and his elbow on his knee, suddenly straightened up and slapped his own knee. "Don't you see?" he said.

The others shook their heads guiltily. They watched Kato, but he only continued to berate himself. Then he stopped and stared fixedly at the center of the floor, pulling at his lower lip, his eyes drawn together.

"Well," Kurimoto said. "What is it?"

Kato stirred and rubbed his palms across the sides of his legs.

"He wasn't afraid of us," Kato said. "He was afraid of one of us."

Oka started to complain, but was interrupted.

A woman said she thought that was absurd.

"After all, none of us even knew the man."

"No," Oka said, "We don't know that. None of us said we knew him. That's what you meant, isn't it?"

The wayfarers all peered closely at the rope maker Kato, as if they might now suddenly discern something significant.

Kato spoke in a lowered tone to the woman as if the others already understood. "If he came to an inn he must have expected people, so we shouldn't have frightened him. But when he ran out he was afraid," Kato smiled and spread his upturned palms apart, "afraid of one of us."

"Well then," the thin man said, "someone's lying. Or maybe more than one of us." He looked about but he did not let his eyes rest on anyone.

"Maybe it's not just that there's someone here who he feared. Maybe there's also someone here who he was coming to meet."

It became clear to the wayfarers that if one or more of them were lying about someone who had acted so strangely, then there must be some reason. They drew their arms to their sides and leaned away from one another as if this would offer some protection. They studied each other's faces furtively.

The youth saw the lips and broad nose of the bearded man and he tried to remember what the man had said in the storm, but his mind was still hazy and he found it impossible to think quickly. He felt that there was something that he should not tell, that the man had been warning him of some evil that would befall him. Suddenly realizing that this evil might be with him in the inn, that the evil might be there even in that room, he jerked himself up on his elbows and pushed back. Rising so suddenly, his head swam, and he had trouble focusing. He opened and closed his eyes a few times so his vision would clear.

Half-raised on his elbows, his face contorting with the effort to clear his vision, he drew the attention of the wayfarers, who turned toward him. Those blocked by others shifted or leaned over to the floor or sat back with their heads at odd angles and their eyes twisted to the side to see. The wayfarers so preferred staring at him to avoiding each other's eyes that they remained fixed in their odd positions while he, trembling on the strained muscles of his arms, stared back.

Kato grunted and, moving forward in a crouch, crossed to where the apprentice lay and sat with his knees almost touching the soles of the youth's feet. This action roused the others, and soon they all sat as closely as they could around the youth, stretched out on the floor before them, while those who could not be right next to him kneeled forward with their heads above those in the front and their hands in the shadows or on each other's shoulders for balance. In the flickering light the sight of so many faces pressing in on him and straining around each other gave the youth a sense of motion. The darkened clothing and shadows merged and seethed unevenly in small rippling movements. Such was the youth's fascination with these motions and the downturned faces that it was some time before he realized that they were all waiting for him to answer someone who had repeatedly been asking if he was all right.

Distracted, the youth let his arms collapse and he fell back. He nodded to show he had heard.

The performer Ueda leaned forward until his face was only inches from the youth and his foul breath washed over the apprentice's face and made him want to turn away.

"How are you feeling?"

"He should rest more," someone blocked by Ueda said.

"Did you see him?" the rope maker Kato asked.

The youth looked around Ueda to avoid his breath and confronted the fire-yellowed faces of the wayfarers gathered just beyond. Some began to poke at his sides and legs so he would answer.

"Did you see Itoh? Did you see Itoh?" a voice asked insistently and then a hand grabbed the apprentice's upper arm and began to shake him for an answer. The youth saw it was the pox-faced hunter. Itoh, he realized, must be the hunter who had followed the bearded man out into the storm. The dead hunter.

"Did you see either of them?" Kato asked again, poking the apprentice in his ribs.

The youth shook his head ambiguously, as if he might be clearing it or he might be saying no. He thought he could feel the eyes of the girl upon him. He needed time to think clearly. He wondered if they could see in his eyes that he was lying, and he looked away to guard himself, but he was pressed by the performer and that gave him a moment to recover.

"Are you all right?" Ueda asked.

"Yes. My head hurts." He felt again the pain in his back, and he shifted to ease it.

Ueda leaned forward and pressed his fingertips against the apprentice's forehead. When he pressed, the youth jerked and drew his breath in sharply through his teeth.

"How did you say you did this?"

The youth looked away. "I fell down a slope and hit a tree."

Glancing back, the youth saw the performer frown.

"I can't believe you couldn't find either of them," the pox-faced hunter said. "They couldn't have been five minutes ahead of you. How far could they have gotten?"

"He couldn't see a thing in that storm," the thin man said. "I'm surprised he found the inn again."

"Why? All he had to do was follow their tracks."

There proceeded above the youth a small debate filled with broad gestures as to whether it was possible for him to have found the men by following their tracks in the snow. There were those who thought the darkness and the blowing snow would have made it too hard. Some pointed to his injuries and repeated his denials. The youth looked once for the girl but wayfarers now pressed close about him everywhere and she could not be seen. It was moments before he was confronted again.

"Didn't you follow their tracks?" the pox-faced hunter asked.

"I fell. I said I fell." Surrounded by so many faces, the youth could not think of any more to say.

"He said he fell," someone said.

"But couldn't you follow their tracks?"

"Yes." In his mind's eye the youth saw the bearded man stepping down on his ankle and turning the knife and cutting his snowshoe. It occurred to the youth that the bearded man had not torn his snowshoe to kill him—that he could have killed him with the knife as he had probably killed the hunter. The bearded man had torn his snowshoe to keep him from following, but also perhaps to give him an excuse for not having found him, an excuse the youth had thrown away when he had taken the dead hunter's snowshoe and discarded his own. He looked away from the guests. "But I fell and hit my head."

"Really?" Kato said. His face was red from sake and his eyes wide and white. "Did you really fall and hit your head and turn back, or did you find them in the snow and maybe see that the man had something valuable? Did you . . ."

"Kato!" Wakabayashi said.

"Did you maybe say, 'If I keep this who would know?'"

"Kato! That's ridiculous," Wakabayashi said, spittle spraying across the youth. "Apologize."

"Why? He hasn't answered. Look at all the blood on him."

"It's from his head!"

"So much? From that?"

"I didn't see him. I didn't see either of them," the youth said.

Kato got up on one knee, but Wakabayashi brought his hand down heavily on Kato's shoulder. Kato glared wildly and half-tried to rise, but Wakabayashi held him down.

Kato hesitated and turned away. Joined by Kurimoto, the two went back to their original places, talking in hushed voices with their heads bent together.

The youth felt the pain in his back again and shifted once more to relieve it. He snaked his hand underneath him and felt something there. With a start, he realized that the pain was from the wallet of the dead hunter that he had placed in his sash. He moved his arm by his side so no one might see it.

From the corner of his eye, the youth watched Kato and Kurimoto whispering one to another. He saw, too, the pox-faced hunter sitting alone, hunched over himself with his arms around his knees, glaring at the fire. From time to time the man turned his poxed face to stare at the apprentice. The man's wrists and fingers were thick and blackened with soot.

❀

In the depths of that night the youth lay in darkness and stared wide-eyed into darkness and in his narrow chest his heart beat in the darkness within him. He had awakened in terror from a dream half-recalled and his arms lay as if paralyzed by his sides. He found himself at last in the back of the kitchen where he slept now that the inn was full, and he began to remember. He heard a bowl, rolling along its rim. He heard someone stumbling on the stairs. He heard a pipe, banged against a metal firepot. He heard his own breathing.

Matsuko, sleeping near him, began to snore. He listened for a while until the snoring was steady and then he quietly lifted his thin bedding and crept with the dead hunter's wallet over the cold, creaking floorboards on the sides of his feet to the dim light of the corridor. The wallet was heavy, and he took care lest, in opening it, it make some noise that would give him away.

He poked into the wallet with his fingers and tilted it toward the light. He hefted it in his hands and poked with his fingers again. There was money, too much money, over a year's worth of money for him. He clutched the wallet in his hands and crouched with the skin stretched tight across his chest in the cold, and he reopened the wallet and poked through it and weighed it again. His breath was shallow.

The youth crept back across the uneven boards, past the smell of the rags and encrusted grease and the mounds of blackened dishes piled askew, past the oil-darkened water with a scum of ice that would harden by morning. Under the cover of Matsuko's snoring, he felt his way to the back of the earthen floor in the farthest corner of the kitchen. Running his hands along the coarseness of a stack of rice sacks he hid the wallet in the lowest one, shoving it deeply into the coldness of the grains. He heard rice spilling and he squatted and scraped at the frozen earth in the darkness to gather it up until his fingers ached and he brushed the rest away. He reminded himself to check it once again by daylight and hobbled back to his bedding. There he lay thinking, and although he was tired and his eyes stung, he could not sleep.

He thought a long time about the wallet and the dead hunter, and he thought most of all about the girl who had worn the cloak of yellow fur. He wondered if she, too, might be lying awake. He wondered if she might be awake in the corridors, or in the next room by the fire, and the thought disturbed him. He heard the coughing spasm of a guest and frozen snow striking against the walls of the inn. When he heard someone stumbling across the floor of the main room, he got up.

The apprentice went carefully into the main room. The guests there lay in darkness or propped in faint light against pillars with their heads lolled to the side. Something slithered beneath the bedding to his left and then was still. He peered in the dim light from the unattended coals in the firepit toward the part of the room where the performers should be. He could make out Ueda, on his side, and beside him, the youth thought, the body of the girl who had worn the yellow fur. They lay quite still. There was no way to tell if they were awake. Staring at the mound of bedding that covered the girl, the youth could feel his blood in his arms and his chest tightened so that it was an effort to breathe. He heard a rat's claws in the rafters overhead.

A voice below him asked for sake. It was the narrow-faced man, who had risen on one elbow. The apprentice said in a voice slightly louder than necessary that he would get some, but there was still no movement from the performers on the far side of the fire.

When the youth returned with the sake the narrow-faced man was sucking on a pipe. The glow from the ash lit his eyes red as he reached up for the vial. "Still blowing," he said, as a gust hit the side of the roof above.

The apprentice waited for the narrow-faced man to bang the pipe against the iron firepot, but instead the man simply set it down and poured more sake. Uncertain whether he could stand there any longer, the apprentice drifted away toward the far side of the room and the entrance to the bath. He passed a body, wheezing into its bedding, one leg exposed and pale against the darkened floor. At the edge of the room, he glanced back toward the fire. He could make little out.

As he entered the dark corridor toward the bath, the youth stood and breathed lightly, listening for the sound of someone rising. But there was none. He was suddenly tired. He felt foolish, and wanted to return to sleep, but he thought it was too soon to cross the main room again, so he continued on down the corridor to the bath.

The room that enclosed the hot spring seemed empty, except for two of the tappers of lac, who sat on a side board near the shallow end. Nearby an oil lamp burned, its wick turned low. The light could not quite pierce the white clouds of steam rising off the water, and the corners of the room were obscure. The lacquer workers looked briefly toward the apprentice and resumed talking. A dark bottle of sake stood near them.

The youth stood at the edge of the room and undressed and splashed water on himself from a small wooden bucket and rubbed at his sides with a coarse bag of bran and stepped into the spring. The water was hot. He bit at his lip and had to ease himself in. There was a slight sulfur smell to the steam. He waded by the lacquer workers to the rear wall of the room. He was tired, and he let his head rest on a wooden ledge and his upper body float. The water soothed him. He closed his eyes.

At length it grew quiet, and the apprentice felt he might sleep. He looked up briefly into the halo of white steam between him and the oil lamp. The walls around him were shrouded in blackness except where beads of condensation reflected the light. The steam enveloped him, set him apart. He closed his eyes again.

The voices of the lacquer workers, suddenly raised, made him open his eyes. The girl who had worn the cloak of yellow fur had entered the far side of the room. She did not respond to the tappers of lac. She began to disrobe.

With only his head above the surface and a wall of steam lying close across the water, the youth knew he had not been seen. He clenched his hands underwater. The lacquer workers spoke to the girl a second time and then laughed. The girl nodded briefly at them and then ignored them once again. She set aside her outer clothes and wore only a white shirt and white slip. She pulled off the shirt and tossed it on top of the outer clothes. The youth could see her upper body more clearly above the steam. It was lit to the side by the oil lamp on the near wall. Her skin was pale. Her arms were thin and her breasts small, and he had seen small nipples when she had turned to throw her shirt.

He lowered himself until only his eyes were above the water and tilted back his head so she might think he was resting if she looked his way, but she was looking down now to remove her white slip. Her hands tugged at a string at her waist. For a moment her hair fell partly before one shoulder and partly behind so that it swayed at the small of her back and lay across her breast until she bent down and stepped out of the slip and threw it, too, on top of her clothes. She walked to a bucket and the bran that the youth had used and, squatting by the edge of the hot spring, nearly lost now in the steam near the water, she scooped the bucket into the sulfur-smelling spring and splashed it over her and scrubbed briefly with the bran at her armpits and sides. She threw water over herself again. Then she rose and stood, her hips and back wet and catching the light, and she stepped slowly to the end of the room farthest from the lacquer workers and dipped her foot in the water and then slowly lowered herself into the hot spring. She disappeared into the steam.

The youth raised his head slowly from the water and looked toward the girl, but he could see nothing through the steam. He wondered if, with the light to the side, she could see him; but he doubted it. In his mind's eye he saw her again standing with the light on her hips and back, stepping slowly to the end of the room, dipping her foot into the water with her leg stretching and her hair falling forward, and then squatting down and lowering herself in, here, to the water that now swirled around both of them, even to the far side where she was hidden. He tilted his head back again against the side and stared into the steam but he could see nothing.

Soon the tappers of lac stepped out of the spring and rubbed at themselves with small cloths. They spoke to each other but looked repeatedly toward the far end of the room where the apprentice guessed the girl would be. He could not tell if they could see her there. Then one turned toward him and he was afraid they might speak to him, but the man merely stared into the steam between them and shrugged. They dressed and left.

In time the water grew too hot for the apprentice and he slipped his arms out slowly so they would make no noise and rested them along the wooden ledge behind him. He breathed lightly. He looked in the direction of the girl, but he could see nothing. He looked up into the white steam rising above him.

He did not now know what to say or do. He could not speak to the steam. He had no reason to wade to the far end of the room. He feared moving toward the entrance, because he did not want to leave.

He felt the water rippling toward him. She was moving. Then there was nothing again. At last he heard her moving quickly and she pushed herself up onto the wooden ledge at the far side of the spring where the dim light caught her. He could see once again her head and arms and nipples and her hair above the steam. Her head hung forward with her arms gripping the ledge beside her. Then she twisted her body to one side and her head to the other and swayed a few times side to side in this fashion. She reached her arms high above her and then with her elbows still high brought her palms down across her forehead and face and he could see the light across her ribs and the darkened concave space below.

The youth looked away lest she see him looking at her and slid his arms back off the ledge and underwater. Then he grew so embarrassed and uncertain that he pushed himself brusquely off the wall with the water making a loud noise. He thought that he might speak to her or that she might say he startled her, but she said nothing and he could think of nothing to say, and so he waded on noisily to the entrance as if he did not know or care that she was there. He lifted himself naked into the light where she could see him and, standing straight with his muscles tensed as if against the cold that he did not feel, he took a small towel and dried himself slowly, his back to her. Then with the briefest of backward glances toward the spot where he had bathed, he swept the edge of his vision past where he sensed she still sat on the ledge. He was surprised to see someone else there beside the girl, and against his will he looked quickly toward them, and he saw that the tiny girl performer was resting on her elbows on the ledge beside the girl. He saw the tiny girl looking at him.

The youth looked away and grabbed for his clothes and pulled them roughly around him and walked back into the corridor toward the main room. He had no excuse now to turn back, although he had thought once more the girl might speak to him to ask for something or to say that he had startled her, but she had said nothing and now he was committed to going and he felt stupid not to have said a word. He thought he could at least have asked her as innkeeper if all were well or if she had what she needed, but he knew, too, that she would see through all that and he distrusted his ability to say it casually.

But then, as he left, berating himself, he wondered suddenly if she had not indeed been awake when he had crossed the main room earlier and brought the narrow-faced man the sake, and whether she had not, after all, come into the bath knowing he was there.

When he reached the edge of the kitchen he walked slowly, listening for a call or a noise that she might make behind him. But there was none.

❋

The youth lay once again in his bedding at the back of the kitchen and stared into the shades of black above him. He listened closely to the sounds of the inn. It struck him as not impossible that the girl might be thinking of him. He imagined he could hear her returning to her bedding in the main room and, unable to sleep, seeking him out. He wondered if she might, even then, be standing in the corridor, guessing at where he might be. He made small noises so that she might know he lay awake inside. In the haze of sleeplessness, he felt yet a certain aching in his limbs.

Most of all, he listened for her footfall, half-hearing one in the midst of gusts of wind and snow flung against the sides of the inn, or in the twisting of the rafters. But he heard only those footsteps that shuffled in the night and headed away toward the toilet. He thought about rising to loiter by the toilet himself in case he might meet her there, but he considered his trip to the bath to have been enough. He thought it was her turn now.

The youth, who was not experienced in love, had wondered at times if this slowness reflected some diffidence in him or something more serious still that he might lack. He had compared himself unfavorably to others, contemporaries from his village, who had mastered such challenges. He thought these others mocked him.

He had wondered most of all about the power of a young girl who possessed so casually those things he most desired. He considered if such a one would not, in the fullness of time, be his. He had questioned why one should be or if, as a matter of fairness, one might not be some day allotted.

He had at times in the past thought about a certain girl whom he had known in his home village, one who had lived in a communal house with some of his friends. He had thought her plain, and largely indifferent to him. But when he left, he thought he saw a sadness in her eyes. Time and again since, he thought about her expression as she sat, crowded by others, on the side of the room. He had in the weeks between imagined that their parting had been different. He had rearranged it in various ways. With a change of her hair and a slight shifting of her features, she had become suddenly quite different and alluring with possibilities he had not then imagined, and soon he felt uncertain which was memory, and which imagination, which was the real girl at all.

It was, he reflected, no doubt true that this girl he had seen in the yellowish cloak and again in the steam of the bath had acqui ed different qualities by virtue of that one look she had shown him as he lay by the firepit. But it was also no doubt true that she was more beautiful than others he had known, and of a deeper, more reserved character. He saw in himself some special qualities if she would be his that would win out over his lesser self and bring him a very different fate in the end.

He knew, of course, of friends who would have urged him to a more tangible goal with her. And he felt for this goal as well, but he was not yet an initiate, and he feared partly to expose this ignorance. Somehow that end alone seemed for lesser creatures. It was for him only part of a transformation.

In her look as he lay by the firepit, he had seen an appreciation of deeds of bravery that he had not thought were his. He imagined over and over, with slight variations, scenes not so far beyond his powers, that would have her see him with awe. He heard her confessions and through his own hesitant ones he aroused the most tender aspects of her desire without diminishing her confidence in him. She blended with him. In the pictures of his mind, she was infinitely tender and sensuous, and she responded to his touch. She was lost in him. She came to him in the hot waters of the bath. She pressed against him. They were together, alone. They were together, traveling free of the endless snows, where he no longer had to dig after every storm. She was smiling. There was sun on the snow.

In his thoughts, she awaited him.

Frozen snow, driven by a gust, hit the sides of the inn. He stared once more into the shadows and listened to the sounds from the corridor.

So raced his thoughts, more pure than carnal, until he fell into a sleep near dawn, and all faded with the motion of morning.

5

In the early morning the wind had died, but snow fell still. The inn had been nearly buried by the storm. The main room lay dark as night.

The youth stirred at the sunken firepit. He moved slowly, for his head and the muscles of his legs hurt. From the kitchen he could hear the sound of a rice tub being moved.

Over the pit the apprentice had lowered a smoke-blackened cauldron, dented through the years, which shone dully where scratches of metal could still be seen. The shifting of the fire jerked the shadow of the cauldron silently about the lower rafters, and waves of heat distorted the air. The upper rafters were in darkness, beyond the fire's reach, except for pale patches of hoarfrost that shone pallid like faces.

The wayfarers lay splayed as though dead in the shadows of their rags. Here and there above the darkened floor could be seen the pale underside of an arm, or features of faces slack with sleep that caught the faint firelight as they hung to the side.

A rat clawed softly on the rafters above, and a thin body at the edge of the room hunched slowly up into a sitting position, looked about, and lowered itself again to the floor.

In the back of the room a man hawked up phlegm and banged a pipe softly to clear the ash. An unkempt woman staggered into the room from the direction of the toilet. A hand or two rose into the firelight and protested as she stumbled across them. From the side came a spasm of coughing.

To the apprentice, tending the cauldron, it was as if the claws of the rat had summoned the wayfarers, unwilling, back to life. The youth looked briefly yet again to the spot where the girl who had worn the yellow fur should have been. He could not guess why she had already risen.

Two men at the edge of the firepit took to discussing how long the cougher might live. One was certain she would not make it through the spring. He invoked other cases he had seen and compared their pallor or the wetness of their coughs to hers.

"She's a factory runaway," the rope maker Kato said, rising from the shadows behind them. He must have lain awake in the darkness, listening.

The two men by the fire looked at the apprentice. A factory runaway, he knew, meant a tubercular, and was, as well, a twofold charge against him, for regulations barred inns from admitting either.

"They'll come for her when the storm breaks," Kato said. His face was largely in shadow, but the youth could see the glint of his eyes.

A fourth voice spoke. "Not one like this. They don't want them back."

A small debate ensued among those awake around the fire-place as to whether the factories hunted down runaways with tuberculosis.

Kato said they chained runaways in the courtyards, an example to others. "Even ones like this," he said.

The cougher lay huddled in her bedding, as if she did not hear.

"Any blood?" a voice said.

If there were blood in her cough, the youth would have to push her out, even into the storm.

"Why don't you leave her alone?" a thin woman near the youth said quietly. She was stretching, her fists balled, and her rotted teeth, blackened in the old style, showed. The iron-shavings of the blacken-ing were wet and caught the light. She had large, deep-set eyes that seemed soft and liquid. Her face, too, seemed soft and liquid. After she spoke she turned away and the skin of her cheeks seemed to sway. A ghost of a blue vein ran from her temple into her hair.

"Go comfort her," Kato said to the liquid woman. "Go ahead. Put her head in your lap. Let her breathe on you."

The woman turned even farther away. She had rubbed charcoal to darken her eyebrows, and the charcoal on one side had smudged during the night up onto her forehead, the painted eyebrow and the real eyebrow no longer aligned.

From the shadows beyond the fire a man asked the woman if she had a daughter. She looked toward the voice and then into the fire.

Someone behind the youth was pulling on his shoulder. The youth set the poker down and started to edge away to give another guest room by the fire, but it was the pox-faced hunter who crowded upon him and would not let the youth move aside.

"The storm's letting up," the man said. "We could go now." The man wanted the youth to help him find the hunter who had rushed out into the storm.

"I can't go until the roof is cleared."

"The roof can wait. The snow's stopping."

The youth felt the guests around the pit watching him. "I'm sorry," he said. "There must be eight, ten feet on the roof. The snow walls have collapsed, the shafts are filling." He looked about at the others.

"We'll come back for that," the pox-faced hunter said, his face close to the apprentice's.

"And where would we go?" the youth said. "The tracks are buried."

"You said you fell down a slope, remember? We could start there. Unless you don't want him found."

The pox-faced hunter had taken the apprentice by the arm and was staring into his face. The hunter's fingers were rigid and made the youth's arm feel weak.

Even if the snow stopped now, the youth knew, the body he had found would have been covered by fresh snow during the night. There should be nothing to fear.

And yet the pox-faced hunter's tone at "remember?" haunted him, and the youth could feel a rush of fear in his blood and in the sudden aching in his chest. He had let the guests think that he had not found the dead hunter in the storm, and although he did not see how anyone could challenge that, he still felt uneasy for lying, and for the fear that he might give himself away.

The apprentice tried to make his own eyes steady. From the corners of his vision, he felt the attention of the wayfarers.

"Once the roof is cleared," he said, although even to his own ears his voice sounded too high.

The liquid woman with the blackened teeth now looked up at the apprentice. Her three eyebrows were drawn together. "It can't keep snowing," she said. "Those men are still out there."

The youth did not know what to say.

"You're not from here," a man said to the woman. It was the transport agent, Wakabayashi.

"We have snow," the woman said.

"No," Wakabayashi said. "Your snows in the south are little snows. They dust the scenery."

"It's still snow."

"Not like here. Here the snows eat us. Seven months a year we live under the snow. And after every snow we dig. We dig because a second storm would crush us. All the money in that bag won't buy you out of a second storm." Wakabayashi pointed his chin toward the woman.

Looking over, the youth saw for the first time that there was indeed a bag next to the woman's leg. She grabbed it and pulled it onto her lap and held it tightly against her.

"You never let that bag get a foot from you," Wakabayashi said. "Where'd you get that money? That old man didn't earn it." Wakabayashi pointed at the old man near her that she traveled with. Wakabayashi smiled. "Where's that daughter of yours? You sold her, didn't you? You're not up here for theatricals, are you? Where'd you sell her? To a factory, like this dead girl here?"

The youth had barely noticed the woman's bag. He looked more closely at Wakabayashi, while the old man with the woman pushed himself to his knees and began to talk unintelligibly.

Wakabayashi spoke over him, "A silk factory, maybe. But they pay more where the conditions are even worse, don't they? Sado Island? To the brothels? Maybe the mines themselves?" He smiled. "Someplace where she'll get a pretty cough just like this."

"I don't have money in here," the woman said. "You're crazy. I didn't sell anybody."

"You don't know anything," Wakabayashi said. "Your little snows are as far from ours as beauty is from pain. The snow must be cleared from the roof first, before anything, before eating, before breathing." Wakabayashi, whose voice had risen, turned now on the pox-faced hunter, whose eyes moved between the woman and her bag. "You want help to find that fool, then help dig off the roof."

One of the tappers of lac said they'd help dig the roof for a free night's lodging.

"Guests shouldn't help," Matsuko said from the side of the room. The youth had not seen her enter. He knew she would not tolerate losing three nights' fees.

"They don't all get sick," said the woman with blackened teeth.

"We'll help anyway," another tapper in the shadows said, "for the lodging."

"Help me out," the pox-faced hunter said to the liquid woman, gesturing toward her bag. "Give me just a little to pay for the digging, so we can find my friend. He didn't ask for anything when he went out after that man."

"Of course," Wakabayashi said, "she sold her daughter so she could give you money to find your dead friend."

"Give me just a little," the pox-faced man said again. He leaned across the fire toward the liquid woman and stuck out his hands. The smoke formed wreathes around them. The coals lit his face from beneath.

"I don't have any money in here. You're all crazy."

"Let me look in the bag, then," the pox-faced hunter said, reaching an arm out, "to set their minds at ease."

The old man with the liquid woman was still talking. He moved up by her and laid a vein-striped hand on the bag.

"Oh, you'd better keep that bag close to you," Kato said, laughing. "It wouldn't do to leave it around."

The youth turned to the tappers of lac. "Have you dug before?"

"Of course."

"Then you've one free night for your help."

"It's too hard work," Matsuko said to the lead tapper.

"Too late," he smiled at her from the dark. "We accept, innkeeper." The three men pushed themselves to their feet.

Matsuko now turned bitterly on Wakabayashi. "Why don't you help, too?"

"For one free night?"

"No. To help his poor 'friend'." She twisted her face at Waka-bayashi and spat the words at him.

"No friend of mine," Wakabayashi said.

"He's dead already," Kato said.

"If they'll dig," the pox-faced hunter said to the youth, gesturing toward the tappers, "we can go now."

"When the roof's cleared," the apprentice said, and he stood up into the blackness.

"Lady," Wakabayashi said to the liquid woman with blackened teeth, "the poor people here sell their children, too."

As he reached the entryway, the apprentice wondered if the girl who had worn the cloak of yellow fur might be in the bath, but it was too late to turn back, and he was not sure, in any case, if he should. From behind him, the youth heard Kato call out, laughing.

"Hey," the rope maker called again, waving his hand and trying to get Wakabayashi's attention, "I didn't know there was a difference between beauty and pain."

❋

The apprentice stood upon the roof of the inn and gazed into the emptiness about. He knew that before him there lay a mountain range, and to the west the sea, but he could see only the low gray sky and a field of gray snow broken in places by the tops of trees. These, too, were soon lost in the haze of lightly falling snow.

He walked the roof trying to judge the work ahead. Near the chimney, just below the ridge pole, an overhang reached nearly twice his height. There were places below where the snow walls had collapsed against the sides of the inn, and places where the tops of the snow walls had eroded, leaving long, open crevices along the eaves. On the drift side, snow had risen in spots several feet above the lower roof.

The tappers of lac and the pox-faced hunter appeared below him. They carried beech shovels and wore the wadded cotton head-gear of the mountain people and one wore a straw vest and one striped leggings and they crossed by ladder to the roof without speaking.

The youth could feel the cold against his skin. He gripped the shovel for warmth.

They dug for nearly an hour. The tappers of lac worked well and after a while they talked as they dug. The hunter kept to himself. At times the youth would turn to see the hunter staring at him.

As he dug, the youth thought about the girl who had worn the cloak of yellow fur. He thought for a long time about how she had looked at him, her mouth slightly open, when he had rushed out into the storm. He tried to read some meaning there.

At one point, bending at the waist, he thought he heard the strings of an instrument from inside the inn. The day before he had seen the girl carrying the case for such an instrument, and so he put down the blade of his shovel and straightened and held his breath to listen. But, under its blanket of snowfall, no sounds from the inn could be heard. There was only the light hiss of the falling snow. Soon he doubted that he had heard anything at all.

When they finished the roof, the youth knew he might see her. But when they finished the roof, he also knew he would have to go with the pox-faced hunter to begin the search for the dead man.

One of the tappers of lac had stopped digging. "Someone's coming," the tapper said, leaning a forearm on his shovel handle for a moment. It seemed a studied pose.

In the near distance, just visible through the lightly falling snow, a group of men in straw cloaks could be seen climbing up the ridge toward the inn. Beyond, the sky and the earth lay close together, and there was no line between them.

"Villagers," the youth said, pausing to count the number he would have to report to the master of the inn, "coming to dig."

Another of the tappers of lac had stopped work and was watching the snow land on the roof just in front of him, his shovel held down across his thighs. "When snow falls on snow it disappears," he said. "It's the same with men."

As the villagers neared the inn, several of them called out to the youth. Their voices had a muffled sound in the cold gray light and the falling snow. They blew on their hands or wiped at their noses with the backs of their gloves and some stomped in place and slapped their arms against themselves and some hawked and spat. Although they were not far away, they called to the roof as though across a great distance.

Two villagers known to the youth joined him on the roof in the snowpit he had dug. From his pit, the heads and shoulders of the tappers of lac, rising and bending, could be seen. The villagers exchanged glances when they realized that guests of the inn were digging.

"Lots of guests," one of them said after a while. His face was hidden in a cloud of breath.

"The storm closed the coastal road," the youth said, unwilling to help them out.

The two villagers exchanged another look.

The youth stopped digging, the blade of his shovel in the air. "The road's not closed?"

One of the two villagers, a good-looking boy named Takashi, worked his way closer. "The river crossing was swept away," he said, but then he lowered his voice, "but it wasn't the storm."

The other villager stood up as if to rub his hands and looked about at the strangers. The tappers and the pox-faced hunter were far enough away that they could not hear. Some of the villagers were already moving packs of snow off the roof. "There have been men in the village and in the forests," the villager said. He, too, had lowered his voice. The youth could not remember the man's name.

"I've heard."

"Not just here. Before the crossing was closed we heard there were men in the village to the south, too."

"And in the forest to the north," Takashi said.

"We say the crossing was swept away, but the ropes were cut."

"Before the storm," Takashi said.

"We think they're waiting for something."

"Or looking for someone," Takashi said.

"Maybe," the youth said, trying to keep his voice casual, "they are looking for a thief," for, indeed, some of the guests had thought the bearded man a thief on the night of the storm.

Takashi tilted his head to the side. "Why wouldn't they tell us?"

The youth thought about what it might mean if the bearded man were not a thief, and if the river crossing had not been swept away, and if the men in the forests were somehow a part of what had happened the night before.

Takashi drew nearer and dropped his voice. "Did you hear they found a dead man?"

The youth shook his head.

"At the edge of the village. Early this morning."

In his mind's eye the youth saw the bearded man splayed out in the snow.

"Who was it?"

The boy Takashi shrugged.

"Didn't they find anything on him?" the youth asked.

Bent over to shovel, Takashi looked up at the youth as if he were crazy. "I don't know. Ice."

The youth pictured again the dead body of the bearded man.

It was true, the youth knew, that the bearded man had probably killed the hunter Itoh, but he had not been a thief. He had not taken the dead hunter's wallet. And while he had fled the inn inexplicably, he had also inexplicably spared the youth's life. He had even tried to warn the youth of something.

Odd, the youth thought, that he felt a vague remorse at the death of this man, and not of the hunter Itoh who had risked the storm with him. Indeed, he could not remember the dead hunter's face. He was not even sure he had ever seen it clearly. And yet he could remember the feel of the hunter's body as he warmed his frozen fingers in its armpits in the dark of the storm.

The youth looked across toward the pox-faced hunter. After a time he realized that he and the villagers had fallen into a silence.

The youth and the villagers bent and rose with the rhythm of their digging. From time to time they looked about. The sky was gray, the ridge was gray, a light gray snow still fell like a curtain around them. They could not see far. They could not see where the snow came from as it fell at them out of the sky. They could not see the trees down the ridge that faded into the mist. In a while they had dug so deeply that they could not see out of their pit at all.

❋

When the youth reentered the inn, the transport agent Wakabayashi was sitting at the edge of the steps in the gloom of the entryway, rubbing his toes through his socks. He could hear the voices of guests in the main room.

Pulling off his cloak, the youth listened for a voice that might belong to the girl who had worn the cloak of yellow fur, but he heard none. The dwarfed creature, snoring, was huddled in the corner.

"Any news from the village?" Wakabayashi said.

"They found a man dead this morning."

"I'm not surprised," Wakabayashi said, pulling the collar of his garment closer around his neck.

The youth hesitated, "It's too bad I couldn't catch him."

"Who?"

"The man who came in out of the storm and ran back out again."

"Oh, do you think it's him?"

"Don't you?"

Wakabayashi shrugged. "I don't know. I hadn't thought about it. Why couldn't it be that hunter who ran out after him?"

The youth looked away. "Of course, it could be him, too."

"Anyway, you did what you could, didn't you?" Wakabayashi said, and he stood and walked back in toward the fire.

The youth, following, wondered suddenly why the man had been in the entryway at all.

A dozen guests sat in the main room by the edge of the firepit. Their heads were bent low and they held things to the light. When the youth drew near he saw that they held near their faces cards of lacquered paper and that other cards lay scattered about their feet and others still passed among them hand to hand. On the cards were painted pictures of naked women bathing and lovers engaged in odd, exotic practices and on some were monkeys with erections and on one a demon and a maid. The top card, facing outward, bore a half-dressed courtesan and a warrior, reversed upon each other, garments hitched to their waists, with swollen, oversized organs and impossibly reddened flesh, and behind her back the courtesan held a dagger and there were scratchings on the card that bore urgent words. The wayfarers about the pit examined the cards with thick and blackened fingers. They craned their necks toward the performer Ueda and stole glances at the images he had tossed casually before him and at those that passed and those that were to come.

"I'll tell you a tale," Ueda said. He stuck his head forward and gleamed at the wayfarers with a tight smile. He said the tale was true and had happened nearby and was worth a bit of sake, and when someone poured he began.

He told the tale of a merchant who took his house to ruin. The merchant had a daughter of some beauty, and some said he abused the child. The daughter grew headstrong, and nothing could be done with her. She scorned the merchant and her mother alike and she would not weave crepe or attend to the duties she was set.

Ueda looked about at the others and he looked at the apprentice and the snow diggers who stood over the fire and reached their hands out for its warmth. He laughed at the taunts of those who said the tale was not worth the sake, and, holding up his hand, he continued.

He said that boys from the village took the merchant's daughter places, and word spread that she had many lovers. There were odd tales of her sexual prowess, and they said she had coupled with dogs and men and several of the boys at once. Then to their village came a young samurai, who spotted the girl as all did, and she folded him into her. He took her away to a village near his home. She began to refuse him. She took other lovers in the village, which enraged him, but he would not be done with her. He was distracted when he was not with her, and when he was. When she refused him he would beat her for the humiliation he felt, but he could not break the tie. At last she grew with child, which she said was the samurai's, and she refused to give it up.

The child was born sickly, and after many months did not recover. None in the village could help. But there was one near the coast known for his medicines, and the woman resolved to go there. The young samurai refused, fearing she would not return. But she begged him, she opened her robes partway and told him she would love him as she once had and no other, if only he would take her and her baby girl right away. Now he refused her. He did not believe her. But she knew him, she watched his eyes gleam as she drew her hand slowly down inside her robe to her thighs and then brought her scent to him. She let him get the taste so strong he could think of nothing else and then she promised him that everything he wanted would be his that night, willingly, if they started right away.

Now Ueda looked at the faces around him in the fireglow and finished the last of his sake. He saw that they were his for a while, and he motioned for another vial, and someone placed coins to pay upon the mat. The girl who had worn the yellow fur had returned during the tale to sit behind Ueda and point her feet toward the fire, and the apprentice stole a look at her and her face half-cast in shadow.

Ueda slowly took another sip of sake before he resumed, holding out his hand. Even though it was winter and the skies gray and the wind picking up, the young samurai and the girl clutching her baby set out to cross the first pass. But soon the wind blew strongly and the young samurai said they must turn back. The girl mocked him and said that they could get to a hut that she knew. Soon a storm raged, and they bent horizontally to the wind. Snow swirled from around them into funnels hundreds of feet in the air. Their hats were torn from their heads and their winter capes flapped about them. The woman's hair blew wildly around her and into her eyes and she could see nothing but snow. Snow blew down their collars and up their sleeves and inside their clothes. They fell to the ground, hands and feet so cold they could barely bend. They called out as loudly as they could but none could hear and they could barely hear each other. Soon they curled up, each alone, not able to find the other, teeth chattering. Every slight movement made them colder. Their eyes grew dim, their hearing faint, they lied to themselves that the wind would soon stop and that they would soon be rescued. The snow swallowed them.

The next day a group of men passed just where the couple lay buried in the snow. They saw only a field of unbroken snow, but suddenly they heard below them the sound of the snow wailing. They looked around and when they could see nothing they fled, but as the cry grew more distant their courage returned and they crept slowly back. Again they heard the cry from within the snow. They were afraid of the spirits of the place. But they began to dig.

Soon they came upon long black strands of hair suspended in the snow like shoots of a plant reaching for the surface. They found a woman's head, and they could see the sightless eyes and frozen face. The woman's mouth was half open and caked with snow. Frozen hair stuck to her forehead and cheeks, and while the edge of a collar was visible, snow was so packed around the neck that they could not be sure a body was attached. Now there was a crying sound, which seemed to the men standing in the snow around the floating head to come from the black, motionless throat. That was how they discovered the baby, still alive, swaddled in clothes and tucked in against the mother's breast beneath her clothing.

Now the guests around Ueda grew derisive for several did not believe a baby could live so long beneath the snow and others claimed to have heard a similar story but with different particulars. Some who knew the tale swore that the baby girl had been replaced by a fox, for it was known in those regions that a fox could take the form of man or woman or animal and so do harm for greed or lust to those they crossed. Ueda shook his head vigorously side to side and spoke to them rudely that the story was not yet done and they had best know the ending if they were to sleep that night in the inn.

The guests looked sharply at the apprentice for some explanation, but he did not know what to say, and Ueda bore on.

A search party from town was sent for and they poked the stave through the snow but they never found the young samurai. His parents and brothers spat on the mother's body and abused it until they were restrained by others. They denied the baby girl was of their blood and gave her roughly to a dirt-poor woman in the town. But as the child grew, the samurai's brothers had her brought to their rooms at night, and they would mistreat her. The young girl-child had the mother's beauty and soon the men in the samurai family began to handle her differently and carried her naked against them in the recesses of the house.

Then the young samurai's mother had the child sold to a brothel, where she swept the floors and oiled the women and watched the secret ways. At age ten the madam put the child in a cage with a bear trained to couple with young girls so the girls would be frigid and not fall in love with their patrons. They fed her through the bars and aroused the bear with a stick when it seemed to lose interest. Groups of men paid to watch. Like other girls who have been trained this way, she learned to handle many men in a single night and her skin turned a milky white.

Stories of this north-country training for prostitutes were apparently well-known among the guests, who made impatient motions for Ueda to continue. The youth, now squatting by the fire, stole a look at the girl who had worn the cloak of yellow fur, but she hugged her knees and barely seemed to listen to the tale.

"Then," Ueda said, "they trained the young whore in all of the finest ways to pleasure men. They gave her wooden penises and taught her how to handle them. They taught her how to sing out in the night and move to finish off her customers more quickly."

This, too, seemed common knowledge among those sitting about Ueda, but as he moved his awkward body and made panting noises they elbowed each other and showed yellowed teeth or toothless gaps as they laughed.

"They taught her how to draw pubic hair on her mound," Ueda laughed, "because she was still too young to have any of her own." A fat woman on the far side of the fire laughed out until tears streamed down her face and her sides rocked. She reached into her clothes while she was laughing and pulled sharply and made a little cry and her mouth opened and then, laughing harder, she pulled her hand out with pubic hairs stuck between her swollen fingers and flung them at the men around the fire. "No ink here," she gasped, laughing, "No ink, no ink" and the laughing men beside her made grasping motions above the fire as if to catch the pubic hair she had thrown. Some clung unnoticed in her moist palm.

"And then," Ueda said, laughing and shouting over the others' laughter, "when she was twelve and ready they gave her to me for her first night, because I had done this for them before."

The others stopped laughing in a series of diminishing gasps and leaned forward intently with glinting eyes to hear the secrets of a man used for the first-night training by a house that could afford a bear.

"Is there feeling?" a bucktoothed man asked. "At least on the first night, even after a bear?"

Ueda glanced at the man and continued. "First they brought her out for me to examine and then they told me of the girl's story and asked me if I was still ready to take her into the first night of her new life. I scoffed at their story, but later when they brought her to my room her skin was so white and cold as I undressed her, and her eyes were as still as a practiced round-heeled, hot-springs whore. But inside," Ueda said, leaning forward and slapping his thighs, "inside she was as hot as this fire and there wasn't a trick she didn't know. I bought her contract on the spot!"

Now he and the guests exploded in laughter, looking into the fire and then looking at each other, and when they caught each others' eyes, laughing louder again.

"Was there feeling?" the bucktoothed man shouted again, laughing too.

Ueda laughed so hard that he couldn't get his words out clearly, although he tried several times. The man asked Ueda to repeat what he was saying, but the harder Ueda tried the more difficulty he had speaking.

"Was there feeling?" the man asked again.

Ueda wiped at the tears of laughter rolling down his face while a man on one side tried to steady him. At last Ueda blurted out, "Ask her," and was torn by laughter again.

Some guests sat back a little and others stretched forward to hear. Ueda looked up at them and, when he realized they had not understood, rippled one more time with laughter. Then he stopped, drew heavy breaths, and his voice grew deep within him. "Ask her," he said and he reached behind him and grabbed the girl who had worn the cloak of yellow fur by the hair and yanked her forward to the fire. The girl pulled back quickly from Ueda's touch, slapping at the air, and then, looking once defiantly around, clasped her arms with her hands and sat back.

Now the guests all turned to her as if a spirit had suddenly appeared among them.

"This is her," Ueda said. "Ask her. Ask her."

There was silence, and then the bucktoothed man snorted. "Well, was there feeling?" Then he made an odd nervous laugh, and Ueda told the girl to answer.

The girl stared fixedly into the fire.

"Well?"

The girl had not raised her eyes. The wayfarers were silent, waiting. "Yes," she said quietly, so quietly the youth could barely hear.

Laughter burst from the throats of the guests so that mucus ran from their noses and spit formed in the corners of their mouths. Their features strained and distorted with their laughter and they slapped each other's arms and beat their hands against the floor and wiped at their faces. But soon, even as they laughed, the wayfarers looked at the girl from the corners of their eyes with a keen scrutiny and they looked at her parts and at the hair on her. Ueda watched their faces narrowly even as he smacked his thighs and opened his mouth wide with more laughter and poked at the others to spur their laughter on, and the girl looked at none of them, but at the fire only.

❀

Five men from the inn stood colorless in the gloom on the rim of the escarpment. They had sunk to their crotches in the snow. The youth, head bowed before them, looked down the slope where he had fallen the night before.

Without the blinding storm, it seemed strange even to the youth that he could have just stepped off the edge. The surface of the slope, covered by fresh snow throughout the night, looked as if it had never been broken. The pine tree that had broken his fall seemed closer to the rim. Then, too, the branches were thick with snow and needles and stood far out from the trunk. In truth, it did not look like a tree on which he might crack open his head. And indeed he had not, yet that was the story he had told the guests the night before.

He glanced at the others. They looked at the pine tree and the place he said he had fallen. None spoke.

Among the five was the pox-faced hunter who looked at the others and looked at the pine and at the youth and made a doubtful sound at the back of his throat. He urged the others to search inward from the rim. He did not speak to the youth, as if, having found the spot, the youth could be trusted to do no more. The others noted this affront and looked at one another and kept their eyes averted from the youth.

The five moved off into the snow. The youth hesitated at the rim. Much of the night before was vivid to him. Much was not. But he knew that he had walked a good ways before he had found the dead hunter's body, and he thought it unlikely that they would find him now.

In truth, the apprentice knew, he had very little sense of where he had found the dead body the night of the storm. He remembered that he had circled ahead, and he thought he could find the spot where he had been attacked by the bearded man, but then he had panicked, he had lost his own trail, and he had only the vaguest sense of where he had wandered. He might have doubted that he had come this far from the inn, had he not now seen it to be so. He had even warned the others, but the pox-faced hunter had urged that they press on.

The youth looked after the five men spread out among the barren trunks of the woods. Already they were passing from view. He looked into the gray snow and sky. Night would come soon. This comforted him. The youth did not want the dead man found.

It would be best, he knew, not to lag too far behind the others. He hurried to catch up.

He could see only three of the men ahead. One man carried a long pole to search through drifts. In the deep snow a dead man was more likely to be stepped on than seen, and the men looked as much at their feet as the horizon. They walked at a mournful pace.

The men called out to one another now. Walking on the gray,

unbroken snow was to them like walking on a shroud of death. A hundred stories from their childhoods whirled about and they looked for imagined hands reaching up from the snow. When their snowshoes caught beneath the surface they jumped quickly away and turned to stare at the spot where they had been. When one did this another would stop and stare and briefly laugh and then look at the snow about his own feet. Each mark on the snow caused them to slow and lean forward at the waist. They bent their paths to walk closer to tree limbs they could grasp.

After a time the man with the long pole stopped entirely. He was looking at a barren tree to the right. Hanging in a lower limb of the tree was a snow-encrusted thing. The man looked around and looked at the thing again.

The youth's step slowed. The thing in the tree was the dead man's muffler. The night before, when he had thought it right to recover the body, the youth had tied the muffler in the limbs of the tree to mark the spot.

He stopped. It was as if the dead man had tricked him. Even when he considered his confusion the night of the storm, he could not believe the dead hunter was this near to the rim.

The others were drawing ahead of the man with the pole. He reached out a hand toward the nearest of them, but it went unnoticed and he hesitated to call out. He started forward and then stopped and turned back and looked again at the tree. His mouth hung slightly open.

The youth, who might now be seen by the man with the pole, stepped forward hurriedly and lowered his head as if the tree held no interest for him. He wondered if he should create a distraction.

The man with the pole stepped closer to the tree, but he seemed to hesitate to touch the thing. The others were pulling farther ahead. The youth passed the man and thought of telling him that he was being left behind.

From the corner of his eye the youth saw the man swing the pole off his shoulders and rest one end in the snow. It sank of its own weight. Suddenly the man picked the end up and looked about at his feet. Then he calmed himself and reached the pole up toward the thing.

The youth felt the beating of his own heart. One of the men ahead stopped and was watching the man with the pole.

"What's that?" the youth said to the man with the pole.

The man had his back to the youth and he grunted. His cloud breath rose and disappeared. He poked at the thing and some of the snow fell off. He poked again.

The nearest man now started back toward them. He looked relieved to be headed back and unwilling to move on alone. The youth feared they would all welcome delay.

The man with the pole now brushed the snow off the tree limb as well, and the knot could be seen. "It's tied," the man said. He looked around to the others. "It's a marker."

"Maybe he built a snow cave," the other man said, hurrying now. He was a short man and he waddled through the snow. "He's alive! Smart fellow."

The two men shouted out into the gloom. One of the others from the inn, who was still in view, turned and then shouted out into the distance himself. In a moment the men could all be seen heading back to the tree.

The man with the pole now stepped back proudly and bent forward at the waist. He shouted as loud as he could into the snow at his feet. "Hey! Don't worry. I've found you."

"We're here!" the short man shouted into the snow, bent forward as well.

"What is it?" some of the others yelled from behind them.

"A snow cave," the man with the pole shouted back. Then he bent farther forward so that his mouth was only a foot from the snow. "We'll get you out," he shouted and the gray of his cloud breath suspended briefly near the surface of the snow as if it could also have come from within.

"Can you hear us?" the short man, too, yelled down into the snow.

The two men now bent lower still until their ears were near the surface and listened closely to the snow for a response.

Soon the others had gathered. "We're here," some yelled, "You're saved," others yelled, and they all yelled down together into the snow.

Together, they listened for a response.

To the youth, it seemed that they called to rouse the dead. He began to shiver.

The man with the pole told the others to step back and, gingerly at first, and then with more force, he poked the pole into the snow around them.

6

Six men squatted in the graying snow around the tree. They dug six holes. They dug with their arms, groping through the snow before them. Their clothing and faces were filled with snow. They shouted joyously into their knees that they were there. They strove to be the one who would first save the buried man. They called out as if to save his soul.

The youth pulled himself far back from the tree and imitated the others. He dug with dread. He had no faith in their ability to save another's soul. He knew they would find the man dead; he was afraid they would find his ruined snowshoe as well.

The youth watched a small, dark man digging near the tree. "You'll be warm soon," he was yelling. Broken snow lay strewn around him. "Hey!" his hand recoiled and then he reached forward into the snow. "I've got him!" He stood and pulled at something. "You're saved," he yelled into the snow where the head would be.

The others now stepped over and lent their strength. A snow-shoe and a bent leg emerged. They pulled on the leg, but it did not straighten. The dark mountain trousers were stiff with frozen snow. The men fell back in silence.

The pox-faced man began to push away the snow where the leg indicated the rest of the body would be. He cleared first a shoulder, then he swept his arm across an ear. The leg, the shoulder, and the ear seemed to indicate that the body was lying in different directions. The men stepped back again. They grew quiet. They could hear one another's breathing. The small man who had first touched the body gripped himself and began to rock.

Only the pox-faced hunter continued digging. He brushed the largest clumps of snow off the body. The head hung forward on the chest, but it had rolled to one side. Snow had frozen around the face and the head and the chest and the snow there had frozen black with blood.

The pox-faced hunter brushed at the snow on the dead man's face, and the men saw with varying degrees of certainty that it was the hunter Itoh who had run out into the storm. They looked aslant at the pox-faced hunter.

In the graying daylight the youth saw the dead man more clearly than he had the night before. Although he had heard many tales, he had never before seen a man killed by sword or knife. Some indistinguishable part of the man had passed through the severed throat and frozen in a mass on the dead man's chest near the head. Ice, stained black from blood, clung to it. Black-stained ice and snow filled the wound and coated the chest. The head, largely freed of the neck's restraints, had fallen to the side and frozen there at an angle life could not imitate. Snow and ice filled the ears, the nostrils, and the mouth. Beneath a thin layer of frozen snow the eyes were open toward the sky. They seemed to contemplate the world from a new and unexpected angle.

"There must have been a fight," one of the men said.

The others edged closer and squatted by the neck to see. They nodded agreement.

One of the men stepped forward and, using the end of a pole, tried to shift the head back where it belonged, or at least to give it a decent repose upon the chest. But it was frozen to the side. The man gave up and stepped away. He wiped in the snow the end of the pole that had touched the body. The pox-faced hunter remained where he stood. None looked at him.

For a moment the men from the inn stood regarding the corpse. The breath of the living formed small clouds before them.

It struck the youth now that it might have been the hunter Itoh who had attacked the bearded man, and not the other way around, as he had first thought.

Digging out the roof of the inn, the village boy Takashi had said that there were men in the forests and that they might be looking for someone. If this dead hunter Itoh had attacked the bearded man, the apprentice suddenly thought, then maybe he was somehow connected to these men, too. The youth felt the intricate workings of others brush by him. He felt alone.

The men had now moved a yard or two off to the side, debating quietly whether the head of the corpse could be freed. Some were afraid that they might break it off from the body. They knew they would have to carry the body back, and no one wanted to carry the head separately.

During this discussion the pox-faced hunter had straddled the body and, bending down, began to pat the clothing. The others stopped to watch him. Soon he squatted upon the dead man's legs and tried to peel the garments open. The cloth, soaked with blood, had frozen to the body and resisted being pried apart, as if reluctant to see the dead man suffer this final humiliation.

The hunter pried with his gloved fingers at the material, but all without effect. Then he cursed and pounded with the side of his hand to crack the ice. As he pounded, the chest had an unexpectedly thick sound. The dead man's garments did not yield.

The pox-faced hunter sat back to catch his breath and rub his hand. Then he drew a knife from inside his clothes and pressed the point into the dead man's chest. It grated on the ice there. The others, watching him, rose to their feet and shifted uncomfortably. One protested, but the pox-faced hunter had worked the blade between the layers of the dead man's clothing and begun to pry them apart. The ice made a cracking sound. The dead man's head, hanging by the side, watched this operation without expression.

With the clothing bent open, the pox-faced hunter reached inside against the corpse. He began to search about, at first methodically, and then more hurriedly. He turned, still squatting in the dead man's lap, and cursed the youth.

"You have it," he said to the apprentice. "You have it." He stood abruptly and waddled backward to free himself of the dead man's legs.

Standing once again, the pox-faced hunter turned to face the youth. "Where is it?" he shouted, and he stepped forward and shoved the youth's chest.

The apprentice was startled and forced back. He set his legs apart in case the pox-faced man attacked again. He remembered now the wallet he had taken from the dead hunter and hidden in the kitchen the night before.

The others stood up and took a half step forward. They looked at the contestants with a measure of surprise. But none moved to interfere.

"Where's what?" the youth shouted back. To his own ear he sounded defiant. He should have sounded surprised as well. He tried again, "Where's what?" and he made his voice sound as if the attack hurt his feelings, too.

"He had money." The man spoke in hushed tones, as if reluctant to admit this, even now, when the money was gone. "He had a wallet of money."

"How would I know? Get away from me." The youth felt the tension build within him. He jumped forward and pushed and the hunter fell back. His eyes opened wide, surprised.

"You took it. You took it." The man's face was red and the marks of the pox held a yellowish color, but he made no movement to attack the youth again.

The youth's mouth was dry. "You're crazy," he shouted back. "Get away from me. He's crazy," he shouted to the others on the far side of the corpse, but they still made no move to intervene.

The hunter and the youth stood just beyond reach of each other, leaning intently forward over their snowshoes, knee-deep in the churned snow. Their hands were raised and clenched close to their bodies. They eyed each other warily.

"I want it," the hunter shouted.

"It? Money? So that's why you dragged us out here. It wasn't your friend. It was his money."

The hunter glanced over at the others. They regarded him impassively. Then one suggested the dead hunter may have dropped the wallet, that maybe it was still nearby, and in a moment the hunter and the others were bent back over the body searching around in the snow.

Soon one of the searchers found the torn, oval snowshoe that the youth had worn the night of the storm. The man regarded it quizzically. "This one's been cut," he said, turning the snowshoe in his hands.

Thinking of the money, the men had lost their fear of the corpse, and now one of them quite matter-of-factly reached into the snow and, feeling around, raised the dead man's legs.

The men saw that one leg had no snowshoe, and that the snowshoe on the other leg was round.

"Hey," the man holding the mismatched, broken snowshoe said, "he was in a hurry."

The men considered this in silence. The youth tried to read their expressions without looking at them too closely. He could tell noth-ing. No one turned on him.

After a moment he told them it would be dark soon and they needed to start back. The pox-faced hunter and another looked about in the snow for the lost wallet still, but the others stood about, awaiting the problem of carrying the dead man back.

The youth regarded with a chill the bent back of the pox-faced hunter. If the dead hunter Itoh were connected to the men in the forests, he thought, then so is this man.

In a while the six set off silently to return to the inn. They took turns together at carrying the corpse. The body hung between them, frozen into the odd, seated posture in which it had been found. They progressed jerkily. The sky and snow darkened.

Still far from the inn, they set the dead man down on his back at the top of a rise. The bent body sank slightly into the snow. The car-riers breathed heavily so their breath formed thick before them and they swayed over their knees or splayed out sullenly in the snow. None spoke. The pox-faced hunter sat apart and eyed the youth with malice, but made no movement toward him. The others looked over dully from time to time, curious to see if the two might go at each other again.

Looking up, the youth saw the lower half of the heatless sun. Only the orange arc stood out from the dull, even grayness of the indeterminate snow and sky. There were no shafts of light, no col-ored clouds. As it sank, the sun grew darker and rounder until at last the very top emerged, and the sun hung whole and blood red in the graying sky.

Looking around, the youth saw the others. Their chins rested upon their chests and their eyes stared into nothingness and they were indifferent to the sun. But the dead man's head, turned impos-sibly to the side, marked well its final passage.

❇

A hunched man in soiled stripes hesitated on the threshold of an upstairs room at the inn. A voice called out to him, and he entered. As the door slid open and closed, the calls of others and a strand of music swelled and faded. The apprentice followed.

The room was dark, and the air stank of sweat and tobacco and charcoal fires that burned the youth's eyes. Guests were scattered about. The brief glow of pipe bowls marked the whites of the eyes and the jowls of men crouched along the walls.

The girl who had worn the yellow fur squatted on the floor near the only lamp. She gripped the wooden pegs at the neck of her instrument and tested the tune of the strings. When the youth looked at her she turned her head slightly away and tightened one of the strings. She plucked at it several times, her face in shadows.

A group of men slumped around the girl. The lamp cast long upswept shadows across their faces, flattening their noses and hiding their foreheads beyond the brightly lit sockets of their eyes. The lips of these creatures moved in uneven sequences lost in the overall din, and as their heads twisted from side to side their features seemed to flow before them from solid to shadow to solid again. One pointed to the youth with his chin and said something, and the others stopped and stared with pale fleshy faces or long shadow scars from which their eyes would glisten. The girl looked up too, and the shadow of her nose reached her ear.

In the center of the room stood the tiny girl. She had been dancing. Sweat gathered on her forehead, and she fanned at her neck with the exaggerated sleeve of her kimono. The men on the floor around her watched through the clouds of their breath as if she still danced.

Men on the far side of the room called out toasts to different body parts of a fat woman from the village who had joined them. She poured them sake and they drained their cups at a gulp and produced more names of parts to toast.

The youth looked carefully about for the pox-faced hunter, but he was not to be seen. The youth took some comfort there, and in the presence of so many others.

When the music resumed, the youth managed not to look in the girl's direction. The tiny dancer began to raise and lower herself beyond the candle flame, her kimono swaying stiffly below her knees and making a slithering sound when she turned. At times she fixed her dark eyes on the youth. Her hair was piled high, in shadow except the very top, which caught the greasy light that hovered above her.

Behind the youth men gambled in the dim corner with the bleached bones of a rat. With each toss sharp voices called out to invoke the fates, and the small bones clinked as they tumbled one across another. The gamblers leaned intently forward into a circle and the shadows hid all but the tops of their heads, like men feeding from a common bowl. Then one player slapped the mat in protest and another grunted in rough triumph and reached forward to gather coins to himself, and the still white bones positioned at the center marked the zero sum of men's fortunes.

The youth felt a chill and looked about the room.

Watching him across the flame of the oil lamp was the pox-faced hunter.

The hunter had wrapped a dark, wadded cloth under his chin and over his head, and so his pale face loomed out of the bleakness. Men on either side talked across him, their arms waving weakly in the air.

The youth turned away, although he felt the hunter's look still. The night before he had thought the pox-faced hunter was concerned for the missing Itoh, and later for the dead man's wallet. Then, digging out the corpse, the youth came to think that the hunters might in truth have been after the bearded man, which tied them in turn to others in the forest, all searching for some reason the youth did not understand. But climbing back to the inn, with the corpse bent between them, its one hand trailing in the snow, the youth also remembered the packet that the bearded man had buried during the storm.

"Something valuable he had stolen," one of the guests had said the previous night. Something valuable, for certain, the youth thought, but whether the packet was something the bearded man had stolen, or something he feared others might steal from him, the youth could no longer be sure.

He thought it possible that the bearded man might have buried the packet so it would not be found on him, should he die in the storm, or should others, like the hunter, set upon him. That a man so near exhaustion might yet value this packet, value it even above his life, struck the youth as something new.

And if it were the packet that the hunters and these others in the forest were after all along, and not the bearded man, then, the youth realized, they would be after him, too.

The youth bit unconsciously at his lower lip. He had thought himself safe, because no one could know for sure whether he had found the bearded man in the storm, or if, as he claimed, he had hit his head on a tree. But if in fact these men in the forest were after the packet all along, the youth saw now that he was their only hope of finding it.

Indeed, he realized, it would not matter much whether or not they believed his version of the night of the storm. Either way, with the hunter Itoh and the bearded man dead, he was the only one left who might know where the packet lay hidden. They would have to come for him.

And if someone were going to come for him, he had no idea who. Or truly why. Of all those around him, he knew only that this pox-faced hunter watched him closely across the room, and that he might be one of them.

And were he the only clue to finding the packet, the youth saw now, finding the packet was also his only clue to them.

He wondered what the packet might contain.

"Something valuable," the guests had said, and so, the youth thought, it must be, if so many sought so small a packet.

He sat up straight. Gold. Gold, he thought. Gold. Gold would be small enough.

But if it were gold, he knew, they would never let him be.

Then, too, the youth thought, there might not be anyone after the packet. His fears might all be imagined. The pox-faced hunter might only seek Itoh's lost wallet. The men in the forest might be waiting for someone else. Indeed, when the youth looked back across the room, he saw the pox-faced hunter talking with a man, and he grew momentarily ashamed of his fears.

But then there would be no danger in recovering the packet. And if there were danger, then it would be because these others already assumed he was their only hope to find the packet. And in finding it first, perhaps learning something, perhaps returning it, might lie his only safety, and the only way to repay the odd debt he had come to feel to the bearded man. For the bearded man had killed the hunter, and yet, exhausted as he was, he had not killed the youth. He had even tried to warn him.

In this fashion, the youth drew cautiously toward a plan of action. But when at last he turned back and looked defiantly across the room toward the pox-faced hunter, the man was no longer there.

An old man to the youth's side suddenly shouted out, and in a moment others joined him. The old man sat with his knees in the air and his elbows balanced across them and gnarled fingers interlaced before his mouth, so that all the youth could see were his crinkled eyes. The old man was watching the tiny dancer sway before him, confiding some secret joke into his palms. "Shallow River," the old man shouted again.

"Shallow River," yet another group called out.

The tiny girl stopped dancing and pursed her lips and shook her head strongly side to side. She looked imploringly at Ueda, who rose slowly from one of the corners. He wore a performer's garment that was dark on the left side and white on the right so that he could play two roles. As he rose from the shadows, only the light side shone, and it seemed there stood only half a man. His light arm waved and his light leg moved and he balanced improbably and called out another song.

"Shallow River. Shallow River," the old man insisted and the men around him began to clap and his bent and withered hands took up the clap, too.

The youth glanced about, but the pox-faced hunter was nowhere to be seen. As he turned his head, something caught his eye. Guests in the adjoining rooms had poked their fingers through the paper screens to peek in at the dancer. In the ragged holes, the youth could see the glistening of their eyes. He wondered if the pox-faced hunter might be there among them.

Ueda had stepped to the side of the lamp, and his white arm tugged at the armpit of the fat woman from the village. She sat in an oily kimono between two tappers of lac. She smoked a pipe, and the smoke seeped from her mouth back up into her nostrils. The lacquer workers held her down by them and yelled to the tiny dancer. One pushed at Ueda to shove him away. The village woman slapped the men on their arms and rocked and laughed and seemed not to notice Ueda, who still clung to the pit of her arm. When her mouth tilted up the youth saw that her teeth were yellow and small, and the white of her makeup lay only across her face and the neck below was coarse.

"Shallow River, Shallow River," the wayfarers cried from where they sat or squatted or slouched about the room, and their wet lips shone.

The tiny dancer had now stopped moving altogether. Ueda stepped in front of the apprentice moving his arm up and down. The youth realized the music had also stopped and when he looked he saw that the girl who had worn the yellow fur had placed her instrument across her knee and was looking at him without expression. Men sat close to her on either side. One, the youth thought, might be touching her leg.

Ueda was still trying to get the youth's attention, and he had grabbed his arm. The youth turned to snatch it away. When he looked back toward the girl, she had already picked up her instrument. She began to play.

The tiny dancer now began to raise and lower herself over her knees and the wayfarers began to slur the words of a song. Some knew only a phrase and others snatches of different verses and each stumbled trying to pick up the words of the others.

Dancing, the tiny girl now did what seemed to the youth an amazing thing. Reaching down to her ankles, she parted her kimono and lifted it several inches off the ground. As she straightened, her eyes fixed once again on the youth, and they were wide and dark. The men were now shouting "Shallow River, Shallow River," and as they did she raised her hem higher and stepped behind the candle as if to cross a stream. Her bare calves in the candlelight were thick and pale as she stepped. She wore low, stained socks.

The music grew slightly faster. The girl who had worn the cloak of yellow fur played with averted eyes. The old man had now rocked forward onto his bony knees and he clapped loudly and without rhythm while the verse came around and the men shouted out and the girl raised her hem higher still. Her shoulders began to shiver as if she were being shaken from within.

One of the men below her reached out and ran his hand up the dancer's leg until it was below the hem and behind her knee. The tiny girl stared down at it but she kept her steps to the music and the village woman pulled the man's hand away and bit it until the man cried out.

"Shallow River," the men shouted, and the kimono was raised halfway above the knee. The dancer's small thighs were plump and pale and the surface jiggled and settled as she stepped. She had gathered the thick kimono up into her arms until her arms seemed borne down by the weight and pinned to her sides. The inner hem of the kimono was red and coarse and stained, and her pale plump legs seemed to erupt from it.

The village woman now threw herself forward on her stomach very near the candle and sniffed up into the shadows beneath the tiny dancer's red kimono. "No smell," she shouted, laughing, "no smell," and the men around her laughed, too, but with a different edge as they looked at the young girl. The tiny dancer pulled the end of her kimono up to hide her face and she stepped blindly in place. "Shallow River!" The music now played very loud and very fast, and the men pounded the floor "Shallow River!" and the floor shook. "Shallow River!" and the tiny dancer now raised her kimono above her waist, her arms filled with clothing and her stomach bare and her thighs shifting back and forth without rhythm, almost in place. "Shallow River!" and she raised the gathered clothing higher still until she was naked from the floor to her child's breasts.

"Her hair's painted," one of the men by the fat village woman yelled and pointed, and the youth saw that the tiny dancer's mound was in fact not covered by hair but by long painted lines.

The tune shifted and quickened so that the singers could not keep up with the words, and the tiny dancer began to spin, near-naked, in place. First hips, then stomach, mound, and thighs revolved, revolved, revolved, and the men clapped until the girl-child lost her balance and stumbled over one of them, and he pushed her back onto her feet and she turned and turned and the men clapped on until the music abruptly ceased.

The tiny dancer stopped. She reeled slightly and threw down the kimono, her eyes wet and streaming. She stood uncertain for a moment, disheveled and dizzy, and then she staggered hurriedly into a corner with her back to the room and huddled there, her shoulders heaving, and tugged at her clothes.

The men called out to her, but none rose to touch her.

Near the corner, the youth was surprised to see, sat the pox-faced hunter. His face was turned toward the tiny dancer, and his eyes could not be seen. The youth wondered if he had been there all along.

The girl who had worn the yellow fur placed her instrument across her lap and stared at the floor mats, shaking her hands at the wrist. She stretched her arms casually and then, placing her fingertips together, bent back her fingers and palms. She massaged her forearms. In a moment she began to play another tune. She did not look at the youth.

The fat village woman rose to the center of the room to dance. She lurched and swung her arms without meaning. Soon a tapper of lac stood and danced awkwardly beside her, and the finely elongated shadows of their legs crossed the floor and stretched up the far wall to where their squat torsos laced and dissipated, one about the other, beneath small and flattened heads.

❀

Passing into the kitchen with some trays, the youth stumbled upon the performers. They held bowls among them and ate cold rice with their fingers. Ueda's hand was in his mouth. The girl who had worn the yellow fur sat with her knees pressed together and against her chest, her toes at the edge of the dark wooden platform. She was looking at the youth, her fingers just above the rice. Behind her was her instrument. The tiny dancer squatted on the earthen floor, her bowl beside her, her head inside a cupboard.

"Innkeeper," Ueda said, half dark, half light, scrambling to his feet, and the tiny dancer pulled her head quickly from the cupboard. She bore a guilty look and, grabbing her bowl, jumped quickly up onto the cold mortar stove.

The man urged the youth to join them. His fingers, held up in greeting, were thick with white grains of rice that stuck to him like parasites. The man sucked them off one by one, still talking. The tiny dancer began to swing her legs, her heels hitting against the side of the stove. The youth could hear the loud voices of guests from the floor above.

"It's a good night," Ueda said, "a good night. And so we sought some sake. Not to add to your worries, innkeeper, but to celebrate for now the easing of our own. We'll pay, of course."

The youth stepped through them, past a post with a bamboo rack and in it metal ladles and spoons of hinoki, stained spatulas with battered ends and half a dozen skewers, bent or straight, and a long-handled knife with rust upon the blade. He pushed aside with his foot a wood-slab bucket bound with cord and oily water spilled from it. He placed the soiled trays near the sink and wondered if he should correct once more the man's calling him innkeeper. Not far from the cupboard was the stack of rice sacks where he had hidden the dead hunter's wallet the night before. He avoided looking in its direction.

"I'll get you some more," the youth said.

"Not too much," Ueda held up a hand weakly, "it's too expensive. But not too expensive to share." His white-clothed arm reached for a second cup and held it out to the youth.

The youth could hear the woman Matsuko snoring at the back end of the room. He glanced into the darkness, but he could not see her there.

"It's not too expensive for me," the youth said softly, and he drew half a vial for the man.

"It is a good night. Thank you, thank you. You're too kind to me."

"He can pay for that," the girl who had worn the yellow fur said from the floor. "You shouldn't let him trick you."

With a start, the youth realized that he had not heard her voice before. It was lower pitched than he would have thought and bore a trace of the north country in it. It took him a moment to adjust.

"I don't mind," he said to her. He hoped she would speak again.

"He doesn't mind," Ueda repeated.

"Don't flatter yourself," the tiny dancer said to Ueda, "he's doing it for us. He likes us. I'd like some sake, too." She thrust out her cup, which the youth had not seen before.

The youth feared the warmth he felt rising in his cheeks. He looked down, surprised, too, that the tiny girl-child seemed to bear Ueda no ill will for forcing her to dance half-naked upstairs only a short time before.

The girl who had worn the yellow fur held out her cup, as well, without rising from the floor. The youth saw her forearm bare and white where her clothes fell back from her hand.

The apprentice filled their cups. He felt their eyes on him while he poured. Careful not to spill any, he held back his sleeve the way the old samurai had done the night before.

The youth thought of complimenting the tiny girl-child on her dancing, but then he thought it might seem lewd. Instead, he turned to say something to the older girl about her music, but at the last moment he held back on this, too, afraid that complimenting one and not the other could itself be a problem. In the end, he stood in the middle turning between the two mutely, as if eager to pounce on their cups once either wanted more.

There was a silence in which he felt foolish. The performers seemed bored and fixed on their drinks. Ueda, his lips wet, held out his cup first. He gestured, vaguely, toward the cup he had set out earlier for the youth. "I saw that hunter," the performer said loudly, and he began to shake his head in an exaggerated manner side to side. "Money bought him no good."

"Money?"

"Oh yes, they say he carried quite a bit, although none was found." The performer leaned far forward and lowered his voice. "Someone removed his head, you know. Of course, you know." He leaned back suddenly. "I forget, you found him."

"With the others."

"Of course," Ueda said.

"They say he killed a bear," the tiny dancer said. "The gall blad-der alone brings a lot."

Ueda swung his cup into the air as if in a toast. "Even the bear has his revenge. In time we all pay for our wrongs, each of us. To the spirit of the bear." He raised his cup higher still and then drank it all and held it out once again to the youth.

"You know they took his snowshoe, too," Ueda said.

The youth, pouring, focused intently on the performer's cup. He felt the man's eyes. "His snowshoe?"

"Yes, they took his wallet and one snowshoe. And, of course, his head. You would have thought the wallet and the head were enough."

The performer ducked his head down near the youth's and lifted his eyebrows high. He wore an odd grin. His protruding eyes were stretched wide and the youth found himself staring into them. He was aware that his mouth was dry, and he did not trust himself to speak.

In his mind the youth saw the dead hunter's round snowshoe and his own oval one, and he tried to recall what had happened to them when he returned to the inn from the storm. Much was blurred and uncertain to him. He recalled only that there had been many feet around him. He knew that his boots and the snowshoes were gone when the guests had moved him by the fire.

The youth wondered what this performer knew, and he searched the man's grinning face for meaning, but there was no clear message there.

"Feed him," Ueda said to the older girl, gesturing at the youth with his chin.

Startled, the youth looked behind himself and saw that the girl was in turn looking at the hunched dwarf. It had pulled to the end of its tether and was staring in at them from the opening to the entryway. Against its dark, unkempt hair and skin, even the dim candlelight made the whites of its eyes glisten. They looked moist. The pupils were still, black points. Then the dwarf slumped and picked up its dirt-blackened feet.

"You feed him," the older girl said, her voice low pitched again.

"Feed him, I said."

The girl ignored him.

"Go on."

The older girl rose reluctantly, holding one arm around herself. The youth saw now that the performers had scraped together some scraps of food and dried millet cake that lay in a clump on the edge of the water cask. She gathered these up in her fingers and left the room for the entryway. In a minute she returned for her instrument and went back out again.

Through the doorway the youth could see her hunched down

by the dwarf. She was partially blocked by the dwarf's body. She seemed to be feeding it by hand.

For the youth, still standing by Ueda and the tiny dancer, the silence held a measure of comfort.

At last the tiny dancer turned her head to Ueda. "You shouldn't talk to her like that," she said in a whisper. She spoke as if the youth were not there.

Ueda waved his long fingers dismissively, and he turned aside to finish his bowl of rice. His dark half toward the youth, the performer nearly seemed to disappear.

The tiny girl-child concentrated on her rice, too, and in a minute Ueda left.

"He shouldn't talk to her like that," the tiny girl said again after he had gone.

The youth stood uncertainly. "What does the dwarf do?"

"We'll use him in the theatricals. In the village."

"What does it do?"

"We put him in a cage."

"Does it need the cage?"

"No. The crowd does. He rattles it and screams and hops up and down. They love it. They wouldn't like it without the cage. We tell them he's part outcast and part Russian."

"Is he really?"

The tiny girl had shoveled a great quantity of rice into her mouth, and as she chewed, the rice began to spill back out so that she had to catch it with her fingers. She stuck her chin far out so that the rice wouldn't fall on her clothes, but some fell on her anyway and landed in her lap. She shrugged and made a noise that the youth could not decipher.

He waited. When, still chewing furiously, she reached down to pick up the other grains, he looked into her lap and thought about the painted lines. Through her clothes he could see the thick outlines of her thighs.

"Does it matter? He lives as he is." The tiny girl looked up at the youth. "Sometimes he makes Yukiko go into the cage."

Yukiko, the youth thought. He looked over his shoulder at the girl who had worn the yellow fur and turned the name over in his mind. "How?"

"How? Are you stupid? Ueda. Ueda does. Is there any more sake? She goes in when he's ranting and raving the most. Crowds love it. Then she calms him down. Once some dumb water-drinking farmer ran in to save her. Ueda's going to ruin it. Thanks."

He filled her vial. "How does she calm it down?"

"Depends on her mood and the crowd. Sometimes she sings. Sometimes she opens up her clothes." The girl looked up. "Once he bit her."

The youth was not sure if it was the dwarf or Ueda who had bitten her, but he was afraid to ask. "How's he going to ruin it?"

"She'll run away. Or she'll get someone to buy her contract. And he needs her."

The youth was surprised by this.

"He needs her music," the tiny dancer said, rolling her head in exasperation. "She can't stand him." The tiny girl lowered her voice. "He tried to touch her once. Then he hit her. So she poisoned him. Enough to make him really sick. Then while he was so sick he couldn't move she beat him with a stick. He's never touched her again. I think he's scared of her."

The youth looked back over toward Yukiko. She seemed to have finished feeding the dwarf and was talking to it. He could not hear what she was saying. "What would she do?"

"If she left? Play. Teach. Find a patron, most likely. Maybe an innkeeper. She likes you, you know." The tiny dancer looked up at him with interest to watch his reaction.

"How would you know?"

"She told me. She tells me everything. Sooner or later."

"When could she have told you?" he asked. He tried to make his voice sound as if his only interest was to show the tiny dancer that he did not believe her.

"Last night. When you got out of the bath. She didn't see you there at first, hiding in the steam." She punched at his arm casually in the manner of a hot-springs geisha of many more years. The gesture seemed practiced and false. "How long were you watching us?"

"I wasn't watching you."

"No? Why not?"

The youth poured more sake. "How much does it cost to buy a contract?"

"Hers or mine?"

"In general."

"Too much for you."

"How much for a rich man?" He thought about the money in the dead hunter's wallet, and about the packet the bearded man had buried in the woods.

"I don't know. I've never seen a rich man."

"Rich men have seen you." Yukiko was returning from the entryway. "What are you two talking about?"

The youth felt again the shock of hearing her voice. A low voice. In his mind he clutched it to him.

"Me," the tiny dancer said, and she slid off the stove. She touched the youth's arm and talked to him with an intimate tone, "I'm going upstairs." Then she gave an odd smile to Yukiko. "Be nice to him. He's going to buy my contract. He's a rich man, you know," and she walked out.

Alone now with Yukiko, the youth did not know what to say. He was afraid she might think he was attracted to the tiny dancer.

"You should make Ueda pay for the sake, you know." The girl sat back down at her former spot on the boarded platform with her feet on the earthen floor. Her legs were slightly apart and she rested one elbow casually across a knee with the soft underside of her wrist and her palm facing up. With her other hand she reached for her cup of cold sake. She sipped at it without looking at the youth, her face turned down in shadow, her hair a mask in the candleglow.

The youth stepped over with the vial of sake. The girl dipped her head briefly and stared with dark, quiet eyes into his. As she held out her cup, the light caught the edge of her outstretched arm.

Looking down, as if he cared more for how he poured, the youth watched the thin stream of sake, glistening in the candlelight, slip the short distance from his hand to hers.

❋

A commotion above drew the youth to the foot of the staircase. He came upon a man running hard down the stairs and slapping the walls with his palms for balance. The man overstepped and skidded down to the bottom with one leg straight and one bent behind him and the underside of an arm slapping on the stairs to stop his fall. The air rushed from him when he hit against the platform below. Hard behind him now appeared a tapper of lac carrying a short wooden club and taking the stairs as fast as he could with his lips pulled back, his eyes wide and staring harshly first at the flailing man and then at the dimly lit stairs. Other men behind him rushed out onto the landing at the top of the stairs.

The fallen man eyed the upstairs wildly and tried to rise, but he saw that the man with the club would be upon him and he thrust his bent arms up to shield his head. The tapper of lac leapt down the final stairs and swung the club with a cry and the club made a cracking noise on the defenses of the fallen man's arm. The man cried out and gripped the arm and began crawling backward in an odd scramble as the man with the club lunged at him again.

Others had now followed down the stairs yelling encouragement to kill, kill, kill the wounded man and yet another rushing down behind them sought to pass and lost his balance, knocking them all into a slide that crashed against the wooden lip of the entryway. The hunchbacked creature that had been hiding in the space below the ledge now began to shriek and wave its arms and push itself out of the way.

The transport agent Wakabayashi had rushed to the entryway and grabbed a pack frame that he swung jerkily back and forth in front of him. He stood near the fallen man yelling at the man with the club to stop. Someone grabbed the man from behind and the two of them struggled awkwardly at the entryway until a third in turn grabbed onto the pair and all three toppled against the wall. The apprentice pulled without effect at arms and legs that stuck out from the group and yelled at them to stop. One man had taken to kicking blindly and the youth, shouting to identify himself, tried to ward off the feet.

At last there came a stillness among the combatants. The man on the ground groaned over his arm. The man with the club eyed an opening. The men breathed heavily and their chests rose and fell.

Then, as if at a signal, both camps began to appeal to the apprentice innkeeper at once. There was much pointing and protestation. It seemed that the wounded man had accused the lacquer worker with the club of cheating.

The youth urged them to part. He turned to help the wounded man rise.

As he did so, something sprang by him and he saw it was the man with the club who now brought it sharply down on the unguarded head of the fallen man. It seemed only a half swing, and only from the forearm, but there was a loud crack and blood spilled out into the wounded man's hair even as the front of his head hit the floor.

The tapper of lac now stood back, his chest heaving, the club at his side, repeating his former charges of being wronged. He said he didn't have any quarrel with the others. He said repeatedly the other man had his due.

The youth tried to take the club away, but the man would not let it go. He pulled it back and saw there was blood and hair on the club, and he wiped these against the wall. Then he looked at the wall and at the club and there was blood on each.

Others now tended to the wounded man with great caution, even as they watched the club. They made ready to spring away if the tapper of lac lunged again. They saw that the club, once swung, had not respected the sensitivities of the crowd.

Much blood flowed from the wounded man's skull and clumps of hair matted in the wound. None among the guests offered cloth or clothing to stop the bleeding, and so they sat about with their hands in the air.

In a moment Matsuko appeared with a rag from the kitchen. The cloth was stained and crusted, and they laid it across the man's head. Soon the rag had darkened and filled with blood. She had only brought the one, and it was left against the wound.

Looking about, the youth saw the commotion had brought other guests to the entryway. The old samurai stood halfway down the stairs. Now he moved back off. Other guests, newly arrived, crowded at the edge of the platform. They looked at the fallen man strangely, as if he were of some other species. Some, not knowing the cause of it all, stood surprisingly near the man with the club.

The pox-faced hunter appeared at the back of the crowd, and the youth noticed that some of the guests edged away from him and looked back and forth furtively between the hunter and the youth. It had not taken long, he realized, for word of their confrontation in the snow to spread.

At the edge of the entry, Yukiko clutched her instrument against her. She, too, stared at the fallen man.

The tiny dancer stepped forward and placed the palm of her hand against the youth's shoulder and pushed with open fingers. "Don't take chances," she said. Her voice was scolding. She looked to Ueda. "He's buying my contract, you know."

The youth looked up at Ueda and then away toward where he had seen the pox-faced hunter and briefly thought to protest that he was not so rich, but he feared the protest might sound forced. He thought then to smile at the tiny dancer's notion, but that, too, seemed wrong, standing above the fallen man. He wore instead an odd expression that bore his doubt.

After a moment, the performers and the hunter and others began to drift back into the recesses of the inn. A few wayfarers remained around the fallen man and engaged in a debate. One thought the man should not have said anything.

"He had it coming," another agreed. "He was a fool."

"I didn't see any cheating. I'd have said so if I did."

"Well, you're a fool, too."

One among these suggested they put snow on the wound. The others looked at him as if he were crazy.

They spoke about the man largely in the past tense. The youth wondered if the man could hear them.

The dwarf had shuffled quietly forward and huddled about the man's feet. Its head hung down and its nose twitched as if to smell out death among the toes. The men saw the dwarf and shooed at it bitterly. It made a noise and hobbled backward a distance and sat once again in the frozen mud, rocking and holding its knees.

The youth looked upon the fallen man. He seemed set apart by his tragedy, even in the midst of others. His eyelids were half closed, but a line of white could be seen between them, and at times the bulge of the eyes jerked within. The youth wondered if scenes of some remorse might not be playing there.

The fallen man had soiled his trousers front and back. No one wanted to clean him. They pushed him farther to the side and placed his straw cloak over him to contain the smell. They left him like that until morning.

The youth hoped the man would live long enough for someone to take him away.

7

The youth stood beneath the morning sun at the foot of a black pine, its needles encased in snow. Through a gap in the snow cover he could just spot the twin trunks of the tree. In the gloom of the storm, he had seen the bearded man bury a packet wrapped in straw at the foot of that tree.

The youth looked about into the forest. All around the snow sparkled unbroken.

Leaving the inn that morning, the youth had been careful not to be seen. He had waited until the pox-faced hunter had gone off to the toilet, and checked several times to be sure no one followed. He had circled around a knoll and come back upon his own tracks, but he saw no one. He had passed through a basin and gone beyond and then, crouching back to the crest, peered back over the rise. At last, still uneasy, he had regained the trail broken the day before while recovering the dead hunter.

But soon he had come to recognize his precautions of the morning as insufficient, for he realized with a start that no one had to follow him from the inn, they could simply await him along the trail he must retrace. He saw that all of his stratagems had only served to leave markings in the snow that others might read as indications of his secretive intent. And, as he had drawn farther from the inn and remembered the snow-filled mouth of the dead hunter and the eyes caked with frozen snow, his spirits sank. He had progressed fretfully, peering around the trunks of the forest ahead, and the way had become strange anew beneath a heavy sun.

Now, the youth knelt down at the edge of the black pine, and snow rode up over his thighs. He bent so close to the surface he could see the scouring of the wind in the clear morning shadows. He reached with gloved hands into the drift before him and dug with long, swimming motions of his arms. He dug deeply, and soon he was half hidden in the snow.

The youth withdrew his hand sharply from the snow. Well below the surface, he saw the edge of a straw wrapping.

The youth drew from the hole a packet and held it up before him against the sky. The packet, bound with doubled cord, was of plain straw. It was thick, but of little weight. He opened it.

A lacquer box fell out into his hand. The surface of the box was a glistening black. He could not judge its age. Engraved in gold on the top was a small man, hopping in the air. His naked belly was swollen with fat and hung low, bulging out above his sash. He wore a smile that hid his eyes.

The youth opened the box. Inside was a block of plain wormwood, nothing more. He saw no gold within. The youth removed the block carefully and turned it around in his hands. The wormwood was also light, and perhaps it, too, was a box, for it seemed hollow and there were lines around the edges that looked like joints. When the youth shook it he thought he felt something move within the heart of it, but he could find no opening, nor pull the halves apart.

He held the wormwood to the light and pulled at it again and held it to the light once more. He studied the patterns of the sightless creatures that had lived and died and all unknowing etched within their crooked paths the full and hollow measure of their being, and although he could find some small beauty there, he could read no meaning in it. He briefly contemplated the distant sky and then he blew on his fingers and pulled at the wood once again. He thought about smashing the block open against the tree.

The youth stood up in the snow hole and looked about, wondering what to do. It was risky, he knew, to return to the inn with the packet. It occurred to him to hide it, to give himself time. If the bearded man came back, the youth could make him prove he had not stolen it. If, more likely, he were dead, the youth could keep his secret from those who had hunted him. The box might yet be opened. There would be time enough then to decide.

The youth climbed out of the hole and began to wander in the direction the bearded man had gone during the storm. He tapped the packet against his chin as he walked.

Listening to the sound of the snow beneath his snowshoes, the youth walked up the hillside, moving farther and farther from the areas he knew. In time he dropped into a barren hollow where he had never been, and he sank to his chest in drifts that seemed bottomless. Struggling, he paddled with his arms and pulled himself to the base of a slope and then surmounted it.

At noon he entered into a tumular field of snow-enshrouded conifers that he could not name. In the silence of the snow he heard the sounds of his own breathing. Head bowed to the snow gleam just beyond his step, he trod as a postulant between the buried tree tops. There were some that did not reach his waist and some that loomed over him. A large, black-eyed bird at the top of one watched him jerkily and jerkily exposed obsidian wings that it twitched, gleaming and rasping at its perch, while its neck stretched taut and its beak worked open without a sound. Clumps of snow broke loose beneath its claws and cascaded down the snow cover, exposing there thin arrays of needles with white-ribbed keels that clenched the snow like exposed bone.

The youth moved on through still barrows, ranged and hushed all around. He stole between them with quick glances to either side and a sense of foreboding of what lay hidden, secret, entombed within. He passed with the blinding gleam before him always un-broken, and the snow-bleached copse all around him still, and sev-eral times he turned quickly and looked along the trail behind, afraid of what he might see.

When at last he left this place, the land ascended once again and he climbed steeply to the spine of a ridge. Beyond there lay an open field with the feel of a false summit.

And in the middle of that field, suspended in a sea of dancing snow so bright he could not look upon it, rose the snow-covered roof of a shrine.

❈

A blanket of snow lay thick upon the shrine, and the white of its roof shone stark against the deep-colored sky. One edge of the building seemed to have collapsed, and the snow there reflected the sunlight straight back at the youth so that he had to shield his eyes with one hand. He looked through his fingers as if to confront some great heat.

The night before, one of the wayfarers had spoken of a shrine on the mountainside above the inn. In the telling there had been something mysterious about the shrine, but the youth could not remember exactly what it was, and he could not be sure if this was the shrine that the guest had spoken of.

The youth peered into the forest around him. The thin shadows of the barren tree trunks rose and fell in long, gray, undulating stripes across the whiteness of the snow. There was neither movement nor sound.

He kicked lightly at the snow in front of him. He listened to the snow fall back upon snow, and he watched as some rolled to a stop with the thin trails of comets. Then he set out quietly toward the shrine.

Crossing the open rise, the youth could no longer see far into the forest, and he could not yet peer into the blackened void below the eaves. Long, uneven icicles, bared and glistening, hung at the edge of the darkness like part of some great open jaw biting down at the earth.

Drawing close, the youth saw no place to enter, and he stopped and circled uneasily partway around as a man might keep his distance from a dreaded thing. To one side the snow wall had collapsed, taking the shutters inward. In the shadows of the dark interior could be seen a pale talus of snow. Aquamarine fissures lined the broken snow above.

The youth saw no better entrance, and he stepped to the edge and over. He slid from the surface in a cloud of powdered snow down below the eaves into the shadows until at the very end his feet slid out and he landed hard on the floor of the shrine. He sat up sightless in the darkened interior, waving his arms before him like some instinctive creature, waiting for his snowblindness to clear. The room had a wet, rotting smell to it. There was no sound but the echo of his fall.

In time he could see a little, just beyond his reach. He stood and took half steps forward into the interior, walking awkwardly, his arms outstretched before his weakened eyes. The floor creaked loudly with each step. The stench grew stronger.

Something cold and sticky attached itself to his face and he swatted at the air in a panic and bent to the side. Lines of cobwebs filled the length of his arm. He crouched on the floor of the shrine wiping his hands around his neck and head much as some ancient priest performing a dry and antique rite of ablution. When next he stood, he raised his arm above his head and swung it down before him so that he moved in the manner more of marionette than of man.

He half-saw a movement farther within the shrine and his heart beat fast, but there was only silence. Stepping closer, he saw a mirror, encrusted with years, and from it he could raise only a tattered image of pieces of himself. On the wall above were faded writings, indecipherable, sketched by an ancient hand. To the side hung two thick ropes that reached halfway to the floor. Twisted in the hemp were bits of yellowed paper with forgotten prayers. Soot clung in the folds.

The youth traced his way back toward the light at the edge of the room. At the very edge of the shrine near the talus, the youth pulled from his clothing the straw parcel. He could feel the box inside. He leaned out into the snow and shoved the parcel below the wooden floor of the structure. He reached well in and pushed the parcel beyond his fingertips. When, a few seconds later, he groped with his hand in the darkness below the platform, he could no longer find the box.

As he rose and stepped away, his foot brushed against a small wire cage. He bent over it. Two dead grasshoppers lay within. They had faded to the color of dust. One was on its side, its legs drawn in. The other rested upright beside it. It could have been praying over a fallen comrade, or eating it. Oddly, the door to the tiny cage was open. The youth blew on the bodies softly, but they did not move. He blew harder, and the torsos tumbled apart, leaving some legs stuck to the floor of the cage as if the bodies rested upon them still.

The youth climbed out of the shrine to the surface. There he stood blinded and blinking with narrowed eyes against the light.

The glare hurt his head. He batted at the snow that had gathered on him in his climb.

A voice called out to him from the shrine.

The youth turned quickly and stared painfully into the light and shadows but he could see nothing.

A voice called out again.

The youth shielded his eyes, but he could still see nothing. He answered to the shrine and waited. He saw a flash of light within.

A man wearing glasses appeared in the recesses of a small upstairs window. It had been a reflection of the snow flashing in the man's glasses that the youth had first seen. Even now only the man's head was visible. The forehead was shaved in the old style.

"Surprised?" the man said, much amused.

The youth wondered if the man had seen him hide the box beneath the floorboards of the shrine.

"Spring again," the old man said from his perch at the window. He looked about, and his eyes settled on the eaves above him. Snow and icicles were melting there, and the wet underside sparkled in refractions of the sunlight. As they watched, beads of water fell from the eaves into the shade beneath.

"Or maybe just an illusion," the old man said, "from the sun." He dropped his eyes, and his gaze fell not far from where the box lay hidden.

The youth was careful not to look down toward the box.

"Look," the man pointed off into the snow.

Yards from the edge of the building there was the slightest variation where something might have been buried in the snow.

"I've neglected them," the man said.

"Neglected what?"

"The dwarf trees, the dwarf trees," the man said. "I'll have to clean the snow off them soon, or the branches may never recover." The man looked over at the youth. His glasses reflected the sun once again. "Maybe you'd like to help?"

"But I am late already," the youth said, and he bade the man farewell quickly and started back to cross the clearing into the woods from which he had come.

"You could have invited your friends to join you," the man called after him.

The youth stopped and looked up at the man and then followed his gaze into the woods. From where he stood, the youth could see nothing. He shaded his eyes and moved his upper body quickly side to side in an effort to see around the tree trunks. Still he saw nothing. He looked back up where the man's head stuck out of the window.

"Can you see someone there?" the youth called up to the man.

"Yes." The man shoved his neck and chin out farther and moved his head jerkily to the left and right, staring off into the forest. "Well, I thought I did," he said, his chin still poking awkwardly into the air. His face brightened. "I see tracks. I'm pretty sure I see tracks."

The youth turned about and left the shrine across the clearing in the opposite direction. He left without looking over at where the box lay.

"Come back," the man in the window yelled twice at the youth's back. It might have been an invitation or a command.

❄

The youth fled from the clearing around the shrine and plunged through the edge of the forest. He looked back over his shoulder repeatedly with his mouth hanging open. His cloak flapped off his shoulder and beat at his sides as he ran, and his hat bounced about his head and slid repeatedly to the side or down over his eyes. The clouds of his breath boiled up around his face, blurring his view through the trees. In his rush he broke off small branches barring his way, and to his ears these cracked with the noise of drumbeats. His snowshoes creaked and pounded, and all of these sounds drowned in the roar of his own breathing.

In his flight he looked at his telltale trail through the snow with alarm. He struggled to form a plan.

Surely if someone has followed me, he thought, surely they'll stop to search the shrine. He knew that would take some time. He could count on some delay.

But in the very next instant he realized that the man with the glasses had claimed to see more than one man hiding in the grove. If they divided, some of them might even then be gaining on him.

His legs felt the exertion already.

The youth saw now that he had been on a fool's errand, and this tired him further. He knew he had stayed too long in the shrine. Thinking back, he realized that the hole he dug searching for the packet would tell a plain tale. Having once uncovered the box, he could not now so readily rid himself of it.

He saw, too, that the box was of no importance to him. He had learned nothing from it, yet he had endangered himself to seek an explanation of events in which he had no place. His conduct seemed to him idiotic, even wrongful, and his pursuers just in their cause.

He resolved that if he were caught by the men who had hidden near the shrine he would tell them readily about the box. He could say he was headed now for someone to tell, that he was glad he had stumbled upon them. But he had no faith in his ability to carry off this tale, and no faith in the goodwill of these men. Better, he knew, not to be caught.

As he ran, the rush of air or his remonstrances brought tears to his eyes, so that the imperfections of his vision further complicated his course. His feet at times became tangled in the snow.

He glanced back at his trail again. He willed it to disappear. He considered plans to double back on it or to leap to the side or climb a tree and drop down again from the far limbs, but he discarded each of these plans in turn, for each would take time, and he knew his pursuers would soon see that his old trail had ended, and his new one would always betray him.

He came to see his own demise. He had never thought that this deserted forest might be the place of his death. His passing alone in such a place seemed somehow more tragic, and his folly all the greater. Fear and anger spurred his pace.

A large bird lifted from a pine to the youth's side and startled him. It flew on ahead. The youth sought in its flight some sign of whether he was being followed. He bitterly compared its speed to his own. It left no telltale trail through the air. He saw that he was not meant to be caught in the coils of this chase, that only his own errors had brought him to this state.

Desperate to increase his speed, the youth turned more downhill, although he knew from games as a child that it would be dangerous to be spotted on the downward slope by others who could close on him from above. He began a controlled slide, and trees around him passed in streaks. A plume of snow filled his face. He lost his balance and toppled, and for a while he let himself go, holding his snowshoes high so they would not be damaged, before his arms reached out to slow his fall.

When he stood again, covered in snow, he glanced quickly back up the slope. No one appeared on the rim above.

In his failure to spot his pursuers, the youth found proof of their stealth and skill. His legs ached. Sweat had formed underneath his headgear and his forehead itched there. He stopped to rub at it hurriedly and wiped with the back of his glove at his nose.

The trees around the youth stood motionless and straight. It took an effort for him to move on again.

The youth began to achieve some focus in the midst of his flight. A kind of plan began to form. He saw now that he had been wrong before to take a solitary course, avoiding all chance of encounters. He had been afraid to meet others when he had the box, but he had also made it too easy for others to follow him. He needed instead to merge his trail with that of others. This would confound his pursuers. He needed to be closer to people. There would be some added safety there.

If he dropped farther down the mountainside, he thought, he would run into tracks from the villagers. If he could find a path from the village to the north, his trail could be hidden within it. He could leave the path later on, perhaps even in the tracks of someone else, and his pursuers could not be sure whether they were still following him.

There was danger, he knew, in dropping down closer to the village. He had heard there were strangers in the forest. But, he thought, they would not know to trouble him, for there had not been time for his pursuers to spread the word that he had recovered the box. And he could keep an eye out for any others in the forest. He would have a better chance of spotting them than he would of shaking off his own tracks through the snow.

He dropped down off the ridge.

While he formed his plan, the youth had grown momentarily calmer, but his doubts soon took a different turn. He grew fearful for his legs and snowshoes. If he twisted an ankle or broke a strap, he would be easily caught, but if he slowed his way to reduce these risks, he might also be overtaken. His legs had grown tired, and being tired, the risks of falling increased. There seemed no simple course between speed and safety.

At the back of his mind tugged the sense that there must be something easier that would spare him, something he had forgotten, some answer that perversely hid itself from him in his peril. But it eluded him still. If only he could stop to rest, he thought, it would come to him. But he vaguely realized that this thought, too, was a trap. He knew he could not stop until he found a way to disguise his path.

❋

Stepping over the edge, the youth picked his way down the side of a gorge where the snow had slid off in large chunks, and stunted trees, twisted and tortured, clung along the face. There were places so steep that the tanned tops of long grasses rose thinly through the snow. At the bottom of the hollow was a talus of snow too deep for wading, and it forced the youth to sidle along the edge of the slope at an angle. His ankles ached and he worried about the bindings of his snowshoes and grabbed at the branches of the stunted trees for balance.

He saw above, at the rim, the remnants of a hut torn and carried forward by the drifts and tilted out over the void. Its walls were aslant and one gone altogether, and on the roof only bits of thatch remained. Between the twisted boards were gaps as wide as his forearm and he could see through them to the snow and the deepest color of the sky. In the hollow of the hut air could be heard, although nothing moved therein.

Soon he saw ahead a line of smoke. It rose like a rope, thin and gray against the sky. He debated turning and climbing out, but he had dropped too low, and it would take too long to retrace his way.

He moved on, and as he drew nearer the smoke there were no more grasses, but only the ragged ends and trees stripped of limbs. Ahead and halfway up the slope, the youth saw a man hacking at the sole branch of a tree that showed through the snow. The man was covered in chunks of snow and wore a dark, wadded cloth around his head. He stopped when he saw the youth approaching and held the thin blade away from the tree. He watched while the youth walked just below him and nodded when the youth nodded toward him, and long after he had passed, watched the youth still.

Now the apprentice approached from below a frozen overhang of snow, twice his height and wider yet, and the smoke rose from the blackness of a cave beneath. He saw two frames of bark hung at the opening. Of the bark doors one was pulled back and one askew, and a soot-darkened child stood in the mouth and watched him silently. The child wore a formless shift of grasses and its hair

strayed around its face. Its dark eyes watched the youth but its head
did not move. In the snow below the cave were long, dotted streams
of yellow urine and some turds that had rolled down and lay partly
covered in snow.

The child watched the youth pick his way around the refuse. In
the shadows of the cave above the child, the youth could make out
something dark hanging from a rack. Just as he passed below the
cave's mouth, the youth saw the broad head of an adult peer over
the edge at him and then a hand yanked the child back inside. There
was a yell and then a child's cry and the open bark door swung
down and closed the cave from sight.

When the gorge had played out, the youth came across a clearing. In its midst lay a half-beaten snow path headed north.

The path looked as if only a half dozen people might have passed.
And yet it would be enough. It would serve to disguise his tracks.

He placed his snowshoes in the path and looked behind him
again. He knew he would need to reach the forest at the edge of
the clearing. Once out of sight, he could leave the trail somewhere
ahead.

So near to the success of his plan, he felt a great need to hurry.

He passed into a grove of fir. He was lower on the mountainside
now, and he watched closely for signs of the men in the forests
about whom he had heard, but there were none. At one point, he
thought he heard a distant shout, but it did not sound again. Indeed,
he could not be sure it had been a cry at all.

In time he came to a place where the snow path traced the edge
of a slope. He paused and looked about. Then he jumped as best he
could and landed partway down the rise. He traced along the bottom to a point where he doubted his tracks could be seen from the
trail above.

At the lip of a hollow far from the trail he heard a noise and
dropped to his chest in the snow. Behind him, through a break in
the trees, he saw two men.

The men were moving along the path single file with their heads down and their bodies oddly shortened in the deep snow and their arms long and ape-like. They did not seem to speak. They wore the common cloaks of villagers but one wore nothing about his head and one the stretched skin of an animal.

The youth watched them through the branches of a beech and waited while they approached the spot where he had left the trail. He gauged their angle to the tracks he had left and judged they could not yet see him.

He looked at the branches of a dwarf cedar near his head that held clumps of snow out into the void like an offering, and he hoped for the men to pass.

In a few more moments, their square backs had passed from view.

The youth had a general sense of where he was on the mountainside. He thought for a moment about the route he should take and waited longer to be sure the two men on the path did not double back. Then, brushing the snow from his chest, he rose to go.

When he stood, he heard a shout from the hollow below. There at the far side of the field at the edge of a rise stood a man. The man held a spear against the pale sky, pointing in the direction of the youth and bidding to others, unseen, behind.

❋

The man with the spear at the far edge of the field turned almost casually about. Those to whom he shouted lay still unseen. When the man turned back, the youth realized that he was not looking at the youth, but at something to the side.

There, in the midst of the field below, a solitary red deer struggled, caught in deep snow.

The deer pitched itself forward. Its thin legs pushed at the snow beneath it like water. But for all its effort the deer moved but a foot and then lay still with the snow lapping up around its body and holding up its chin. After a moment the deer shook from side to side, and, bending its body, lurched itself forward another few inches and lay panting once again.

Coming slowly through the trees at the far side of the clearing below were two more hunters. They bore spears and heavy packs and they followed the snow trail of the deer and called to it like some lost friend.

The deer turned its head as far as it could to either side as if it could not get a clear view of the creatures approaching from behind. Then it shook and tried to leap again. When it lay still once more, its face, tilted upward by the snow, seemed to beseech the sky.

The hunters did not change their pace. As they drew near, two of them set down their packs and began to search inside them. The third plodded on until his snowshoes almost touched the animal. He stood talking to it in tones too soft for the apprentice to decipher. At length he walked around to the deer's head and, reaching into his pants, struggled for a moment and then pulled out his penis. He began to piss in the snow just in front of the deer's nostrils.

One of the hunters, looking up from his pack, shouted at the man not to piss near the throat.

Still holding himself, the man plodded around to the back of the deer and squatted down close to the snow. The deer twisted its head to each side to see him and then bucked forward a few inches. When the deer lay still once again, the man pressed his free hand against its haunches. A soft steam rose around its sides.

The man called out to the others that the deer was warm. He asked if they should fuck the deer.

The other two men spoke to each other over their packs. One said something that the youth could not hear.

"It can't kick when it's dead," the man by the deer called back to the other two.

All three men gathered at the head of the deer. Their backs hid its head from the apprentice's view. One of the hunters now held a knife and he moved to the side and lay across the deer's neck. The deer cried out for the first time in a low, guttural call. The rear of the animal shook violently.

When the man rose from the deer, the three men stepped slowly to the side and watched a red stain spread in the snow close to the deer's head. Steam from its blood rose off the snow around its neck.

The men broke into an argument, the details of which the apprentice could not discern. The youth could see the death-glazed eyes of the deer.

The man who had pissed walked around behind the deer again.

The youth pushed himself back, watching the men. When he was well out of their line of sight, he stood and moved away.

❀

Pausing at the front of a ridge, the youth could see smoke from the inn. The sun had slipped beneath the earth and thin clouds held the orange of its passing.

He looked about into the forest and ruminated on his chances. On the open mountainside his path had been unpredictable to most, but in the end he must return to the inn. There lay his greatest danger.

Then, too, he knew that once again the girl who had worn the cloak of yellow fur was near. He wondered if she might be thinking of him. She would not have known that he would be gone so long. She might have found excuses to wander about the inn, hoping to run into him, growing more perplexed that he was not there.

In his mind he saw her again on the step in the kitchen as she was the night before when he had poured sake for her. He saw the light on the hair of her arm and the darkness of her eyes and the slant of her eyebrows as she looked up at him. He felt again the sudden rush of blood in his chest and arms.

It struck him as odd that he could see so clearly the eyes of the girl at the step and the slant of her eyebrows, but that he could not conjure up the rest of her face. Hard as he tried, it eluded him. Rather, what he saw was not truly her face, but the features of others that he constructed there. And even though they were beautiful to him, he knew they were not hers. He felt a touch of sadness. A touch of eagerness, too.

He grew aware that the sky pressed down darkly on the redness in the west, and the orange of a high cloud had passed to a deepening gray. A single bat flashed quickly into the gloom to the right and then jerked suddenly downward and farther right and disappeared into the forest. In a moment the youth saw others, following. He felt a growing chill in the air and in the silhouettes of the barren tree tops. He sank down off the crest.

The snow on the far side of the slope, moistened during the day by the warmth of the sunlight, had already begun to freeze. The surface resisted and then cracked under his snowshoes, but the snow beneath was still soft and light. He slid unexpectedly down a steep grade and fell to his hip toward the bottom to slow his fall. Rising, he saw that the trees around him now were gray as shadows against the snow's dull light.

When he could see through the trees the darkened sides of the inn against the snow, he also saw a man. The man stood still in the forest and made no sign of having seen him.

The youth slowed. He tried to skirt the man quietly, using the trunks of the trees and the growing darkness.

The man was standing in the clear with bowed head, his back to the youth. He held his hands down around his waist. His body was motionless.

As the youth approached, the man lifted his head and one arm, rigid, as if to touch the heavens.

The curved tip of a bow appeared. The youth ducked down near the snow and looked to the nearest tree, but the man seemed still unaware of the youth and lowered his bow off toward the hillside beyond. He held the bent bow level, his lead arm still rigid, his draw hand anchored at his throat. The youth shifted slightly in the snow, but he could not see the target.

The man stood immobile as the trees in the graying light, the bow drawn full and nearly invisible against the snow. Time passed.

At length, the man lowered the bow and stood at rest, his head tilted down once again. He turned sideways to the youth and adjusted his feet with care. He looked off into the slope the youth had just traversed. The youth saw now that it was a guest from the inn, the one whom Matsuko called the old samurai, but as far as the youth could tell, there was no arrow in the bow.

The youth stood slowly. He was afraid to startle the man, and so he called out. The old samurai twisted his head sharply about before he saw the youth.

The youth approached. He looked, to be certain that there was no arrow in the bow, and he bid the old man a welcome and the old man bid him one in return.

"Is it easier without the arrow?" the youth said as he drew near.

The old man smiled and blew on the fingers of his draw hand. "It's more accurate."

"What were you aiming at?" The youth looked off into the hillside.

The old man shrugged. In the dying light, his face was difficult to read.

Soon the youth had gained the edge of the clearing behind the inn. He could hear guests through an open window and see a pale square of candlelight cut into the darkened wood walls. Music played, and he knew it must be the girl who had worn the cloak of yellow fur. He picked up his pace.

As he neared, the head of the tiny dancer appeared in the window, looking out into the dusk.

She saw the youth and yelled to him. Waving broadly from the shoulder, the sleeve of her cloak fell down around her arm. "Well," she called out into the room behind her, her head wagging and her voice slightly slurred, "it's the innkeeper returned." She waved again and reached hurriedly to catch herself on the windowsill.

The playing stopped and other heads appeared in the window. He dimly saw the head of the girl Yukiko who had worn the yellow fur. She was looking out at him, too.

"Where have you been?" the tiny dancer called out loudly, so loudly that the youth grew fearful that her calls would alert the hillside, and although he was not so far away, he hurried closer still. She had leaned far out of the window and called with a plaintive tone as if they had long been friends, and he wondered what the girl Yukiko might think.

Drawing closer, the youth could see the tiny dancer's breath in the dim light of the window. She rocked forward with her stomach over the edge of the windowsill, and one of the men behind her grabbed at her clothes to be sure she would not fall out. Her head, hanging down, swayed at the end of her neck.

"Hurry up," she yelled loudly, picking up her head again. "There are only stiffs in here." She slapped at the hand that held her back and squealed shrilly. The man laughed. It was the dealer in winter cloth.

The youth guessed that they had been drinking for some time. He was afraid Matsuko would be angry that he had been gone so long.

Nearer now, the youth saw Yukiko. She was looking at him. Then her head disappeared. He waved to the guests remaining at the window and hurried around the corner of the inn.

When the youth turned the corner to the side of the inn he was hit fiercely in the stomach so that the breath rushed in a gasp from his lungs and he collapsed to his knees, staring stupidly at the bluegray snow. He was hit again, hard across the base of his neck, and his vision scrambled. He started to topple and someone forced a sack over his head. Then he was pushed and something smashed across the side of his face and spun him around and he sprawled out on his back in the snow. A great weight held him down and he could see only a vague quilt of light through the coarse sack lying close across his face. A hand gripped his throat. Hands felt along his clothing.

"Where is it?" There was a deep rasping voice that the youth did not recognize.

A hand smashed the youth's nose and lips through the sack. His eyes filled with tears and he could taste blood and he was maddened because he could not see if he was about to be hit again.

"Where is it?"

The youth felt panic rising in him and blood choking him and he coughed into the sack, the blood and phlegm falling back on his face or stretching between himself and the mesh. He tried to speak, although he could not tell if he had the air to be heard, and he shook his head as best he could from side to side in denial and stupidity and self-pity and tried to say he did not know.

He was hit hard near the bottom of his rib cage and he screwed up his legs and tried to force himself to breathe but the pain there was too large to breathe around. It pushed up into his lungs, and he could not move. He was suffocating, and there was not even air to cough to clear the blood that gagged him.

"Where? Where?" The same voice, higher, more insistent than at first.

The youth felt a hand grip his groin and his eyes opened wide within the sack and the hand squeezed hard and jabbed inward and the youth called airlessly in pain.

"Where?"

Through the desperate need for air, the youth tried to think of what the men would do to him next. He imagined the hand on his groin crushing downward. The hand lifted and the youth tried to drag his legs upward to protect himself, but something smashed down into his stomach that jarred him all the way to his back and he was hit almost at the same time along his cheekbone. There was a distant scream, not his, and then he was hit again and his head crashed with white light. He felt himself slipping away. The sack was blurred and wet and seemed far from his nose. As if from a distance, he heard running steps in the snow crust.

In a moment he realized he was on his side, coughing, and drinking air again.

8

The youth struggled with the hood as a man fighting demons. When at last he had cast it off, his face ran with sweat and he sucked painfully at the air.

Two men in straw cloaks and sedge hats were running away from him around the corner of the inn. To the youth, propped up in the snow, they seemed even farther away. Turning his head, the youth saw the old samurai approaching through the dusk with an odd, duck-toed gait. He hooted like a younger man at the backs of the two who fled, and he shook his empty bow in the air.

The old samurai seemed much amused. He looked down at the youth and said something the youth could not make out.

The youth, slumped forward in the snow, wanted nothing more than to breathe easily. His throat felt swollen. He tried to spit blood, but it mostly ran down his chin. He shook his head to the old samurai as softly as he could so it would not hurt. Large clumps of snow filled his lap. He stared at them dully.

The old samurai was smiling. He extended his hand. "Arise, you are reborn."

The youth could only look at the hand.

Just then they heard a muffled scream from around the front of the inn. The old samurai rushed toward the corner. The youth rose unsteadily and stumbled after him. His head hurt as he tried to run.

As the youth reached the corner, he heard a second, hollow cry. It seemed to come from the snow beneath them.

They stepped to the edge of the snow wall. There, a dozen feet below, wedged between the snow wall and the wooden snow blinds of the inn, were the two girl performers. The girl Yukiko was on her back in the snow, her black hair spread about her. The tiny dancer squatted over her in the dim lamplight from the inn. Stopping suddenly and bending to look down at them, the youth felt dizzy.

"Yukiko. Yukiko." The tiny dancer tugged at the girl's leg.

Yukiko did not move or answer.

"Is she all right?" the youth called down, and at once felt foolish for asking.

The tiny dancer craned her neck to look up at them and lost her balance. "They pushed her." Her voice was high-pitched and shrill.

The youth lowered himself carefully down the steps cut into the snow wall. A deeper gloom descended upon him, and his vision did not seem quite right. The old samurai's upper body appeared in silhouette against the dark sky above and then disappeared again. The youth hoped he would keep watch after the two men.

The tiny dancer had bent back over Yukiko and gripped her by the hand. "We were coming out to see you," she said to the youth without turning around. Her words were slurred. The youth realized that she was still slightly drunk.

The apprentice stood uncertainly. His head throbbed. Over the tiny dancer's shoulder he could see that Yukiko had not moved. Even in the faint light of the snow crevice, the girl's face seemed pale. Her eyes were closed. Clumps of snow had followed her fall and lay across her body.

"Help me get her out of here," the tiny dancer said, but she made no effort to get out of the way, and in the narrow crevice there was no room to get around her.

"Crawl over her," the youth said, although talking hurt his head. "I'll carry her feet."

Stepping around the girl Yukiko, one hand against the snow wall, the tiny dancer made her way unsteadily to the snow beside the girl's neck.

The youth lowered himself carefully and picked up Yukiko's ankles. He had trouble getting a grip and when he tried to lift her she was heavier than he expected, and the footing in the crevice was uneven. He worked his grip to the back of her knees and although he was aware of holding her there, his head hurt him too much to take pleasure in it.

He tried to step back toward the inn, pulling the girl with him. The tiny dancer struggled under the weight of the shoulders, so that the curve of Yukiko's back dragged in the snow.

In small steps they made it to the edge of the wooden platform in the entryway and set the girl down with her head at an angle to her neck and her arms askew. One leg fell back down onto the earthen floor.

The hunched dwarf came out of the shadows to sniff at the fallen foot and squatted there with dark eyes.

The youth sat. His head hurt in a way that disrupted his vision. He wanted to think about the men who had attacked him and what it might mean, but he felt nauseated and he had trouble focusing his thoughts. He could not remember clearly the order in which things had happened.

"Yukiko, Yukiko," the tiny dancer shook the girl harshly.

There was no response.

"Yukiko, it's me," the tiny dancer shook her again. The girl Yukiko's head lolled to the side and rested on one cheek. The wooden floorboard pushed the skin of her cheek up around the nose and deformed the open lips.

"Maybe she just needs to rest," the youth said. He gripped his scalp. He tried again to think through what the attack on him might mean.

"We need to warm her. She'll start shivering."

"She's not shivering now."

The tiny dancer shook her head and her head kept wagging after it should have stopped.

"She just needs rest," the youth said.

"The bath," the tiny dancer said, as if to herself, and then to him, "The bath. Help me."

The youth had stretched out on the boards on his side. His vision was still not right. He knew the girl would be heavy, but he did not want to argue so he stood and took Yukiko's shoulders, and they carried her into the inn. He held her under the armpits with his forearms clasped over her upper chest and her hair pressing against his chin. He could smell in her hair smoke and tobacco and sulfur from the hot spring.

The tiny dancer called to one of the guests coming from the toilet. He joined them and helped with the feet. Even so, carrying the girl was awkward, and her arms hung limp and slapped from time to time against the wooden walls.

They set Yukiko down fully clothed at the edge of the bath. Water from the wooden floorboards ran up into her clothing. The steam from the hot spring rose beyond her.

Even after setting her down, the youth's arms shook and his neck and back hurt. He sat on the steps with his elbows on his knees and his hands hanging free. In the heat from the hot spring his undergarments stuck to him. He pulled them away from his skin.

Sprawled at the edge of the bath, Yukiko's face was turned away from him. The tiny dancer bent over her and struggled with a knot in the sash at the girl's waist. She bent her head down quickly and bit at it with her teeth. To the youth, it looked a little as if she were suddenly biting at the girl.

When the knot freed, the tiny dancer began to undress her.

The youth stood.

The tiny dancer spread the clothing away from Yukiko's stomach and, reaching forward, struggled with the wet fabric caught under her back. The sides of the garment that had been peeled off the girl darkened quickly with water and sank down into the floorboards with wrinkles like veins. In the center, Yukiko stretched out slim and pale.

The youth, breathing softly through his mouth, stepped closer.

"She's too heavy for me," the tiny dancer called over her shoulder. "Can you help?"

❀

Restless, the youth wandered stiffly to the main room. His body was sore, and he carried his head a little to the side.

Listening closely, the youth could just hear Yukiko playing for the guests in a room above. He wanted the music to stop. If she were busy playing for others, she would not be able to speak to him. Then again, he did not know what he would say to her.

"Can you help?" the tiny dancer had said earlier at the edge of the bath, and together they had finished removing Yukiko's clothes. He had held her slim white shoulders while her head hung down.

Strands of her hair, wet from the steam of the hot spring, had clung along the sides of her neck.

With a strain, the tiny dancer had pulled Yukiko's clothes from under her back and, suddenly freed, one arm had fallen to the floorboards. The back of the girl's wrist had smacked against the wood.

From behind her, where he supported her shoulders, the youth could see the pale skin of her upturned forearm and elbow. Her hand, palm upward, was slightly curled.

He was looking over the girl's shoulder, just past the tip of her breast. The skin of the nipple was dark and uneven. With the tiny dancer facing him, he tried to look only at the lines of the upturned palm.

The tiny dancer had untied Yukiko's padded mountain trousers and pulled them off. The girl's hips had lifted with the trousers and fallen back, her legs stretched out against the dark, wet wood of the floorboards. An undergarment, wet from the steam, pressed close around her and took on the pallor of her skin.

Yukiko's neck and face had a slight snow tan, but her shoulders and the rest of her looked all the more pale. It was a little as if the head and the body did not go together.

Now, lingering in the main room, the youth recalled that the girl had also seemed slimmer than he had thought, slimmer even than she had seemed to him two nights before when he had watched her stepping into the bath. It was not an angular slimness, but the slimness of a younger girl.

Was it, perhaps, her long, intent looks that had made her seem older? Or was it the illusion of a state like sleep that made her seem so young?

Then again, the downy hair on the back of her forearms had been thicker than he would have expected on a young girl. It was that way, too, at the back of her neck, just below the hairline.

When they had lowered her, feet first into the hot spring, that down-like hair had brushed against him. He had pressed the side of his face against her neck to steady her, and he felt her hair against his cheek as he let her go.

As he had watched her slip into the water, he had an urge to take her shoulder in his mouth.

The girl had made a small noise at the back of her throat when the water reached her breasts. She turned her head toward him and her eyes, already closed, tightened.

But later, when Yukiko came to herself, it seemed she did not even suspect he had held her.

At the tiny dancer's request, he had gone for hot tea, and when he returned he bent down to them from the edge of the bath. Reaching for the cup, Yukiko had kept the water up around her neck, and only her forearm broke the surface.

The youth had been forced to bend awkwardly to reach her.

"You needn't be so modest," the tiny dancer had said to her. "You don't think I undressed you by myself, do you?"

The girl's mouth had opened, and she had turned and splashed with her hand at the tiny dancer. "You. What have you done?" she said to the tiny dancer, and she splashed again, but to the youth it did not seem as if she were truly displeased. It was more as if she did not yet know how to look at him.

Some of the water she splashed had hit the youth as well, and when she turned back to him and said, "I'm sorry," the youth chose to refer to this instead. "It's all right," he had said, pretending to misunderstand, "I've been wet before."

He had wanted to hear her thank him again.

The girl had wrapped her free arm around herself under the water and sunk down until the water was just at her lower lip. She held the cup of tea above the water like a torch. "I mean I'm sorry for all the trouble we've caused you." She emphasized the "we" and glanced briefly at the tiny dancer.

"That's enough of being sorry," the tiny dancer said. "He didn't seem to mind."

And before the youth could protest, the girl Yukiko had looked up at him with wide, bright eyes.

He had not known then if he should still protest.

It was that bright look, more than anything else, that made him restless still. Even now, in the main room, he could see it before him.

But that look, too, had seemed more the look of a younger girl.

The youth heard a door slide open upstairs and footsteps on the staircase. He realized the music had stopped. Not knowing what else to do, he took up a pair of metal tongs and searched for coals in the ash of the firepit. Then, uneasy, he rose and, quite against his prior plans, stepped through the guests who were scattered around the firepit. He paused at the edge of the passageway at the far side of the main room.

He was suddenly unwilling that she should think he was waiting for her.

He left just as he could hear a pair of feet at the bottom of the landing. He stood in the shadows of the hallway around the corner from the main room and listened for her voice. He could hear Ueda working on the guests. He heard the tiny dancer, but the girl Yukiko did not speak. He stood there for a while, breathing through his mouth so he could hear better.

When after a while a guest with a towel stumbled around the corner and greeted him, the youth hurried along the corridor toward the bath. From behind him he could hear Ueda offering an entertainment. He heard at last the music of the girl Yukiko who had worn the cloak of yellow fur.

Once he reached the bath, he did not want to be caught there either. He looked at the empty spot where they had undressed the girl. The smell of sulfur hung heavily in the air.

On the far side of the bath, two men sat facing in the same direction, one behind the other. The one in the rear had a knife in his hand. He had lanced a boil on the first man's shoulder. The youth could see a trickle of blood on the man's back. The man in the rear was pressing with his fingers to bring out the pus. On the floor beside them was an overturned bucket that the man took up and filled and used to wash off the wound.

Above the two men on the wall of the hot spring was a faded sign. It read, "The Waters Of This Bath Cure All Known Ailments But Love."

❋

In the depth of that night, the youth stepped to the entrance of the main room a candle in his hand. Before him squatted a dozen guests, more resting on their haunches, lips apart, and among those wayfarers, all turned so their dark eyes were upon him, not a one moved before suddenly they erupted into laughter all. The youth turned quickly to look into the darkness behind him, and the way-farers hooted and shrieked and laughed harder still. When he faced them once again, he saw that they were laughing at him.

The youth opened his mouth to speak, but as nothing he could say would pierce the general uproar without the greatest effort, and as he was not sure what to shout, he closed his mouth again. The sight of his jaw flapping open and shut without effect set the group to point-ing and snorting and falling upon one another more hysterically yet.

He saw that Yukiko was among those laughing at him. Rocking uncontrollably, she had set down her instrument and covered her mouth with both hands. In the candlelight, her eyes glistened with tears.

The youth looked away, and was immediately confronted with the sight of Ueda in his black-and-white costume gripping his sides in pain, spittle dripping from the corners of his mouth, his face wet with tears. Ueda staggered forward and took the candle from the youth, his chest heaving so hard that hot wax tipped and spilt on the mats. With great concentration, Ueda then handed the youth a small purse of money in its stead.

When the youth took the purse and looked at it, the guests dou-bled over in new convulsions and pounded the floor and slapped each other on the shoulders and saliva came to the corners of their mouths and their noses ran with mucus that made their upper lips shine. The tiny dancer, next to Ueda, had fallen to her knees in a high-pitched fit and now, slipping farther, began to roll on the floor cackling and kicking the air.

In a moment one of the guests began to applaud, and then, as best they could while wiping at their eyes and crippled with the pain in their sides, they all began to applaud. Other guests, drawn by the noise, had slid open the doors to the room and, while not quite certain why, joined the applause as well. Even the girl Yukiko and Ueda had taken to applauding. Only the tiny dancer remained seized by hysteria, rolling on the floor and gasping for breath.

Eyes lowered to suppress a new round of laughter, Ueda bowed with mock respect to the youth and, turning his white side to him, motioned him to sit next to the girl Yukiko, who had already taken up her instrument and pick. She shifted a bit to make room for the youth next to her, although there was room enough already.

Other guests, still wiping the tears from their faces, nodded to the youth. The nearest touched him on the shoulder or pushed his head. They drew deep breaths to calm themselves and avoided one another's eyes.

When the youth looked up again he saw that Ueda and the tiny dancer had resumed the performance of a scene from a masque that, the youth soon realized, had been underway when he made his sudden appearance. In fact, in a moment the youth saw that the scene took place at an inn, and that he had appeared just when Ueda, playing the part of a guest, was about to make payment to Ueda, also playing the double role of innkeeper. It was the youth's appearance then that had set the guests laughing.

At a break in the music, Yukiko leaned close to the youth and apologized for their laughter. He felt her scent against him even before she spoke.

She looked into the space between them and said they weren't laughing at him. The youth looked at her in profile as a thing of wonder.

As she prepared to play once more, the girl shifted her instrument toward the others and moved her leg slightly so that it just rested against him. The touch was so slight he could not be sure if she were even aware of it. He strained to see her expression from the corner of his eye, but she was watching the masque intently, her fingers bent over the strings.

His leg where she touched him felt alive. It was as if he could feel her heat through their clothing. Keeping his eyes straight ahead, he wondered if others saw that they touched.

She began to play. She struck at the strings harshly, her upper body jerking with the effort, and when she did her leg pushed against his. He was afraid to move even slightly and afraid not to move at all. If he pressed closer, he might startle her, and he could not bear the thought of her pulling away, shocked. If he moved away, she might think he was angry at her for laughing, or worse, that he did not welcome her touch. If he remained as he was and she suddenly realized why, she might mock him.

Her leg warmed his whole side. The longer the touch continued, the more certain he felt that she had meant it, or, at least, wanted to touch him still. He might otherwise have risen and taken to his duties, but held by her touch, he stayed and pretended to concentrate on the masque.

It was an ordinary drama. Doomed lovers had come to an inn to take poison together. In the myths of that mountain region, it was said that two such lovers lived on in the heavens as stars.

Still thinking about the girl's touch, it was some time before the youth realized that the masque had taken an odd turn. Ueda, playing the male lover, had diluted the poison for himself. And the tiny dancer secretly spilt half of her portion into her palm. Not having seen what came before, the youth could not tell if each had plotted from the start to kill the other, or if they were truly lovers who, in the end, lacked trust in one another.

Playing loudly at the beginning of the final scene, the girl Yukiko's leg moved away from the youth's. He waited to see if it would come back, and when it did not, he shifted his leg slightly toward her, but she was no longer close enough to touch.

In the candlelight before him, Ueda and the tiny dancer pantomimed the passion of their final moments. They gripped each other and shook in mock orgasm. They slipped to their knees and made wide gestures of sorrow and eternal love. Then, with sly looks to the side, they each swallowed the half potions they had secretly diluted and waited with feigned devotion for the other to die. They grew sick, and then violently sick. The actors pantomimed vomiting and writhing on the floor. Then, sick as they were, each realized the other's betrayal. And, sick as they were, they crawled about the floor beating one another.

The youth sat straight up. The night before the tiny dancer had told him that Yukiko had half-poisoned Ueda, so that she could beat him while he was sick. He tried to remember just what the tiny dancer had said. Was she trying to tell him that Ueda and Yukiko were once lovers who attempted double suicide? Surely not. Perhaps the masque had given Yukiko the key to her revenge, or the revenge had given Ueda the idea for the masque; in either case, might the tiny dancer be offering this masque as further proof of what she had said?

Or, the youth realized, might the story she had told him about Yukiko and Ueda be just a lie? If so, she must have realized he might see the masque. Indeed, she may have suggested they perform this masque, no doubt one of many in their repertoire, tonight. It was as if she wanted him to see that much about the girl Yukiko was mere illusion, or as if she wanted to confuse the illusion Yukiko deserved.

Or perhaps the tiny dancer was just a liar, a stupid one who didn't bother to think about being caught, or a brazen one who enjoyed lying and the thought of being found out. Perhaps, more simply yet, she had just cast about for any story that would hold the youth's interest and win her the little extra sake that he had so willingly offered.

Before him, the tiny dancer, her face in shadow, rolled about the floor, kicking at Ueda. And Ueda kicked at her. She rolled closer to the candle flame, and her bloated shadow self obscured the far wall with vain and frantic strikes. She rolled away, and she was nothing.

❉

The apprentice awoke with a start. The room was cold and so black that he could not see.

His heart raced painfully within him. An unpleasant dream had come to him and, confused, he could not now be sure if he had dreamt or felt that something had bumped into him.

A hand pushed roughly on his side.

"Is it you?" a female voice whispered hoarsely.

He turned quickly toward the voice. He smelled smoke and sake.

"Is it you?" the voice whispered again.

The youth could see just the palest oval of a face hanging over him. The features, even the vague outline of the face, could not be distinguished in the blackness.

"Is it you?" a hand shook him roughly through the covers.

"Yukiko?"

"Ah, it's you." The girl now seemed to sit back and the pale faintness of the face moved away, shifting slowly from side to side. "I'm dizzy," she whispered, and the voice grew and faded as it seemed her head swayed. "Is there any water?"

The youth had come awake now. He could hear Matsuko snoring lightly across the room. He pushed himself up on his elbows. The smell of sake was stronger.

He whispered, "Matsuko's here."

The girl bent her face down almost to him and there was a small space in the darkness not as black as the rest. "I know," it was less than a whisper, almost a breath. "Careful."

He could not be sure if this last was a statement or a warning. The smell of sake was so strong he made a face in the dark.

"My hand hurts. It's too cold to keep playing. Here." Something small and pale was near his face. "Here." He felt a cold hand touch his forehead, then his chest, then his shoulder, then work its way down toward his hand. Then she took his hand and moved it to the pale glow before him. It was her other hand.

Her hands were ice cold. He could feel the callus from the hard bit of tortoise shell she used to pluck the instrument.

"Ah, your hand is warm," she whispered in a cracked voice. Her lips were only inches from his cheek. Her breath fell across his face. "I have to go back," she whispered, and he could see her pale unformed face recede again and turn to the side, but she did not take her hand from his.

The youth rolled to his side and placed his other hand over hers as well. She made a small pleasured sound. He groped in the dark for her other arm, but he could not find it. Instead, he brought his hand back and rubbed at her wrist. Her skin was so cold it chilled him.

There was a moment while they remained like that, but then his neck began to ache from holding himself up so long without his hands, and the pale, indistinct face swung back toward him.

The youth let himself lie back on his side and took her hand with him. He placed it inside the covers against his chest.

He had unbalanced her, and she began to topple into him. He could hear the rustle of her clothes and smell smoke and sake and her scent intermingled.

Her forearm landed painfully in his side. He giggled.

"Is it so warm in there?" she whispered, and he felt her wriggle free of him and lift the covers. Cold air rushed in along his side and then, fully clothed, she tried to slip underneath beside him. Her clothing was stiff and cold. She made a small noise in the top of her throat when the warmth began to cover her. They breathed quietly and moved the covers with as little noise as possible, but still they made a slithering sound in the dark.

She seemed to have trouble getting the covers over her feet, and he half sat up in the dark and helped her. The shifting covers made little gusts of wind as they fell back over them.

Almost as soon as they had settled together, facing each other invisibly in the dark, she whispered again that she had to go, but she did not rise. They lay there quite still, barely breathing in the blackness. He thought her eyes might be open, inches from his, but he could not tell. The silence in the room filled his ears. The faintest pale of light seemed to rise in the darkness at the edge of her face.

She moved her hand from his chest, and he felt an emptiness there. Her hand moved slowly to his shoulder, the covers barely moved. She found his hand and moved it to her throat and he heard her inhale. Her throat was as cold as the air. Lifting his body slightly, he slipped his other arm free and brought his other hand up against her throat as well.

Her hand left his, and he heard and felt her moving something between them. He could hear her breath. It came more quickly now. He felt her clothing move away from the heels of his hands and when he slid them slightly down he found only skin. He brought his hands slowly lower until the heels of his palms rested on the broadness of her chest.

He felt invisible there with her, in the darkness, under the covers, silent. Even if Matsuko awoke she would not know he was not alone.

The girl lay perfectly still. Only her chest rose and fell heavily with her breathing. He could feel her heart beneath his hands. He moved his hands slowly lower still and she arched her back to help him and her lower leg came against his. He held her breasts in his hands. Oddly, he thought, the lower one might be larger. He could hear his own heart.

The girl's upper body now rose slowly above him with only the small sound of the covers and for an instant he could see again the pale, featureless oval of her face and then strands of her smoke-filled hair fell cold across his cheek and her head came down with her lips on his neck. Even her lips felt cold and clean and she brought them up along his neck slowly to his ear.

One of her breasts now hung loosely in his hand near his face and he knew not how best to touch her. The sleeve of his other arm was pinned under his side, and this arm he could barely raise. He stretched to touch her with his fingertips, and as he did she slid one leg over him and kissed his ear. Her breath there was warm and moist and then she licked inside his ear. He was startled. He had never been touched like that before. The feeling at first was good, but then it was wet and cold and unpleasant. He could hear her breath just above his ear, but he could no longer see even the ghost of her. She bent down once more, and he lowered his head for the thought of being licked again disturbed him, and she misunderstood and pressed his head down below her throat.

He kissed her on the breadth of her chest. She held his head in her arm tightly and pulled painfully at his hair. He felt her head swaying above him. She moved her leg between his awkwardly and the covers made more noise, but he felt her against him now for the first time and he ached and he thought the noise would go unnoticed. He bent his head roughly to kiss her lower still, and her hold around his head tightened again and she pushed him against her chest so tightly that he could barely breathe.

Suddenly he felt her stiffen, and when he continued to move she squeezed her arm sharply around his head so that he held perfectly still, although his neck ached from the angle of his mouth and the dampness of his own breath against her was displeasing. She was listening. He could feel and hear her heart beating very fast, but she was as still as ice.

He heard footsteps on the stairs above them and the noise from the guests was louder, as if a door had been opened.

She remained still. His face inside her kimono was bathed in her warmth and the moisture of her skin. Her clothing and her skin smelt of her and of the sulfurous water of the bath. He felt he had to move his head slightly to ease the cramp in his neck, and her grip on him, which had loosened, tightened once again but not so painfully as before. Unwilling to show his discomfort, he kissed her softly as he moved so that she would think that was his purpose and he felt her body soften, but she remained frozen as she was, her head above him in the air.

Buried in her clothing, he knew he could not hear what she heard. He remained still. He felt her lowering her face slowly, and she kissed the top of his head. He could feel her heartbeat slowing, he could feel the moment slipping away. The air inside her clothing was stifling him.

"Yukiko." From the corridor came the deadened sound of Ueda calling.

A shaft of fear ran through the youth. He started to move, but she barely breathed the sound of "no" and lowered herself in the dark until she was pressing over him and held him down. As silently as she could, she pulled the covers up over her.

"Yukiko." The call was more insistent. He heard it through the walls and the covers and the girl's body and clothing as if at a great distance.

His arms pinned beneath her hurt, and the heat and dampness from his breath and her sweat made him feel as if he were suffocating. He tried to shift slightly and she squeezed him to be still.

He heard the door to the kitchen open roughly. There was a long silence. He heard the door close, but still the girl did not move. He could hear her breath faintly. He felt her arm muscle quivering near him under the covers, but outwardly she was perfectly still.

He heard Ueda hiss, "Yukiko," from what seemed very near. There was another silence. He heard a foot scuff on the floor. There was yet another small silence, and then the door to the kitchen sounded again. In a moment, as it was closing, he heard Ueda ask someone if they had seen the string player. He could not hear the answer.

The girl relaxed slowly. She pulled the covers back softly, and they lay apart. The cold air bathed him. He drew it deep inside his chest. Because the door was not quite closed, there was more light and he could see her fanning her open clothes against her chest. For the first time he realized the dampness had been unpleasant to her, as well.

Behind him, Matsuko breathed heavily as if in sleep. The youth and the girl looked toward each other, and they began to make short giggling sounds that they cut off quickly so that they sounded like snorts, but that would not stop, and so she leaned forward and put her fingers to his mouth to stop him, even though she was struggling with herself, too.

He wanted to kiss her fingers, but he did not, and in a moment she drew them away.

They listened to the corridor for a moment, and then quickly and quietly, lit from the side by the light of the door, she pulled her clothes together. To the youth watching her, they were movements of infinite sadness.

Strands of her hair hung forward and shielded her face from the light of the corridor. She swept them away.

For a moment the youth and the girl looked at each other without moving. Then the girl placed her hands on the wooden floorboards and rose awkwardly to go. Leaving him, she stumbled toward the light. She listened at the door before she slipped out.

Although he watched carefully, she did not look back.

The youth pulled the covers around him. He lay awake until close to dawn.

9

"Setsuo!"

The youth hurried toward the entry from the rear of the kitchen. He had heard the woman Matsuko call.

In search of the night before, the youth had lingered at the platform in the rear of the kitchen. He had looked at the spot where his bedding had been, and where the girl sat to straighten her clothing. Lowering himself to the floor, he had sniffed at the floorboards for her scent.

Earlier still, he had slowly put away his own bedding, inhaling through his nose for her as he gathered the sheets into his arms. As he closed the closet, he had hoped the smell of her would last until the sheets were laid out again at night. In the scent he could recapture for an instant the passing feelings of the night before.

"Setsuo, the assistant headman is here to see you." As Matsuko spoke, a middle-aged man stuck his long face around the corner. He bowed slightly toward the youth coming down the corridor. The man's lower lip hung down as if it had been pulled and never shrunk back into place.

"I'm sorry to disturb you," the face in the entryway said.

The youth had not met the assistant headman before. It was not usual for village officials to call at the inn, especially now, on the morning of the day when the winter theatricals would begin.

Confused at his presence, and confused at having been caught in the kitchen when he had other duties, the youth lapsed into silence and bowed. Behind the assistant headman, some guests, laden with belongings, were leaving. The youth bowed to them, too. He was glad to see that the man who had been clubbed was no longer by the entry. He wondered if the man had been taken off, or moved somewhere within.

Without asking, Matsuko took the youth and the official into the small room off the entryway where they could talk alone. She placed an oil lamp between them and then brought a thin tea for the assistant headman. While she moved about, the assistant headman apologized for never having had the time to come up to the inn to meet the youth before. He asked about the headman of the youth's home village, a man he somehow knew. Then he spoke about the snow.

"It's hard to have such a big storm just before the festivals," he said.

He was walleyed, and for a while it seemed to the youth that one eye was fixed on him, and then he would suddenly realize that, for no apparent reason, the other eye was watching him instead. Or perhaps not watching him at all, for in one position the assistant headman's eyes pointed at both the youth and the entryway behind him at the same time, and the youth could not be sure where the assistant headman's attention lay.

When Matsuko finally left, the assistant headman was looking down. His one eye seemed to watch steam rise off the tea. He said he was glad to see the inn had survived the storm so well.

The youth nodded and waited.

The assistant headman pulled a letter from his clothing and placed it on the floormats. "There's a letter for the old charcoal maker from Akiyama."

The youth nodded and bowed. It was one of the duties of the inn to deliver mail to some of the people who lived on the mountain ridges. The youth knew the old charcoal maker's hut, although he had never delivered a letter there before. For a brief moment he felt relieved, but then he knew the assistant headman had not come all the way to the inn for this letter.

At last the assistant headman glanced one eye at the bruises on the youth's head and asked if everything was all right with him.

"Yes."

"They say you were attacked yesterday afternoon."

"Yes. But this," the youth motioned his chin upward toward the bruises on his own forehead, "happened during the storm."

"Ah. But they say you were attacked yesterday."

The youth realized the assistant headman was not concerned about his bruises. "Yes."

"You seem okay now."

"Yes."

"Do you know why you were attacked?"

"No."

"Maybe a fight over a girl."

The youth blushed slightly. "It wasn't a fight. I was attacked."

"Over a girl, perhaps."

"It wasn't over a girl." The youth hesitated. He looked at the assistant headman's tea. "They wanted a box."

"Who?"

"The men who attacked me. I don't know who they are."

"Did they look like they were from around here?"

"I didn't see them." The assistant headman seemed to switch eyes looking at the youth, and in truth it sounded odd even to the youth to say that he hadn't really seen the men who attacked him. He wondered if he should take the assistant headman's time to tell him that the men had thrown a sack over his head.

"What box?" the assistant headman said, looking into his hands.

"I don't know. A box. They said a box."

"Why do they think you know about their box?"

"I don't know if it is their box. I don't know whose box it is."

"But you know there's a box."

"They said there's a box." For a moment the youth was uncertain whether the men had in fact mentioned the box. "Why would they bother to attack me if there weren't a box?"

"You see? Isn't it much easier if this were all a fight over a girl? Or maybe you gamble?"

"I don't gamble."

"Well, a girl then." The assistant headman lowered his head with a certain finality that did not bid the youth to speak further. "There was a girl who was attacked, too. Yes?"

"Yes."

"You see. Often people fight over a girl and they are ashamed to admit it afterward. I understand. I was once in such a fight, but it was some time ago." The assistant headman pulled at his lower lip and watched the youth with one eye. "I can put it in the official reports discreetly."

The youth had not thought of official reports. He wondered now if that was the purpose of the assistant headman's visit.

The assistant headman drew a pipe. The woman Matsuko had brought a tobacco tray, and he pinched some tobacco off the tray and placed it carefully in the pipe bowl.

Outside, the youth could hear the woman calling farewell to some more guests. The sound reminded him of the morning cold. He heard the shuffled steps of wayfarers in the entryway. He hoped the performers were not leaving yet.

Wanting to see the girl before she left, he hoped the assistant headman was through.

"I understand you brought a dead body back to your inn?" the assistant headman said at last.

"It was a guest. A hunter. He had gone out into the storm."

"So he was no longer a guest."

"He would have stayed at the inn that night."

"Had he left anything at the inn?"

"I don't know. He had a friend, another hunter, who was still at the inn."

"Where is he now?"

"Which?"

"The other hunter."

"I don't know. He's disappeared."

"Disappeared?"

"He wasn't here last night."

"So he left, too." The assistant headman spread his hands apart, palms up. "Now they are two men who decided not to stay at the inn. They're not your problem anymore."

The youth said nothing. He thought of his fight with the pox-faced hunter.

The assistant headman shrugged. "Some of the villagers came to the inn after the storm to help you dig out."

"Yes."

"You didn't mention to them anything about this missing hunter."

"No." The youth was amazed the assistant headman had spoken to the villagers about him. Had questioned them.

"Because anyone can leave an inn, and then he's no longer the inn's concern. You see?"

"Yes."

"It's really just the same standard you apply every day, isn't it?"

"Yes."

"It was kind of you to help bring the dead man's body back to the inn, but it wasn't your responsibility. Maybe it would be better if the inn weren't involved in any of this. Sometimes even good deeds bring troubles we never imagine. Troubles not just for yourself, but others."

"It would make no difference to the village," the youth said, "if he were found in the forest."

"Found? After a blizzard? Many people aren't found after a blizzard. Maybe in the spring. Maybe the wolves or the birds find the body first. Maybe he can't be identified. Maybe by spring no one cares."

The youth said nothing.

The assistant headman sighed and banged his pipe. He turned the bowl toward him and then banged it again. Neither eye seemed to really look at it. "How was he found?"

The youth blinked in surprise. "I worked my way back toward the point where I lost his trail. During the blizzard."

"You tried to follow someone during a blizzard?"

The youth stared back at him.

"Why were you following him?"

"I wasn't really following him. We were both following another man, a man with a beard, who had come to the inn and then run back out into the storm. We thought he would die out there."

"And this is something you thought this man with a beard hadn't considered?"

The youth once again said nothing.

"Did you find this man?"

"In a blizzard?"

The assistant headman looked hard at the youth with his left eye and then gave a sort of smile. "I'm still not clear how you found the dead man."

The youth looked to the side. "We came across him. In the same direction I had been going."

"Wasn't he buried by the storm?"

"Yes. There was a muffler."

"A muffler?"

"Tied to a tree limb."

"By the dead man?"

"I don't know."

The assistant headman packed his pipe. He had long, thin fingers that matched his face. His eyes were more intense when he looked back up. "I'm told this hunter's throat was cut."

"Yes."

"Completely?"

"Yes."

"It doesn't seem likely he stood up to tie the muffler, does it?"

"No."

"And I doubt the man who killed him was anxious for him to be found."

"No. Not likely." The youth tried to smile.

"Would you slit a man's throat and then mark the spot?" The assistant headman's right eye looked straight into the youth.

"No."

"No. It's said that the dead man was robbed. That he carried a lot of money on him."

"That's what the other hunter said."

"But when you found the body yesterday he had no money."

"No."

"And the snow was undisturbed? No one had dug around him?"

"No."

"So he would have been robbed during the blizzard."

The youth's mouth was dry. "Maybe the man who killed him robbed him."

"Of course," the assistant headman said. "How many people would be out in a blizzard?" He nodded several times to himself and lit his pipe. He sucked at it noisily for a few puffs with his eyes half-closed, exhaling the smoke through his nose. He sat quietly. Then his head tilted to the side and a long questioning sound came from the back of his throat. His eyes popped open. "But then there's still the muffler. A murderer wouldn't mark the body."

"No."

"And a thief, if there were a separate thief, wouldn't do that either, would he?"

"No."

"Who would mark a body? Someone who wanted to come back and find it later. That's not the act of a thief or murderer."

"No."

"No. It's the act of someone who means well."

The youth looked directly back into the assistant headman's eye.

"But you didn't find the body during the storm, did you?"

"No."

"No. I didn't think so. But when I asked you earlier you only said, 'During the storm?' and I wanted to be sure."

"No."

"No. So the murderer took the money."

"Or maybe there wasn't any. Maybe his friend made it up to avoid paying his bill."

The assistant headman grunted and tapped the ash out of his pipe. "But there's still that muffler. If it wasn't the murderer and it wasn't the robber, if there was a robber, and it was someone who meant well. . . . Has anyone come forward to say they found the body during the blizzard?"

The youth shook his head. "I haven't heard of anyone."

The assistant headman sighed and bent his head and tapped the mouthpiece of his pipe lightly against his forehead. "So someone marks the body during the blizzard, but then doesn't tell anyone. A well-meaning act, followed by a thoughtless one. Odd, isn't it?"

"Odd."

"Unless the well-meaning person also perished in the storm."

"Yes."

"But that's a well-meaning person who stumbles on a body in the storm, takes the time to mark it, but then can't make it out of the storm themselves. And no one's missing from the village."

"There are lots of others in the woods."

"Yes," the assistant headman said. "The other possibility is a well-meaning person marks the body, takes the money to safeguard it, and then sees it's a lot of money and changes his mind." The assistant headman looked at the youth and sighed.

The youth said nothing.

"What am I to put in the official report?" the assistant headman said. "I suppose I don't have to mention the money. We don't really know he had any, as you point out."

The youth nodded.

"And how you found the body's not that important. Maybe the wind blew the muffler into the tree. Or maybe I don't need to mention the muffler at all."

The youth said nothing.

"It's a dangerous time," the assistant headman said. "There are many strangers in the village and the forest. Groups of men. Many of them. They don't seem to leave. They hang about. We don't want any trouble with them. We don't want anyone reading our reports to think we're causing trouble either."

"Maybe you should report the strangers."

"Some thought we should. There was a girl raped just before the storm. But we discovered it was a fox-spirit that raped her. Someone even saw the fox-spirit. It had taken the form of a man. She's not right yet, but that is common with such things." The assistant headman shrugged. "We have the theatricals and the festival. People come. We're not like the villages just to the south and the north, where we've heard there are men hanging about too. And if we were, with so much going on, what would really be done for us?"

The youth had no answer.

"They say there was a riot over food last month south of us along the coast. And there are rumors of an assassination, or at least an attempt, in the capital. Some say the fighting headed north. Who knows? We're a long way north. These things should not concern us. But you know there were even peasant revolts near here last year. In ancient times the Heike fled here. Things were not good then. There's trouble with our army, and trouble in China, and some say there'll be a war with the Russe soon. Some want it. We're in between, you know. There are so many things in this world that are not part of our world. They have no part in our village. Our winter crepe will sell well this year, and tonight we'll have a big celebration. You should come. You haven't been here long, but the inn has always been a welcome part of our village, although it is removed, and some say it really isn't part of the village at all.

"But you should come tonight." The assistant headman mentioned the master of the inn. "He has always been a favorite of many of the villagers. His parents, too. They've always taken care of the village, and the villagers of them. Since the time of the Heike, people have come through the inn. Spies and entertainers, lovers on the run, suicides, adulterers. Even conspirators, maybe. These things happen. But the trouble's never touched the village. Do you understand?

"In the old days when the village had to petition the authorities, we'd sign it in a circle, so no one could know who the leader was. No one would be punished above the rest. But times are harder now. Now they punish the whole village. There's everything at stake today."

The youth nodded.

"These topics are much too heavy for today. You know, you've never been to our theatricals. Maybe you should stay in the village for a while."

"Leave the inn?"

"Only for a while."

"How can I?"

"There is a family you could stay with. I'll arrange it. Matsuko can manage here."

"I can't leave the inn."

"Don't be worried about your master. I will talk with him when he returns. He loves the theatricals himself."

It was true, the youth realized, that in the village he would have more chance of seeing Yukiko, who would be in the village for the theatricals and the festival that surrounded them. But staying with a family, he would have no chance to be alone with her. He would be watched. Besides, the youth thought, whatever the assistant headman might say, it could not be a good idea to leave the inn the first time it had been entrusted to him.

The assistant headman nodded and looked down once again at his pipe. "There's not much I can do to help you up here if there should be more trouble, say another fight over a girl. Maybe a villager can come up now and then to see how things are."

"We'll be all right."

The assistant headman smiled and nodded. "I can see you are a responsible young man. There's a place for you here. The last one was not as strong."

"The last one?"

"You're not the first apprentice for the inn. You knew that, didn't you?"

The youth sat silent.

"Oh, yes, four, maybe five years ago. There was another apprentice here. He didn't work out."

The youth wanted to ask why this earlier apprentice had not worked out, but he was ashamed that he had never thought to ask if there had been an apprentice before him. It seemed such a basic question to have asked, and so close to his own affairs. He saw for an instant the master and the woman Matsuko in a different light, for they had never told him.

"We're only a small village," the assistant headman said. "Talk to Matsuko. She knows a lot about us here."

Some ash from his pipe had fallen in the folds of the assistant headman's mountain trousers and onto the soiled and worn mats between him and the tobacco tray. With his forefinger and his thumb, the assistant headman picked the ashes up carefully so that they did not fall apart and placed them in a line on the tray before him.

"There," he said, finishing, "I wouldn't want my brief visit to leave even a trace."

When the assistant headman finally rose to go, the youth followed to the entry. He hoped the girl had not yet left. He thanked the assistant headman quickly and wished that he would quickly leave, but even then the man had something more to say.

When at last the assistant headman turned his back to depart, the youth bowed low, but he could barely bring himself to hold his bow.

Then he caught his breath in surprise.

Before him, in the center of the frozen mud of the entryway, lay two snowshoes. One was oval, the other round.

Still bent low from his bow, he stared at them as if they might move.

The two lay slightly askew, and the edge of one rested upon the other. It was as if they had been placed in haste, or by the hand of a child.

The assistant headman, departing, had seemed to take no notice of the snowshoes.

They were not the very same snowshoes the youth had worn back to the inn the night of the storm. It was not the same round snowshoe that he had taken off the dead hunter. But, the youth knew, they had not simply fallen there, either. They had been left by someone for him.

Perhaps, the youth thought, they had been left as a threat. Or a warning. He could not be sure which. But it meant that someone knew. Or thought they knew.

Or was it but a test?

The youth glanced quickly about, but no one was to be seen. He regretted staring so long at the snowshoes.

He walked quickly through the inn. The girl and the performers and most of the other guests had already left. He rushed to a window on the upper floor to see if he could see them on the snow, but they had already passed from view.

Looking out upon the hillside, he wondered if he should have moved the snowshoes, or if he should even now leave them where they lay.

Later, passing by the entry to the kitchen, he saw in the shadows there the woman Matsuko fulling a cloth spread before her. She squatted in the frozen mud by an open port of the stove where wood burned within and smoke spilled out about her. She gathered upon a block folds of cloth, and with a stick she beat at it to give it texture. Her broad back was bent flat to the earth and her chest had sunk down between her knees. The back of her head shook when she struck the block, and although she neither turned nor rose nor stayed her hand, she knew that he was there and she spoke to him.

"Well," the woman said and struck at the block. Her voice quaked with the strike. She paused to rearrange the cloth upon the block. "This morning you've even put away your bedding." The woman's reddened fingers, wrapped around the fulling stock, rose into the firelight to strike again.

❀

Squinting against the sun, the youth stepped out into the huge winter field before him. The letter for the old charcoal maker from Akiyama rested in his sash. A sky without fault arched high above and around him. It was of a deep and even blue. The snow stretched out white to the sky and the mountain and into the azure shade of the pine trees around the meadow's edge. The air was dry and crisp and cold enough to sting his cheeks when a slight wind blew.

When he reached the middle of the field, the youth rolled back his head and, still walking forward, turned a circle in the snow just to see the world spin. He looked along the line of his footsteps, which ran back into the woods. He stopped.

A figure, running, pursued him through the trees.

The youth bridged his hand up over his eyes and squinted against the glare, but he still could not tell who it was. The figure was moving awkwardly through the deep snow, which the sun had already softened from the night's crust. Running in and out of the shade of the pines, the figure waved its arms up and down for balance. It lurched from side to side.

The youth drew deep breaths and looked around and behind himself to the far edge of the field. Beyond, the pine trees spread out thinly among the barren trunks of the forest. Other than the running figure, nothing moved. He picked a route in case he had to flee.

Squatting to rest his legs, the youth watched the running figure for a while, and then he touched the unbroken snow around him. Small, wind-driven waves had formed and frozen and softened once again on the surface.

The running figure had almost reached the edge of the forest. For all its effort, it moved slowly. The youth saw he could lose it quickly in the woods, if he must.

"Setsu-o-o-o-o!" A high-pitched call.

The youth exhaled sharply through his nose and smiled.

"Setsuo. Setsu-o-o-o-o!" In the winter silence, the words floated out cleanly across the open field. It was Yukiko.

"Setsu-o-o-o!" she called out again. Her voice rose in the first and fell in the last moments. The calls, flowing after one another, seemed like echoes of themselves.

The girl waved an arm with something in her hand and ran toward him. The tips of her snowshoes barely cleared the snow. She ran awkwardly, and twice almost slowed to a walk.

"Hurry!" The youth yelled. He waved back and watched her run to him. He had not expected to see her until the theatricals, and even then he had feared he would not get to speak to her alone. But now she had followed him here, into the snow. As she drew nearer, he saw clods of snow kicked off her snowshoes rise into the air and scud across the surface of the snow waves around her.

"Look! Look what I found," she yelled.

She stopped again about ten yards away. A field of snow glistened between and around them in places too bright to see. The surface lay unbroken, save for the snow trails that traced their separate paths to this point. Snow clung in the wrinkles of the girl's baggy mountain trousers and caked around the tops of her boots. She wore the yellow fur cloak in which he had first seen her. In places he could see where it was worn and frayed.

"Look," she said. She bent forward with her hands on her knees to rest. Her cheeks were red. Her breath appeared in pale clouds and her shoulders shook with the effort of breathing. In her hand, pointing toward the snow, hung a blossom, slightly purplish in color, surrounded on a short stem by claw-like leaves.

"It was just poking through a drift," she said, breathing with difficulty. "It's the first. The first I've seen."

She walked the final gap between them and offered him the flower, swaying on tired knees. Strands of her hair stuck to the sweat at the sides of her temples.

The youth took off his right glove and took the stem from her. The bite of the fresh air felt good on his hand, still flushed from the warmth of the glove. The stem was cold and the petals were sprinkled with snow from when she had stumbled. The leaves were pale green, still slightly curled, with a hairy, rust-colored texture beneath.

"There were two. I had to bring you one."

"I saw some, too. The first of spring. I wonder if they're the same."

"You saw them, too?" Her breath was just beginning to come back naturally. Her chest still heaved as she breathed.

The youth nodded. "Perhaps the same. To the left. In the shade."

"And you didn't pick one for me?" The girl folded her arms. "I'm sorry I brought it, then."

"But I didn't expect to see you here. I thought you'd be working."

"That's right," she said, "you wouldn't have." She smiled again.

"Why aren't you working?"

"You sound like Ueda. And what about you? You don't seem to be doing much."

"I have a letter to deliver." Then he laughed, "Not hard work today."

The girl, facing him, laughed too. Her shoulders moved inward and she lifted her chin. In the daylight he could see she had a slight snowburn and her teeth seemed white. He wanted to touch them. Her laugh made him feel awkward, standing there so close to her. It was too big a laugh, with her eyes and her mouth open wide, and he was afraid that they would stop laughing and he would have nothing to say.

The girl bit down over her lower lip and looked up into his face. The last touch of laughter shook her and trailed off into a sound almost like a hum. He could not think when he looked into her eyes.

He found himself standing square to her, front to front, and even though she was beyond his reach he could feel a sensation reach out across the snow between them, pulling at him, as if he were pressed against her. He could feel her on his skin, he could feel the blood in him. The sensation distracted him, and he did not want it to break. He searched for some sign that she felt it, too.

He looked at the flower. "Maybe not the same," he said. He felt stupid.

He wondered if she would say anything about coming to him the previous night. He remembered touching her hands and the cold skin of her neck and the smell of sake on her breath. It amazed him that he had touched this girl.

He realized there was a silence. "How is your head?"

The girl shrugged and stepped forward closer to him. "It hurts some," she said.

"You were drunk." He wanted her to touch his arm.

"Not drunk," she said, and then she seemed to realize what this would mean and said, "Some, maybe."

She was so close that the youth looked down into his hands. He was still holding the stalk between them, and as Yukiko stepped forward, the head of the flower, which had pointed toward her, bent up against her body. The girl looked down toward the flower, too.

"So they didn't need you today," the youth said. He turned to the side. "Would you help me take the letter?"

"Yes." She stepped after him. Then she paused as if to think. "Where'd you get it?"

"Oh, someone from the village," the youth looked out across the field toward where he had been headed and searched for something to say. "It's not too far."

"Setsuo, did you tell anyone about those men?" the girl said. "I'm afraid they might come back."

"They won't be back."

"How do you know?" The girl stopped and squinted to see his face better. "What did they want?"

He turned back to her. "It's not important," he said. He started to walk again, but she had not moved. "Besides, I don't know what they wanted."

"Then how do you know they won't be back?"

"I just don't think they will."

The girl looked down at the snow and continued walking again. The youth twisted the stalk between his fingers.

"How did you find me?" he said. As soon as he had asked, he regretted it.

"I followed your tracks in the snow," the girl said. "Matsuko started me out."

"Matsuko?"

"Yes. You don't think it has anything to do with that man, do you?"

The youth looked off again. He guessed that she meant the bearded man. "Why should it?"

"I don't know, but it all seems to have started with that."

The youth forced a laugh. "How would you know? I only met you then, too, you know." He saw that the whites of her eyes were as clean as the snow and they watched him. He looked away. He could barely think near her, and it bothered him that she seemed to think clearly.

"I know. But it did start from then, didn't it? When you went for that man during the storm and you hurt your head somehow."

"What do you mean 'somehow?' I told everyone, I fell down a slope and hit a tree. I even showed the others where it was."

They walked a distance in silence.

"Why do you let Ueda tell those stories about you?" he said at last. He had tried to think of something else to say, and his thoughts had wandered to Ueda's tale about the girl.

"Which part do you think is a story?" she said, and she looked at him without expression.

The youth did not know how to respond.

"I'm sorry," she said. "Ueda says it's good for business. He says the stories excite men more. Like Sumiko crying at 'Shallow River.' You didn't realize that she was faking?"

The youth had stopped.

"She cries every time. Once she cried twice at the same party. They loved it anyway. She hides hot peppers in her hem and rubs it under her eyes." Yukiko rubbed her knuckles just beneath her eyes.

To the youth, the movement made Yukiko look like a little girl.

"Why do you think Sumiko makes me paint those lines on her?"

The youth realized he had not known the tiny dancer's name was Sumiko, and he had not stopped to ask himself why she had painted lines to mimic pubic hair if she had not expected to dance "Shallow River." But, most of all, he hadn't thought about how she had painted on the lines. He would have thought, if he had thought about it at all, that she had done this herself, but he saw now that it would be difficult, bending over for so long. He imagined for the first time the tiny girl standing naked with Yukiko kneeling in front of her, perhaps naked as well, carefully painting the lines with slow motions, perhaps resting her other hand for balance on the tiny dancer's hip.

"I shouldn't have told you," Yukiko said. "Now you won't buy her contract."

The youth waved his hand about.

"Why not buy mine instead?"

He glanced quickly at her, but the girl had turned her face toward the snow. Even so, he could see that she was watching him from the corner of her eye.

For a moment he wondered again how much a contract would be. He thought of the dead hunter's wallet, still hidden in the kitchen, and of the packet he had found in the snow. He wondered what would happen if Yukiko did not have to leave with Ueda. But he knew it would sound odd for an apprentice to seem even to consider such a sum.

"You'd need a rich man," he said, still hoping that she might say that a man need not be so rich. Perhaps even name a price.

She was looking off into the snow. When she turned back, she looked straight into his face.

"So," she said, "is Ueda right?" After a pause she raised her chin. "About the stories."

The youth had pretended not to understand.

"Do they excite men more?" She asked again.

"I suppose."

"You know they do. You could see how those men looked at me once they began to think that the girl in the story was me."

To the youth, it seemed the girl spoke with some pride. "And do you think they believe it?"

She shrugged. "They believe it excites them. I suppose that's belief enough for them."

The girl tilted her head to the side, "Did you?"

"What're Ueda and Sumiko doing today?" It sounded odd to the youth to hear himself say out loud the tiny dancer's name.

Suddenly the girl called out. She bent down and, scooping up a handful of snow, threw it at him.

"What!" he blocked the snow with his hands and the flower was hit.

"You! You won't answer me."

The youth raised the blossom to his face. Some of the snow that Yukiko had thrown was collected in the middle of the petals. The small flakes glistened. The youth blew at them, but they would not come off.

"Here," the girl said, grabbing the flower from his hand. "I can put it in my shirt." And she turned her back to him.

Then, standing in the snow field with her back to him, the girl began to open her clothes.

The youth watched silently from behind her. He could see her breath rise. The hair at the back of her head shone from the sun. Her cloak lifted partway up her back, and her outer clothes fell open from her body and hung on either side of her. He watched her elbows move as she untied her inner clothing.

"Oh," she gasped and her shoulders moved quickly inward, "it's so cold."

The youth imagined the petals pressed up against the wall of her stomach. From behind, he watched her replace her clothes.

Turning back to face him, her cloak still gathered up under her chin, the girl smoothed her clothing into the top of her mountain trousers. There was a slight bulge where the flower lay against her. To the youth, it seemed a little as if she were pregnant.

At noon they mounted an unbroken knoll where the scrub trees lay nearly buried and a line of smoke lifted, fitful and translucent gray from the snow itself. On all of that bald, gleaming rise there were no marks save the wind-driven ridges of frozen snow and the ancient three-toed tracks of birds, shallow, passing, beginning and ending without known reason or reference.

They approached the smoke in silence. Climbing, they breathed heavily. A flaw of wind brushed the smoke aside and they stopped and stared as if it were a message.

Even stopped, the youth could think of nothing to say, nor did the girl speak to him. He moved ahead again.

Soon they drew near to the spot where smoke emerged from the snow without sight of home or fire or man. There lay instead before them a great hole with a mound in its middle, and at its edge gathered large black birds that paced back and forth like sentinels about it, and these watched the wayfarers' primitive progress with shifting eyes. The youth cawed at them but they did not move. He threw snow, and they jerked their burnt umber eyes and their bent feathers twitched and they stepped aside in displeasure. But at last when he neared the edge they lifted heavily with slow, stiff movements of their wings across the line of smoke and flew with trailing feet a distance away.

Looking down into the hole with the girl beside him, the youth saw the charcoal maker's hut just below, buried by the storm. Thick icicles, moist from the sunlight, began at the edges of the eaves and ran down into the hole. The youth leaned out over the gap between the snow wall and the eaves and called down into the shadows within.

In a moment there were noises below and the upper body of the charcoal maker, bent at the waist, shuffled into the light. He twisted and shielded his eyes and looked up out of the hole at the heads of the youth and girl that broke the line of sky above.

"Do you carry the pox?" the charcoal maker called.

The youth said he had not left the mountain all winter.

"Have you?"

The girl said she had not been in a village that carried the pox. The charcoal maker seemed surprised to hear the voice of a young girl and moved his head and reddened eyes from side to side to see more clearly.

"I have a letter for you," the youth yelled down.

"Letter?"

"Letter. Yes."

"A letter," the man said to his feet.

"Yes."

There was a pause. The small man withdrew into the shadows. They were bidden to enter.

The youth took a look around him as they left the surface and climbed down the snow wall to the hut. Strips of bark bound with grasses formed one side. A woven sedge door tied with bark hung askew. The icicles dripped on them as they passed under the eaves. Things lay in the darkness about the doorway so that it was difficult to step within.

It was much colder in the gloom of the straw roof. As their vision adjusted to the shadows, the youth saw the charcoal maker huddled by the kiln. His face held the red of the fire. He watched them, squinting, with narrowed and smoke-ruined eyes.

About the youth's feet were strewn straw sacks filled with charcoal and, to the side, dead branches. To his left was a grass pallet under a pile of rag blankets. A plank shelf ran above, largely empty save for a tin on its side. The back of the hut, near the kiln, was totally open, and the charcoal maker was silhouetted against the snow wall. He was weaving straw into yet another sack. When he saw them looking at the branches, he lowered his weaving, but did not put it down. The youth wondered if he had paid for the branches. He stepped closer still.

There was a wave of warm air near the kiln, but smoke spilled out around them and stung the youth's eyes. The charcoal maker's eyes were yellowed and small and the rims were red. Soot clung in his pores and in the wrinkles of his flesh. He wore an odd costume of bark and charcoal sacks woven with twisted grasses. To his side was an empty container of sake, the bottom scuffed with use.

The charcoal maker watched the youth with an expression that groped toward speech. The youth had seen him once before, but from afar. It had been on the ridge.

"Where's it from?" the charcoal maker said.

The youth reached into his snow vest and held out an envelope.

The charcoal maker stared at the envelope as if its contents could be discerned at a distance.

The youth pulled it back and looked at it. It was from an army unit. He said so, and tendered it again.

The charcoal maker lowered his eyes. "I have no money for a letter," he said at last. He turned from it and stared into the coals of the kiln. Red and yellow lights passed back and forth across the surfaces.

There was a long silence.

The charcoal maker picked up the straw bag again, but he did not look at it. He put the bag down. "May I hold it?"

Uncertain, the youth nodded. He tried to read in the man's eyes whether it would be a problem to get the letter back. If the charcoal maker did not pay the postage, the youth could not leave the letter with him.

The man wiped his soot-blackened palms on his thighs before he took the envelope. Then he weighed it in thick and cracked fingers, turning it over and over, and put it to his forehead and closed his eyes as if to pull the words from the paper into his skull. His eyes opened. "So much to say." His head moved back and forth from the youth to the girl with an odd expression somewhere between the start of laughing and crying. The paper bore the smudges of his forehead and fingertips.

The youth glanced at the girl. The sun's glare at the edges of the eaves, refracted a thousand times in its cascade down the snow walls, cast a soft light on the girl's face that caught the youth unaware. It was as if the cold, clear air had purified the light that remained. Her features at that moment, slightly turned away, seemed to him the echo of a dream.

"May I hold it a little longer?" the charcoal maker said.

The youth looked around for someplace to sit. He and the girl squatted on half-filled sacks of charcoal. Some coals spilled out onto the floor beneath them.

Although he wanted to look at the girl again, the youth was afraid he might be caught. From the corner of his eye, he saw that she was picking at some woodchips on the floor.

The charcoal maker was staring at the writing on the outside of the paper. In the last years, when crops were poor, many sons had left to join the army. The apprentice reminded himself to ask the woman Matsuko if the charcoal maker ever had a son.

Turning away, the youth stared up toward the surface. The underside of the eaves of the hut was blackened with smoke and shadow, but the snow at the edge of the snow wall shone a blinding white, and icicles there glistened where they caught the sunlight. The blocks of sky between them were of the deepest blue, deeper it seemed than the sky could be.

"It's strange," the charcoal maker said, "but I don't dream anymore."

The youth and the girl Yukiko looked at him.

The charcoal maker had been staring down into the kiln for several moments, but now he slumped down heavily with one hand just touching the letter in his lap and his free hand on his knee. The air left his lungs.

"Odd," the charcoal maker said, rubbing his palm on the knee. He looked up at the youth. "I can't even remember when the last time was."

The youth did not know what to say. He wanted to be gone.

"I was trying to remember yesterday. The old woman always remembered."

To the youth it was not clear if the old woman always remembered the charcoal maker's dreams, or her own. He stood and reached out to take back the letter, but the man was still rubbing his hand on his knee.

The old man's face turned jerkily toward Yukiko and the ancient crevices of his skin were dark with soot and shadow. "What do you dream about?" he said to her.

Perhaps from having squatted so long by the kiln, the girl's face was flushed.

❋

At the edge of the village the youth and Yukiko ducked into a small teahouse. He would leave her there, for now. She had said she would join him that night at the inn, when everyone was down at the festival, when the inn would be empty. She would slip away. She would join him. The thought beat within the youth's chest, and the joints of his arms and legs felt tight as if he had to run to clear them.

The woman who worked in the teahouse passed thin, soiled cushions to them. In the middle of the cramped room there was a small, open fire that sputtered. Above the fire hung a kettle and two soot-stained ropes frayed for much of their length. Something hissed in the kettle. The straw floor mats around the firepit were grimy and torn. After the clear air of the snowfields, the smoke from the fire burned the youth's eyes and he could taste it in his throat.

The woman pressed on them some squares of beaten millet. The squares sat on a small lacquered plate with a piece of oil-stained paper. Her fingers were thick and red and cracked from work or cold, and dirt filled the crevices. After she set the plate down, she re-arranged the paper with her fingertips.

In the corner behind the woman sat a barefoot child picking inside her clothes for lice. When she pulled one out, she rolled it in her fingers and looked at it and then flicked it past her outstretched legs into the fire. She looked up with dull interest when the woman carried the plate by her. Then she stared at the millet.

The room was so small that a ladder to a loft almost touched the firepit. The lower part of the ladder was blackened with smoke. Behind the ladder was a shelf, the underpart of which was also blackened. On the shelf were odd bits of tobacco and a stack of firepots, cracked or missing handles, and there were dried cakes of pounded root with small wooden pieces that proclaimed their price. At the edge, surveying all their small realm, stood two painted idols, gods of fortune and age.

The woman was talking about the festival that evening. People were coming from miles around, she said. People were coming even after the storm, although she thought the storm had hurt business. She was talking mainly to a fat man who sat wedged in a corner by a covered charcoal burner, but she would regularly nod for emphasis to the youth and the girl, as well. A cloth that faintly bore its original pattern was wrapped around the man's legs.

The youth ate the beaten millet hungrily, holding it to his mouth as he chewed. He looked over the food toward the fat man in the corner. The man watched him and the girl with slow eyes.

The woman poured some tea. The youth and the girl cupped their hands around the sides for warmth and held the steam below their faces. When it seemed the woman had stopped talking, the fat man in the corner asked another question and she began again.

A villager stuck his head in the door and called out, and the woman went to the back without hesitation and produced some rice balls. The villager had been working on the snow stage for the festival, and the woman asked after it. The man thanked her and called to some others who waited for him outside. There were large cracks in the wallboards, through which the youth could see sunlight on the man as he left.

A chill of colder air had followed the villager in, and the youth looked at the fire, which had begun to fade. He was not paying enough to ask her to rekindle it with more wood.

The woman, who had followed the youth's eyes, began to tell a sad story about the villager's wife as if it were certain to be of interest. Although he was annoyed by her constant talking, the warmth of the woman won the youth over. The girl Yukiko, too, seemed amused. She smiled secretly to the youth when the woman was not looking and asked questions to egg the woman on.

Then, too, uncertain what to say to the girl with others about, the youth came to welcome the distraction of the woman.

On the walk from the charcoal maker's hut, he had managed to tell Yukiko of his life at the inn and of the village farther north where he was raised, and she had spoken of performing and festivals and of the road. But here, among others, he could think of little to say.

At a pause the girl Yukiko asked if the woman knew any tales about a shrine up the mountain above the inn. The youth looked at her quickly. The night of the storm one of the guests had talked of sinister tales about the shrine, but the youth had forgotten that the girl had been there for the discussion.

The woman did not seem to know the shrine.

"To the northeast," the youth said. "A two-story shrine."

The woman frowned, as if she were trying to remember. From the corner of his eye, the youth saw the girl Yukiko look at him strangely.

The child in the corner seemed to know the shrine and when she said something involving a man's name the woman seemed to recollect it, too. But she knew no tales.

"What about this?" the youth said. "There's a tale about a snow demon. I can remember the first part, but I can't remember if there's more." He told them the tale of the snow girl who blew on one porter and killed him, but was so taken with another that she saved him. It was the story he had remembered the night he was caught in the storm.

"I know that," the child said, sitting up. Her eyes were bright. "She comes back and marries him. As a human. She comes back as a human."

"He marries a demon who becomes a human," the woman said. "It's usually the other way around."

"He doesn't know she's a demon," the child said.

"And they marry?"

"Yes. And they have children." The child said this last with great amazement and nodded emphatically, but although her head bounced, her eyes remained fixed on the youth. "But then she leaves him, and he's so sad he dies."

"He dies of grief?" the youth said. "She doesn't blow on him and freeze him to death?"

The child said she didn't think so, again without taking her eyes from the youth.

"She doesn't just leave him," the woman from the teahouse said to the child. "Why does she leave?"

The child was silent.

"Does the man break his word to her?"

The child, biting on her lower lip, stared at the woman.

The woman turned back to the youth and the girl. "When she spared the man's life in the snowstorm, she made him promise never to tell her story to anyone. She says that she'll kill him if he does. But one night, long after they're married, something reminds him of that night in the snow—I think maybe it's the moonlight on his wife, and he tells his wife the story, not knowing it's her."

"Just that?" the child asked. "Just that he breaks his word?" She seemed disturbed.

"I agree," Setsuo said. "Wouldn't they fix things?"

"But now he knew," the woman shook her head.

"Does she just leave or does she kill him?"

"Hmmm," the woman seemed to consider this. She looked to the fat man in the corner for help, but the man offered her none. "I think I've heard it both ways."

"No," the child said. "She leaves. She becomes like smoke."

"Oh, yes, I have heard it that way. The husband holds her and cries to be forgiven, and she cries, too, but while he's holding her she turns to smoke or fog or something and soon she just fades away from him and there's nothing left to hold but air." She turned back to the child, "You remember the story well."

"So he lived with a demon," the youth said, stretching his legs.

The woman nodded with a serious expression. She had thick cheeks and, when she was not smiling, her eyes looked small. "Not a demon to him," she said. "It's too bad. He was happy. It's too bad he ever found out."

A wave of sadness broke across the woman and washed against the youth. She seemed to him to have shrunk inside herself. He turned away toward Yukiko, but the girl did not seem to have noticed.

"Don't be too sad," the youth said, looking back. "He was the cause of his own unhappiness."

The woman shook her head. "We all are."

"Anyway," he said, "in the end, what else could have happened? If he had never said a word, would she have stayed and gotten old?"

The woman shrugged.

"We know only one path," the child recited happily. She sang, more than said the words, a chant taught by adults. She smiled at the woman, who laughed and nodded back.

"It's a silly story," Yukiko said, lifting her tea. "No one dies of grief anymore. No one has the courage."

The youth looked at the girl's smooth, thin fingers holding the cup.

"You're right," the woman said. "We die of hunger first." She nodded her agreement with herself, and the movement seemed to break her spell. "Anyway, I think maybe he doesn't die." She looked to the child as if for help. "I think he lives with his grief."

The child looked at her hands in her lap. "He didn't mean to do wrong," she said.

The youth arched his shoulders back and then pushed himself to his feet.

He nodded to the child, who nodded back. "We'd better be going," he said.

As the girl Yukiko moved to stand, the youth saw beneath her clothing the outline of her breasts.

Turning to leave, the youth noticed for the first time a daguerreotype photograph placed on its back at the edge of the shelf near the ladder. In the photograph, a soldier posed against a wall, but he had taken a step just as the picture was being taken, and the image was blurred into two. Together, the two had an odd effect, as if the photograph showed at once him and the ghost of him, as if even when he was there he was also elsewhere, or never really there at all. As if the meaning was found in the motion, not in the eyes.

"Take care," the woman said to the youth as they reached the outer door, but the tone in her voice made him look back.

The woman was staring at the bruises on the youth's face. It was the first time she had made any reference to the marks at all.

The stare was quite pointed.

She closed the door against the cold air before he could respond.

His last glimpse through the closing door was of the small painted idols above the firepit. From his angle, they were turned away.

❀

Heading alone back toward the inn, the youth liked to think that the girl Yukiko might be walking among the trees ahead of him, her hood thrown back upon her shoulders. He could almost see the soft red light of the late day sun reddening her cloak, reddening her hair.

He knew, of course, that he had left the girl behind him in the village. But he clung to the illusion just the same.

And even though he knew she could not be there in the forest before him, he hurried his pace. He felt the pleasure of his movement and the pleasure of overtaking her. He reached his hand out over the snow to touch the ghost of her shoulder. There was great confidence in his touch. He saw her expression as she turned, surprised.

He repeated the scene to himself. He reached his arm out over the empty snow and she turned, surprised. Her eyes widened. She said his name.

The youth laughed out loud at himself and walked even faster and reached out once again. This time she would throw her arms around him, this time she would be demure.

He passed through the barren forest reaching forward into the air like a man too eager for his fate. He passed laughing and shaking his head to some inner humor, at one moment stopping and at another clutching nothing, and to one who might spy him there he would seem a fool altogether, and a fool he knew himself to be.

Something stopped him suddenly. He had heard the sound of bells approaching. Listening, he heard the bells again. In the cold, clear air, the bells had a brittle sound.

Near to the youth was a tree twice his height in the snow. He stepped behind it. Waiting, he looked off into the rose-colored snow made soft by the passing sun.

In a few minutes a penitent could be seen in the distance ahead climbing slowly up a clearing in the direction of the youth. Bells hung from the top of his walking staff. He wore pure white leggings beneath a straw cloak. He moved oddly. Soon the youth realized that the penitent was walking backward, facing the direction from which he had come, the direction in which the youth would go.

When the penitent drew nearer the youth stepped out from behind the tree and called out to him so he would not be startled. The penitent looked briefly around the corner of his hood in the direction of the shout and, seeing the youth, smiled and shook his bells in answer. Then he turned his back once again and continued his backward climb. The youth, too, resumed his way.

Soon the penitent and the youth had passed one another, and the penitent could look more easily at the youth. He smiled again and stopped and bowed and shook his bells twice in greeting. The youth saw that the penitent was surprisingly young, his features finely formed and almost girl-like, and he stopped, too, and spoke a greeting. But the penitent merely shook his bells in response.

"Have you vowed silence?" the youth asked.

The penitent shook his bells up and down to indicate "yes." Glad evidently for company, he smiled broadly back at the youth.

"You have a long way to go," the youth said, knowing only that there was no place close to stop.

The penitent raised and lowered his bells quickly and smiled again at the youth.

"Do you know the way?"

The penitent raised and lowered his bells and smiled.

With the penitent looking at him eagerly, the youth tried to think of something else to say. "Deep snow for walking backward," the youth said at last.

The penitent smiled and bowed.

"Or is it easier when you don't see how steep it is ahead?"

The penitent shook his bells weakly "yes."

"Only somewhat," the youth interpreted.

The penitent smiled more broadly and moved his bells up and down again.

"And is it more comforting to look back at where you've been?"

The penitent shook his bells vigorously side to side to indicate, "No."

"Ah, perhaps that's why you do penance."

The penitent seemed to have no answer for this, and, indeed, seemed too young for penance, and the two merely stared at each other for a moment. To the youth, talking to the penitent who had passed him and stood higher on the slope, it was a little as if he were already a part of the penitent's past.

The youth raised his hand and turned to go, when he remembered to ask if the penitent had seen anyone else on the mountainside.

The penitent shook his bells "no," and then stopped to think, and then shook them weakly up and down and, pausing only briefly, harshly from side to side.

"Not for a long time?" the youth said.

The penitent shook his bells "yes" and smiled and bobbed his head. The youth smiled back, and for a moment they shared the triumph of their communication.

Reluctant still to part, the youth thought for a moment and then asked where the penitent was headed.

The penitent pointed his staff up the ridge.

"Where up the ridge?"

The penitent pointed up the ridge again and then motioned the staff farther forward. At the end he moved the head of the staff in a jerky circle.

"Over the ridge?"

The penitent nodded and moved the top of his staff in an awkward circle once again.

"And then . . ."

The penitent repeated the jerky circular motion.

"You do know where you're going then?"

The penitent shook the bells up and down emphatically.

There was a silence in which the youth did not know what else to ask. The penitent moved his bells again forward over the ridge and around in a jerky circle, or perhaps, the youth realized, a triangle, and looked keenly at the youth to see if he understood.

The youth shook his head "no," and the two stood staring at each other for a moment longer. Then the penitent, growing angry, repeated the movements with his staff twice and, when he saw no reaction from the youth, moved sharply closer to him and shook his staff a third time. His brow was lowered and darkened and his penitent's cloak and white clothing that had looked so pure even against the snow could now be seen to be smudged and stained almost everywhere.

To the youth, he seemed out of balance, and when the youth shook his head again, the penitent stomped curtly and began walking angrily backward up the slope, ever farther from the youth, still shaking his staff in the same odd, jerky circle.

Walking backward, the penitent faced the youth for a long time while the distance between them widened. The bells announced his departure to the youth, his coming to the woods beyond, and his presence to the fallen trees that seemed to take no notice.

In a while the sound of his bells had faded into nothing at all, and the air seemed still.

10

By the light of the rising moon the youth reached the inn and by its light reentered. He descended from the night-blue snow into the darkened entry and groped about and smelled the smoke that clung in the wood forever. The inn was still and silent. He removed his snowshoes and boots and leggings and placed them on the edge of the entryway and placed his cloak on a hook. He looked in the darkness where the dwarf had once huddled and to the vague edge of the platform where the girl had lain. Stepping up from the earthen floor to the main room, he stumbled over the riser.

In the pit in the center of the room embers smoldered half-hidden beneath the ash with a glow so faint it barely reached the mats about. Neither the walls nor the rafters could be seen. He sat beside it on his haunches and coaxed a flame and picked up a wire sieve and with that sieve he searched the ashes absently for bits of wood or charcoal that might yet burn.

The silence of the inn crouched around him in the darkness like a thing. Matsuko and guests and vendors and visitors all had gone to the village for the theatricals, and only the youth had slipped away.

In a short time the girl who had worn the cloak of yellow fur would follow.

Squatting in the near-dark at the edge of the firepit, the youth sniffed at his fingers. He could still just find there the scent of the girl.

"I could slip away," she had said. "I could meet you at the inn."

He had not known what to say.

When the theatricals ended the performers would move on, probably north, but certainly on, and it might be long, long before he saw her again. As he reached the village with the girl beside him he could not set that thought aside. He could not think of when he might see her again, alone.

"I could slip away," she had said. "I could meet you at the inn," and she had fixed him with her eyes in a way that made him feel he was looking deep inside her. He had looked so deep inside that even her hair, where it hung by her face, seemed at the very edge of his vision.

"I could slip away," she had said, "I could meet you at the inn."

They had been talking of the night to come. He had sought a way to see her that night, the night of the theatricals, but he could not bring himself to ask. Instead he had told her that he would lead the remaining guests at dusk down to the village before the opening and wait to bring them back to the inn by torch late at night.

"All of them?" she had asked, and she had said she could slip away, she could meet him at the inn.

If she should slip away, he had thought, if she should slip away, then they could be alone at the inn for hours. For hours. They could be alone for hours, and there might not be another chance.

He had asked about Ueda and the plans he had made, and she had repeated so quietly and so seriously, "I could slip away," that he had not asked again.

"Good," she had said, and she had taken his hand for an instant as they parted.

He had tried to see into her heart by the way she had touched him and by the way she had let him go. And for a time thereafter he had curled and unfurled his hand in just the same way and he had wondered at the meaning there.

The youth took his hand from his face and, by the weak light from the firepit, stared down into his palm. Above him rats scrambled the length of the rafters. Their claws on the wood had the rushing sound of time. He waited for a moment to freshen his sense of smell and imagined that his palm might be hers and how it might touch him and then he brought his hand back to his face and sniffed at his fingers once more.

In the scent he found his heart within him. He felt the blood move in his legs and arms. He knew she might even then be nearing his door. In his mind he saw her glances of the forenoon, he saw her half in profile, he remembered her skin the night before.

He heard the outer door of the inn.

There was a call for the innkeeper. It was a male voice.

The youth jumped up quickly and went to the entryway. Two guests stood in the darkness there.

"One moment," the youth said, and he reached for an oil lamp in the place he always left it, and lit the lamp. He saw two men.

"We'd like lodging," the first said. He was smaller than the other man and dark, and he had an accent from the south. His legs were improbably bowed. His face, too, was round.

"Have you been to a village with the pox?" the youth said, and he held the light up to study their response.

"None of us will die of pox tonight," the man said.

The youth greeted them unhappily. The girl should have been there by now. Perhaps, seeing the men coming, she had hidden in the woods. But now they would not have the uninterrupted time he had sought. If she had come on time, he might have thought to bar the door.

"Are we the only ones?" the round-faced man said. On the side of his neck there was a mole from which hair grew.

"The others are at the theatricals. In the village. It's the first night. Perhaps you'd like to follow the path to the village now, and come back up with the other guests later? There will still be room."

The round-faced man turned to the taller one, "No, we've come a long way."

The tall guest smiled at the youth.

"I'll get the register," the youth said. He realized too late that he should have said the inn was full. Matsuko would never have known.

With a flick of his arm from the elbow, the round-faced man reached out and grabbed the youth's shoulder before he could turn away.

"Why don't we do that later?"

"Of course." The youth had been surprised by the speed of the man's touch. "Forgive me. You'll want to rest."

The round-faced man smiled briefly. He had thick cheeks that seemed to block the smile from reaching his eyes.

"One second."

The youth turned back to them. It was the first time that the taller one had spoken. There was something familiar in the voice.

"I have something valuable. Is there a safe place for it?"

"There is someplace I can put it."

"Good," the tall man smiled again. He had his hands clasped behind him, but now he took them from behind his back.

The youth frowned.

The man held out a small, brass coin of almost no value.

The youth glanced quickly from one man to the other, but their eyes were dark holes in the lamplight, and there seemed nothing in them to be read. He felt his stomach tighten.

When the youth did not reach out to take the coin, the tall man thrust it toward him.

The youth saw now that he had been a fool to be caught at the inn alone. He reached out slowly and took the coin without looking at it. He felt stupid for even doing that.

And he knew.

"Is there anything wrong?" the tall man said.

The youth's mouth was dry. The coin felt moist in his hands and so small he feared he might drop it. Even so, his arm felt too weak to hold steady. For the first time he noticed how the round-faced man's clothes pulled across his shoulders. The man was so stocky that he had not seemed at first as large as he now did. The youth found he could not swallow.

The youth started to speak, but in the end just shook his head, "No."

The round-faced man motioned out toward the youth with his hand. He had short, pudgy fingers.

The youth could not keep his eyes from that hand. He was sure it had touched him, beaten him. He wondered if it had been the small man who had hit him in the face when he had been attacked outside the inn, but perhaps the first blow, yes, the blow in the stomach that had first doubled him over, yes, that would have been the taller one.

The round-faced guest pointed at the coin. "Where would you put something valuable?"

The youth tried to avoid the man's eyes. He gestured behind himself. "We have a place," he said.

"Where's that?"

"Well," the youth tried to sound casual, "I can't tell you that." He was afraid to tell them that there might be other valuables in the inn.

The tall guest leaned over toward the youth. His lips and yellowed teeth caught the lampglow. "You wouldn't hide our own property from us, would you?"

"I . . ."

"Maybe we'd better keep it with us after all," the round-faced man said. He opened his darkened palm upward for the coin.

The youth reached over and placed the small coin in the man's hand. As he reached he felt a drop of sweat slip out of his armpit and glide slowly down his side. It was cool. He feared that it might betray him. He feared the man might grab his arm.

The tall man had bent down and was going through some frame packs in the shadows at the edge of the entry. He straightened up, holding a pack from which hung a long hempen cord. Then he stripped the pack of the cord. The cord slid off easily, making a slithering sound and ending in a sudden snap.

The man dropped the pack down in the corner and, taking the cord in both hands, tugged sharply outward as if to test its strength.

"Maybe you'd better turn around," the man said.

The youth nodded. He turned around and faced his own shadowed figure on the wall. He was slightly dizzy.

The youth's hands were yanked behind him and pressed together with the palms facing out. The first turn of the rope cut into the bones at the sides of his wrists, and the veins on the underside were pushed inward. His fingers felt large. The hemp tightened quickly around him.

The youth saw on the wall the darkened image of the tall man's arm sweep upward and felt the shadow hand reach into his hair. The tall man pulled sharply backward, and the youth gasped.

"Maybe you'd better show us upstairs."

The youth nodded. Behind him he heard the bar on the main door fall into place. He heard the oil lamp scrape against the floor, and then it was lifted and their shadows twisted as if the world had turned about.

Looking up into the blackness at the head of the stairs, the youth led them up. The rising shadows of the three swung and clashed against the walls.

❋

The youth led them to the room near the head of the stairs where once the old samurai had stayed. When they had crossed the threshold, the tall man loosened his grip in the apprentice's hair and let his hand slide down to the neck. The movement gave the youth a chill. Then the man slowly spun him around and, placing a foot casually on the outside of the youth's, threw him forward headfirst into the wall.

The youth had a glimpse of the grain in the wood approaching much faster than it had reason to do and then he could barely close his eyes before he hit the wall. He heard his own grunt. He found himself bent double on the floor looking into his knees and his head hurt him greatly.

When he glanced up again, the men were searching in the closet by the light of the oil lamp. He could see their broad backs, silhouetted against the light. Soon both men turned to where he lay. As they approached, the lamp, held below the tall man's face, lit the bottom of his lips and nose and left his eyes in blackness. Their shadows grew up the far wall.

The youth tasted blood. Something stung his eyes. He guessed it was blood. He knew he was bleeding from the forehead, but he could not tell how badly.

The tall man squatted down on the balls of his feet so close to the youth that he could feel the moisture of the man's breath. He shrank from its odor.

Drawing closer still and slowly reaching up, the tall man pressed his fingers to the wound in the youth's forehead. Pain clattered within the youth's head and made his skull feel paper thin and drew the breath from him. He saw the man's hand removed long before he knew the pain would subside.

Looking up, the youth stared into the tall man's face. The man had opened his mouth, and the edges of yellowed teeth could be seen, but not anything within.

The thought struck the youth almost casually: he had seen the man's face. This time the men had let him see their faces. He had seen their faces. He grew afraid.

"You have something we want," the man said.

The youth looked up at the round-faced one. He let his mouth hang slightly open.

"Where is it?" the tall man said again.

The youth shook his head carefully, for there was still pain within it. "If they didn't hide their faces," he thought, "if they didn't hide their faces, if they didn't hide their faces, then surely this time they will kill me." That was all the youth could think.

The tall man slapped the youth's head sideways into the wall.

The youth, his cheek pressed against the wall and his jaws jammed together, was afraid to draw a breath. He heard the men shifting nearer. His head slid off the wall.

"Well?"

Slowly, the youth opened one eye. His chest was tightening so he could not breathe and he knew it was fear that caused it but he could not breathe just the same. He tugged secretly at the cord behind him, but it would not give. He felt helpless in a way he had never felt before. He had always imagined that through some great exertion he, unlike others, could always free himself from such dangers. But he could not. He felt the fear seeping deeper through him, paralyzing him. The tall man raised his hand to hit him again and the youth could not move, could not even flinch away.

"Now wait a second," the round-faced man said. He squatted down beside the youth and put a hand on his shoulder.

To the youth, the hand felt large and moist. He had watched the black palm descending toward him. He felt his stomach shrink.

"There's no reason for us to hurt you," the man said.

The youth said nothing. His mouth was very dry, and he could not bring himself to speak.

The round-faced man shrugged. "Maybe smoking might change your mind. Don't you think smoking might change his mind?"

The youth looked up quickly.

The tall man nodded and stepped across the room where the youth could not see. When he returned, he held one of the inn's tobacco trays. On the tray were a small firepot and tongs. Crouching by the youth, the tall man poked into the darkness of the firepot with the tongs, and with its blackened fingers he lifted a charcoal ember free of the ash and cradled it in the air as if he held some treasure there. The ember glowed orange through the ash that clung to it and as it rose its color deepened. The tall man twisted it from side to side in front of the youth's face like a small, oddly shaped sun.

Against his will, the youth stared at the charcoal bit. The light, now closer to yellow, tugged within it like the heart of a living thing. The tall man brought the tips of the tongs closer to the youth's eyes. The youth could feel its heat.

"Well," the round-faced man said, "have you ever smoked?" He had a broad grin, the edges of which dived into the bulges of his thick cheeks. There was sweat at his temples.

The tall man pursed his lips and blew on the charcoal so that the cloud of his breath engulfed it briefly. It fired incandescent in the cloud.

The round-faced man sat on the youth's outstretched legs and, pressing with one hand against his chest, fixed him firmly against the wall. With his arms tied behind him, the youth could barely shift his hips side to side. He looked down at himself.

The tall man pursed his lips and blew again on the ember in the tips of the tongs. He twisted to the youth's right foot and removed the sock. Then he swung the ember like a dying star in the blackness slowly toward the center of the youth's sole.

The youth held his breath and shifted his eyes between the tall man's face and the ember to see if they were bluffing, but there was no bluff there. As suddenly as he could, he tried to buck the round-faced man off his legs, but he could not lift his hips and the round-faced man's smile dug deeper into the bulges of his cheeks.

"I don't know anything," the youth said. "I don't."

The round-faced man shrugged.

The tall man brought the charcoal and the edge of the tongs down toward the youth's foot.

Downstairs, someone began knocking at the door.

The tall man tossed aside the tongs so that the ember scudded away across the mats. He reached into his clothing and pulled out a knife and swung the blade quickly to point into the youth's throat. As he moved, the round-faced man rose awkwardly off the youth's legs and stumbled across the room. He crouched at the doorway, looking into the darkness toward the head of the stairs.

The knocking had already ceased.

Neither man moved. Their heads and the elongated shadows of their heads pointed toward the sound of the door. They breathed lightly.

The youth looked up into the face of the tall one. The man's eyes made quick darting movements.

"Hello!" From below the voice was muffled, but the youth knew it. It was Yukiko.

"Who is it?" the tall man whispered. He dug his fingertips into the youth's neck. "Who?"

On the floor the ember glowed.

"I don't know."

The tall man released the youth's neck as if he were throwing it to the ground.

"Send them away," he said to the round-faced man.

The round-faced man left and walked quickly down the corridor to the stairs. The youth heard his footsteps descending the staircase.

The charcoal had begun to singe the mats. There was a small darkening spot beneath it.

The youth used his shoulders to straighten himself against the wall. The tall man looked warningly into his eyes. From below, the youth heard the indistinct sounds of voices from the entry.

When the round-faced man got rid of Yukiko, the youth knew there would be no more interruptions. It was possible she would realize something was wrong and think to go for help, but it would be too long before she could work her way down the ridge to the village and longer still to bring back help. More likely, she would think he was still at the theatricals, or maybe that he had even changed his mind. He tried to imagine the feeling of the charcoal burning into his foot.

Something about the sound of the walls made the youth look up just as the round-faced man reentered. Stepping over the threshold of the room, he reached back into the darkness and pulled the girl Yukiko in after him. She still wore the cloak of yellow fur and straw leggings. Above the leggings her snow trousers bunched thick at her knees.

She rubbed at her elbow.

"Setsuo," she said. The tone of her voice was not one of surprise, but appeal. She wore a strange expression. To the youth, it seemed she had understood with amazing speed.

"She insisted," the round-faced man said, smiling. "She knew he was here."

The tall man shrugged. Reaching down to the floor, he picked up the tongs and, with the tips, the ember. "Does she smoke?" He smiled at the youth.

The girl, standing in the middle of the room, looked first at the youth and then at the man blowing on the tongs. The round-faced man slapped the girl across the face. Her neck snapped so suddenly that the bones made a cracking sound.

The girl screamed. She brought a hand to her face and, as she realized she might be hit again, she brought the other hand up too and stepped back and stepping back stumbled. The round-faced man pushed and the girl fell heavily to the floor with her feet in the air. The man dropped down over her and cupped his hands upon her breasts, and she hit the man across the arm and the side of the head. She pulled at his hands to move them off her and then she twisted over and tried to scramble away, but he hit at her and she fell forward on her hands toward the youth.

The tall man pointed his knife at the youth. The round-faced man reached toward his eye. The youth watched Yukiko, who stared into the air between her hands and the floor, her hair sprayed wildly and her body convulsed with crying and the effort of drawing breath. Lines of tears struck down to her jaw. Her mouth hung open, and the pink underlip quivered and glistened with saliva that caught the light and strung like a thread toward the floor.

The tall man asked the youth if he was ready to talk to them now.

Yukiko looked quickly up at the man and then at the youth. Her throat made a sucking sound and she looked at him in disbelief as if he were her enemy and the tall man her friend.

The youth looked back at her and then away. Only she had known that he would be there, alone at the inn. Indeed, she had arranged it. She had been late. She had been there the first night and again right after he was attacked by the two men in the snow. Indeed, he realized, it was the tiny dancer calling out so loudly to him when he was behind the inn that may have alerted the two men that he was near. True, the two men had pushed the girl down the snow steps by the inn, but in fact he had not seen that, and once on the steps the two girls would have impeded any others coming to help him. It might even be said that by crying out they had helped the two men to escape.

But above all, the youth wondered again how the girl could have met him in the snow field earlier that very day, the day when travelers were gathering in the village, and Ueda was no doubt performing for the crowds? And especially this evening, as the theatricals began, when Ueda would need her most of all? And now that he could not tell, now that he had risked being burned rather than tell, she showed up, and his pity for her was to move him to speak.

He looked down at her. Her nose was red. The composure that she wore, once so clean and distant, was broken. She seemed a sorrier thing.

As he looked at her he saw the round-faced man, smiling secretly to himself, lean over from behind the girl with his palm turned upward beneath her legs. The man jerked up. His hand appeared through her legs at the front of her crease.

The girl's eyes narrowed inward and her mouth opened wide. She brought her hands to her crease and pushed down on the man's hand. His hand twisted between the girl's thighs. To the youth, there was something about the way the man placed his hand that seemed he was familiar with that spot.

The girl squirmed and pushed at the hand and pushed again and then she looked at the youth in disbelief. And with hate.

The youth suddenly wondered if he could be wrong to doubt her. He told the men to stop.

The round-faced man removed his hand slowly and sat away from the girl. The girl rolled into a ball.

"I'll tell you," the youth said.

He looked across at the girl. Her shoulders were shaking silently.

Still, he knew he had not been wrong to keep silent so long. He could not let them find the box. After all, they had let her see their faces, too.

❀

"Go ahead," the tall man said.

The youth pushed himself up a little by pressing the back of his head against the wall. As he raised himself, he pulled briefly on the cord at his wrists, but his hands were too numb to feel if there was any real movement.

"You'll leave us?"

The tall man grunted.

The youth did not believe him, but he concentrated on making his face look as if he were weighing the idea of being free. He darted his glance around the floor before him and bit on his lower lip.

The tall man took the tongs and the glowing coal and stood above the girl. The fingers of the tongs cast a long, bent shadow on the ceiling and the wall.

The youth made himself stare at the coal. "I hid it. It's at the edge of the village."

The round-faced man had come over to the youth now. Below the men, he could see the girl. She was lying quite still.

"At the teahouse at the northern edge of the village. It's in the snow. Under the platform at the front." The youth stopped and looked straight up at the taller man. "It's under the steps. On the side."

The youth expected the men to show some sign of excitement, but neither moved. The round-faced man rubbed the fingertips of one hand against its palm. The tall one stared down at the youth. The image of the candle flame burned in his eyes. There was a si-lence. The youth did his best to stare back at the men.

The jaw of the tall man worked and the muscle there hardened so that a shadow lay thin across his face and he began to wave the tongs slowly until the ember in the tips of the fingers glowed brightly and cut a pattern in the darkened air. "You lie," the man said and all the while he shifted his glance from one eye of the youth to the other as if to discern the secrets hidden there.

The youth looked at the coal, yellowed and tugging in the

gloom, and he wondered if he should change his story or protest its truth. He could not decide which was best, but if he changed he could not see the end of it, so he said it was all true. He made his eyes look back and forth between the men, but he could not bring them to the tall man's eyes and his own voice sounded strange even to his ears.

The tall man stood regarding him as he might some lower form of life. He weighed the silence and weighed the tongs as he kept their odd rocking motion. The light pulled within the ember ready, expectant. Then the man crouched down and grabbed the youth's ankle and slapped the charcoal against his sole.

The youth watched the coal streak in the black air until it disappeared below his foot and he tried to pull his foot away, although in the first instant he felt nothing, and then all at once he was screaming unbelievably and unbelieving and there was darkness and then he saw the lines in the tall man's face straining to hold his leg and then darkness again. His body had taken to jerking about and his head banged against the wall and above his own screams he heard dimly the screeching of the girl. Through the blur of his tears, he saw that she had brought her hands to her face and she was yelling into them so that the yell was choked and the sounds bounced around in the dimness of the room.

When some time had passed and the youth was no longer screaming and the walls of the inn had echoed into silence save for the sobs of the girl, the tall man flexed his cramped hand and waggled the tongs and the ember in the air again.

The youth's foot and leg throbbed, and he could not focus his vision well. He found that he had bitten into his tongue, and his mouth was filled with the taste of blood. He coughed and spat out some of the blood onto the mat and onto himself and some ran down his chin. He could not see the men clearly but only the shapes and colors of them, and he thought that might help him deceive them. He tried not to blink away the tears that blurred his sight, and he said once again that he had told the truth. He tried to sound resentful, and the blood in his throat and the pain further distorted his voice so that even he found it strange and compelling.

He saw the smeared shapes of the men's heads look from one to the other and then the tall man pushed away from him.

The youth kept his eyes out of focus. He tried to think through the pain in his foot. He guessed it would take nearly an hour for the men to reach the village and determine that he was lying. Maybe longer, if some of the people in the village were near the teahouse, and they could not search right away. Given the hike uphill, not much less coming back. He figured he had perhaps two hours or more.

In that time, something might happen. Looking up toward the tall man, the youth thought about trying the cord again, but he was afraid they might see.

The tall man hesitated for a moment longer, then he reached down and, grabbing the youth's ankles, jerked him onto his stomach. The youth looked down into the frayed weaving of the mat. He smelled the dust embedded within. The man yanked at the cord on his wrists.

The round-faced man had stepped over to the closet and moved things in the darkness there, and when he turned he held before him two shapes like serpents. One he threw twisting across the lamplight. When it landed it was a cotton belt that the tall man took up and lashed about the youth's ankles. A second belt had been tossed at the girl. She lay curled on her side, facing away into the corner. The belt had landed across her back, but she did not move.

When the tall man stood again, the youth's face was only inches from his foot.

As soon as the tall man had left the inn, the round-faced one went to tie the girl. He bent over her for a long time, but the youth could not see around the man's back to tell what he was doing. On one side of the man he could see just the back of the girl's calves and feet. Her thighs were still bunched up by her body. Twice her legs moved slightly. The youth looked around the room. He had hoped both men would leave.

The man lifted the girl up to her feet with one hand on the inside of her arm and propped her, facing out, against the doorway. She did not resist. She did not once look at the youth. Her hair hung around her face, and her clothes were disordered. The man checked the youth with a glance and then he picked up the tobacco tray and placed the lamp and the charcoal and the tongs and the firepot on it and led the girl downstairs.

The youth lay alone in the almost total blackness. Once, as she headed down the stairs, he thought he heard the girl. A sound almost like a laugh. Then he guessed they had reached the firepit in the main room, and there was no sound at all.

He became aware that he was thirsty. His head and leg throbbed. The taste of blood was thick in his throat, and he had to swallow some. At the same time he knew it was foolish to worry about his thirst.

He looked around into the darkness of the room, but he could see nothing. The cord on his wrists and the cotton belt on his ankles were tight. When he tried to move more they cut into him. His hands grew numb.

The youth waited for his eyes to adjust. He lay still without dimension or reference, save only, after a while, for the faintest light along the edge of the door at the corridor. When he was sure of that, he gauged it carefully, and began to squirm to reach the other side of the room. He twisted on his stomach and he rolled to his side and he crawled with the back of his head and his hips and he rolled to his stomach once again. Yet even with this his progress seemed slight. He moved as quietly as he could, afraid the floor would creak.

As the lamplight had faded down the staircase, the youth had looked across the room to fix in his mind the angle to the post by the closet. In time he could barely see, or at least imagined he saw, the lighter color wood of the post, just visible against the dark.

He had led the men into the old samurai's room because it had been near the top of the stairs and because of the post. For at the base of that post lay a nail with a decorative head in the shape of a crane, and on the bent wing of that crane several days before he had accidentally torn some bedding. He tried now to remember exactly how the wing bent into the room, and considered how he might best make use of it.

Pressing his face against the floor, he heard a brief noise from downstairs. He stopped and listened. He thought it might have been the girl, but he could not be sure of even that. He wondered if the man would have tied her legs apart. He tried to think of something else. Still, the image came to him. The thought of her lying with her arms crossed over her face and her thighs facing upward spread a sudden warmth through his body. For an instant longer he rested in the dark with his cheek to the mats and the dust in the floor rising up into his nostrils, and he breathed lightly in order to hear.

When he hit the edge of the room he twisted himself around and searched with his foot for the post. With the bottom of his good foot he felt for the nail, and then he swung up his legs and lowered them in the dark so that the cotton belt around his ankle caught something, caught the bent wing. He pressed the belt in against the nail head and concentrated on hooking into the material. He felt the strain of holding his legs in the air. He jerked slightly against the cloth and heard a small tearing sound, and then the belt slipped away from the nail head and the side of his foot hit against the mats.

He rested briefly before he tried again. Breathing in the darkness, concentrating on the muscles of his legs, he wondered how much time he had lost and how much time he had left.

On the third try he hooked the belt again. Pressing down carefully, he felt another small tear.

11

When the cotton belt around his ankles first began to give, the youth lost all track of time. His thighs cramped and the muscles of his stomach and neck shook from holding his feet so long in the air. When he rested, his legs quivered in spasms. He knew he would do better if he rested more, but he no longer knew the hour and he was afraid of the passing time. He lifted his legs again.

A moment later the cotton belt tore through. His ankles came free.

He rolled onto his left side and stared into the darkness and listened to the downstairs and listened to his breathing and listened to the pulse within him. For a short time he waited and stretched his legs and calves so that he could get to his feet soundlessly and walk without stumbling. In that time the slightest noise from below made his heart jump and tears welled up in his eyes. He could not bear the thought of being discovered now with his feet untied and his arms still lashed behind him.

At first he had thought of trying to free his hands and going down for the girl and taking on the round-faced man before the taller one returned. But he knew the man was too strong, and the stairs would groan and give him away before he could get near. Then, too, trying to free his hands would take too long, for the rope was stronger than the cotton belt. He would be discovered before he was ready. Or the tall man might return.

But if he could leave the inn, he knew he had a chance. He had no snowshoes, but the snow had been warmed by the sun during the day, and it had started hardening with the cold even before dusk. On his walk back to the inn that night, a crust had already begun to form. With luck, the snow would be hard enough for him to work his way down the ridge and into the trees before the tall man returned. He could hide there. They would try to follow his tracks in the snow, but there were lots of tracks now, and the snow was harder, and if he made it to the snow path that lay down the hillside from the inn, then they might well lose his trail.

And if he could escape, he thought, they would be unlikely to hurt the girl. For he knew their faces, too, and they would still need her to make him talk. More likely, he thought, they would tie her up and search for him.

He even thought it possible he might bring back help for the girl before the men gave up on him. It was possible. It was, in any case, all he had.

Escape. The thought made his heart work hard within him. It would have to be out of a window in the back of the inn. He dared not risk the stairs or the front door. Against the back wall of the inn was a drift. He could trust himself to that.

Pushing himself up with his shoulders, the youth worked his way to his knees. His arms and hands, still tied behind him and numb from the ropes, tingled painfully as he moved. Careful not to press too suddenly on the mats, he rose to his feet. The pain from his burned foot shocked him. He tried to put his weight on its edge. He took his first step and then listened in the dark with his mouth open. He doubted that the round-faced man downstairs could have heard him. He took his next step, fearful that the shift of weight might make the floor creak. If the round-faced man came up while his hands were still tied, he would have no chance.

He thought for a moment of hiding somewhere in the upstairs of the inn, but they would be too likely to check. He could not bear the thought of being caught so near to being free.

Then, too, the window might stick or creak. But if he could get it open, he could throw himself out, and if the evening cold had hardened the snow enough, he just might get away.

He tried to slow his breath, both to hear, and because he was afraid even of the noise of his breathing. He worked his way across the room.

The youth reached the corridor above the stairs. He stopped and held his breath to listen. It was difficult to hear. The blood pounded in his ears. Then he moved on toward the window at the far end.

There was a sound from below, and he stopped again. Someone was moving on the mats. Then it was quiet once more.

He reached the window.

The youth put his forehead to the wooden sill on the window and listened again. He thought about how best to open it. He wanted to open it very gently, so that if it stuck he could think again before it made any real noise. But he doubted he would have that kind of control. He could hear his heart in his ears.

The youth pushed up and out with his forehead, and the window opened slightly. The night cold came through the window and bathed his skin. The window made a small, wooden bumping sound as it had opened, but probably not, the youth thought, enough to be heard below. He turned and pushed with his shoulder until the window was just wide enough for him to work his way out.

Outside, the snow was a luminous silver and it was blue in the shadows from the moon. He looked up. A full moon touched above the ridge and there were thin gray continents upon it, and in its light the sky was clear and starless. He saw there would be no witness save the moon.

The youth pulled the night air into his lungs. He wondered if the air from the window would work its way downstairs and tug at the flames in the firepit and alert the man. He saw about him the stark trees in the forest.

Just beneath the youth, alight in the moonglow, was the drift. He worked one leg hurriedly over the windowsill and, with a last brief effort to listen for something from within, he tossed himself out into the night.

Almost at once he knew he was tumbling over too far. He saw the sky for an instant and then the rushing, pock-marked surface of the snow and then he hit, face first, and broke through the snow-crust and plunged into its depths.

❋

The youth hung head down inside the drift. He struggled to right himself, his hands tied and useless behind him. Snow filled his eyes and ears and chilled his head and when he opened his mouth to breathe snow choked him. He could not see or hear what might be happening above. He expected at any moment to feel the round-faced man's hands upon him. But when at last his head broke free of the snow and he shook it clear, there were no shouts, no pounding on the stairs or floorboards, no one approaching from around the corner of the inn. There was only the silence of the silver-blue snow, which stretched around him and filled his clothes and lay cold against his skin.

In the midst of that moonlit drift he felt exposed. He looked around into the shadows of the grove of barren trees not far from the side of the inn. He twisted himself to stand, but as he tried to step the crusting snow broke beneath his foot. The cold had not yet hardened the snow as he had hoped and it made his way more difficult. He knew it would make his trail more obvious. They might see he had no snowshoes. They would if they knew the north country.

He began to wade toward the shadows that lay across the grove like a striped cloth. His burned foot pained him greatly from the cold and from walking on it and his arms rode awkwardly behind him. He moved through the snow with a lurch. To anyone who might see him there sunken to his crotch, his eyes white with effort and fear, he would have seemed a creature half-crazed.

By the time the youth had reached the edge of the trees, his chest drew air audibly and he had lost his one remaining sock to the suction of the snow. He turned to look once more at the back of the inn. The moon shone on the snow of the roof and bleached the wooden walls where they dipped silently into the drifts. Still nothing moved at the window from which he had jumped, and, except for his darkened trail, it might have been that he had never been there at all.

Wading slowly to catch his breath, screening himself from the inn with the tree trunks, the youth headed to the far edge of the grove. He knew the tall man could be heading up to the inn at any moment. He kept to the shadows. He sought to favor his injured foot, and he was glad to feel the snow begin to numb the pain. He thought briefly about the girl and hoped she would be all right.

As he reached the edge of the grove and the start of the clearing below the inn, the youth saw the tall man break out of the trees down the hillside and stand out into the moonlight. For a moment the youth remained quite still, then he lowered himself slowly and lay into the snow, partly in the shade of the trunk of a beech.

The tall man was walking quite quickly back toward the inn. He followed the beaten path that led north from the village and south toward the valley and coast. His hands were balled at his sides and they made tight arcs in time to his steps. A small cloud of vapor rose from his mouth.

For the first time the youth felt the cold of the air. He had no boots and no coat, and the snow clung in his hair and melted against his skin from his fall into the drift. He found he was shivering, and the chill struck him with the force of life.

The tall man left the track and turned farther uphill toward the inn. He walked quickly by, only thirty yards away. He was muttering as he walked, and his lips moved oddly.

The youth wanted to laugh. A hope began to swell within him. But then he caught himself and shook his head and cursed at his own stupidity, for he saw all that lay before him and he saw all that might mean his end.

It had been the youth's plan to cross the clearing and reach the beaten north-south path before the tall man returned. With the coastal road closed, many travelers had used the old track in the two sunny days since the storm. The path would be hardening in the cold. On the far side of the track, the open hillside ended, and a ridge plunged down through a pine forest into a ravine. He had planned to leave the track a distance ahead to hide in the cover of the ravine. If he could make it to the path, the youth thought, the men might lose his trail.

But the tall man had returned too soon, and the youth knew he would have no time to follow the track. He might not even have time to reach it. But if he did not, they would spot him there in the clearing in the moonlight. It would take them only moments. Without snowshoes, he had no chance to outrun them. He had to reach the track.

The youth lifted himself in a crouch out of the snow. He edged his way toward the far tree line just beyond the track.

A loud bang startled the youth, and he threw himself forward into the snow. The tall man had reached the inn and was kicking at

the door. He had descended the snow wall and, when the youth
dared to look behind him, the man could not be seen, but the sound
of his kicking, echoing between the snow wall and the inn, carried
cleanly through the moonlight to him.

"Open up!" the youth heard. "Open it!"

A line of yellow light appeared on the snow along the edge of
the roof above the door.

"Damn!" he heard the round-faced man say and then the door
closed and the light disappeared.

The youth stood straight and dove forward across the surface of
the snow. He began to roll over and over down the open hillside toward the track and he twisted his body and pushed with his hands
tied behind him to increase his speed, and the crust held beneath
him. Looking up as he spun, he saw the distance between himself
and the trees just beyond the track narrowing, although being so
low in the snow, he could no longer see the track itself. In his mind
he saw the men rushing up the stairs. He heard them calling out
their revenge to him. He knew the tall one had thought of nothing
but beating him, perhaps burning or cutting him, since discovering
he had been tricked. He imagined their faces when they saw the
cotton belt on the floor.

And then they would tie the girl or check her bonds and turn and
come for him. They would know he had not come down the stairs.
They would spot his trail in the snow. They would come for him.

Rolling faster downward, the youth could hear only the snow
crushing around his ears and the rush of the wind as he turned. His
mind became dizzy. They might be watching him already. If they
looked to the clearing, they could not miss him moving across the
snowfield. He cursed the full moon that blurred above. He thought
he could feel the men running down the field toward him even as
he rolled. He imagined he would land up against them when he
stopped.

The youth dropped through the snow to the beaten track and

landed hard on his back against it. He lay there while he tried to get his mind to clear. He could see only the lips of the spinning track and above, the spinning sky, and he felt as if he were in motion still.

In his haze he heard a shout. He tried to raise his head and it hit into the frozen snow and he raised it again and this time he managed to peer over the edge of the lip. Within the twisting world he saw two men clearing the snow wall at the front of the inn and running through the snow to the grove on the side. They wore snowshoes and moved well. In a moment they disappeared into the shadows of the grove.

The youth pushed up into a crouch and dove from the track, but he crashed almost immediately into the branches of a fir tree just beyond. He had sought to pitch himself over the lip of the track and into the ravine, but he had not looked and so he had not seen the tree. He lay now much too near the track. He saw that he had knocked the snow off the darkened needles in the lower branches of the fir, and they lay suddenly exposed like the inverse images of bones. He feared they might betray him. He struggled to get his feet underneath him but he could not free himself from the limbs of the tree. More snow shook down around him, and before he could work himself loose, he knew he had run out of time.

He backed himself deeper into the branches and lowered himself into the snow. He felt the snow cup around his chin. His head began to clear.

He could see through the fir needles and up the clearing. Soon the men had emerged from the shadows of the grove running one after the other, after his trail. In the distance they moved blue and dark and silently through the snow. Their arms pumped up before them and the blade of the tall man's knife flashed in the moonlight at the height of each pump. The round-faced man, too, carried something. It was long and dark and the man gripped it in the middle and it swung in the manner of a knife, although at one point, lost in the glory of his run, the man waved it up and over his head like a sword and then up and over his head he waved it once again.

The men ran directly down the youth's trail in the snow, right toward where he lay.

The youth sank deeper into the branches of the fir tree and dug with his feet to lower himself further into the snow. The branches and the shadows of the tree covered him. The snow slid up under his clothes against his stomach and chest. It hung in the folds like an extra belly.

He thought about throwing himself farther down the steep of the ravine and hiding behind a tree not so close to the track, but it was already too late, and he did not want his trail to be visible if the men spread out along the track and looked down into the forest.

He waited. He held his eyes just above the snow in the shadows of the fir, and he looked away and down the hillside. Everything was still. He tried to quiet his breathing and listen for the men, but his heart beat loudly in his ears. Even so he could hear them now running in the snow. The trees below him loomed up beautifully from the moon-bleached snow and the dark. Clumps of snow in the needles of the evergreens glistened. The silence of the snow swept up all around him. He felt it slowly begin to cover him up in its depths.

Footsteps landed on the cold-hardened track above. The youth held his breath. He dared not turn his head to look. He heard their breathing. Then the footsteps continued. Running quickly. The youth peeked out. The two men were running down the track away from him. One ran north, one south. The youth could still hear the sound of the air rushing from their lungs as they pounded on the track.

The round-faced man brandished his long, dark weapon in an arc over his head once more as he passed amidst the trees and the moon shadows of the trees. Rounding a bend in the track, he disappeared.

After a dozen more yards the tall man stopped and peered into the snow down the ravine. He looked vaguely toward the fir where the youth hid, but the youth knew he could not be seen through the branches and the shadows on the snow, and the tall man looked away. He ran several yards back and forth along the track, looking down now into the woods, now back along the track. He craned his neck to look around the sides of trees as he moved. Then he turned and ran quickly farther north along the track, ever farther from where the youth lay.

The youth drew in a great breath of cold air. He watched the tall man disappear into the trees a long way down the track. He felt an urge to flee, but he made himself wait for a while to be sure neither of the men would double back. He looked about. The night was truly beautiful to him. He looked at the tree gratefully and felt once again like laughing and began to disentangle himself from the branches to slide down the ravine toward the village. He felt the cold again. His hands, still tied tightly behind him, had gone numb.

"Setsu-o-o-o-o!"

The youth's eyes widened and he pushed himself as best he could back up toward the path.

"It's not possible," he thought.

"Setsu-o-o-o!"

He saw the girl Yukiko running toward him from the inn.

They would have tied her up, he thought, she could not have escaped so quickly.

"Setsu-o-o-o!"

In the still night the voice floated clearly out to him as it had once before. He looked up and down the track. He could no longer see either the tall man or the round-faced one, nor could he hear them running. He wondered if they could hear the girl. He feared they would return.

Hidden in the shadows and the branches, he lifted his head just above the snow bank. Yukiko ran down toward him through the snow, stumbling forward. Her arms swung up and down awkwardly at her sides.

The girl reached the snow at the very edge of the track and stopped.

Moonglow reflected off her hair and when she stopped her chin lifted briefly up and the light fell across her forehead and nose and cast her eyes in shadows.

"Setsuo," she said quietly. She looked up and down the track. She was unsteady, and she wavered back and forth over her knees. Her small shoulders shook in around her neck. Her breath formed pale in the night air. Clumps of snow that she had kicked off the lip of the track had floated up into the light of the moon and then scudded down the sides of the ravine around the youth.

In the branches of the fir, the youth thought about calling out to her, but he remembered the damp feel of the girl in the darkness of his bed as she squeezed his head against her and held his face down into her clothing and against her skin. He remembered the cold, wet touch as her tongue licked his ear. And he did not call to her.

Yukiko pushed up off her knees and, jumping out into the track, began to run down the path in the direction the round-faced man had taken.

The youth balled his fists tightly. He thought again about calling out to her, but no sound came. He could not understand how she could have gotten free. He tried to think, and as he did she drew farther away.

As the girl ran, she caught the pale rays of moonlight between the trees. The heels of her boots kicked in the moonglow and her snowshoes sounded against the track.

The youth stared through the branches after her. For a second he looked back down the ravine behind him at the snow and the trees and the moonlight in the branches. All was still as before. Far below there was a place on a drift where the crystals shone. Then once again the silence of the blue-gray snow cascaded all around him until his ears filled with the sound, and soon he could no longer hear her running at all.

❀

The youth descended the ridge. Snow from past falls lay upon his shoulders and along his arms and thick in his frozen hair, and the crystals of this snow caught the moonlight so that he glistened as he lurched like some ancient apparition.

He judged his way from the moon and so judging moved on, a figure pale like the snow. He looked about into the night and then looked about again. In time he chanced upon a place where steam rose off the surface of the snow and the silver light fell upon it like a membrane breached only by the reaching limbs of trees and the shadow limbs of trees, and he hesitated before he crossed it and held his breath when he did, and when he looked back it could not be seen.

As the night deepened and the snow glaze hardened, the way of the youth grew easier and mostly the snow supported him, although often he would stumble across the crust. When he broke through he had to crawl with his knees or twist himself with his chin against the surface to force himself once again to stand. His toes and ankles had long ago gone numb and his feet felt like blocks. He could not feel his hands, behind him, at all.

Near the last ridge that lay above the village, the youth slid down a short slope into a stand of trees. At the bottom tumbling snow fell all around him and filled his collar and he blew it from his mouth and blinked it from his eyes. He struggled to rise. When he had made it to his knees, he saw a form moving in the distance, and he realized it was a man.

The man was hurrying toward him. He wore a rounded straw hat more common to the south and layers of straw hung loose like thatch about his shoulders and these flapped noisily against him in his haste.

By the time the youth had regained his feet, the straw man had begun to run. The youth stumbled back up the base of the slope with his arms useless behind him. He heard the sound of the beating straw grow louder. Looking back, he saw the strain in the man's face, and the man gaining closer still. Soon the straw man was hard upon him.

A shout came from above the youth and when he looked up the slope he saw close at hand a second man, and it was the old samurai from the inn. The old samurai stood thin and washed of color in the full light of the moon. He held a bow fully drawn, and he pointed it at the youth.

The youth fell to one knee in the snow. The clouds of his breath and the beating of his heart astounded him. His vision was blurred with tears. He could not see the arrowhead, but he imagined it there, death within it, thin, blended, seeming to lack substance against the old man. At his back he heard the rush of the straw man come to a halt and the thatch clashing against him. He heard the man breathing hard.

The bow fired, but the youth had not been hit. There had been a thick sound behind him, not loud. The old samurai was looking there.

The straw man had fallen backward in the snow. In the dim light, the shaft of the arrow could barely be seen against the straw thatch, and the feathers of the arrow seemed to hang improbably in the air a few inches from the man's chest.

"Move," the old samurai said.

The youth stepped slowly to the side. He did not know whether to run from the old samurai before another arrow could be drawn, but he doubted he could get very far.

The straw man's eyes were open, and he wore a puzzled look. He seemed to stare into the air as if something surprised him there. His mouth worked slowly and his breath was shallow, carefully drawn. His eyes lowered and he looked dully down at the feathers of the arrow.

The old samurai squatted over the man and took away a short sword that lay by the body. He put his hand lightly on the end of the arrow shaft as though he might feel the man's life within. The straw man stared up at him, but the old samurai said nothing in response. Then he rose and told the youth to turn around.

The youth turned uncertainly. He felt the old samurai cut away his bonds.

The youth drew his arms painfully from behind himself. He found he could not raise them or get them to bend. He stood stiffly like a puppet looking wide-eyed at his arms and his heart beat hard. He bent and pressed his chin against his upper arm but there was little feeling. Then he leaned his body forward at the waist and twisted until his mouth was near one of his hands and he tried to blow on it, but the hand was still too far away. He tried to swing his arms closer and all that resulted was an odd, jerking motion. Bent in half, his mouth straining toward his own fingers, he looked like a man trying to eat himself.

With his head down by the snow, the youth found himself close to the fallen man. The man breathed still. His eyes moved and he looked at the youth as though from a great distance.

"You must go," the old samurai said.

The youth straightened up. Pain was returning to his arms and he found the right one would bend. For a moment he contemplated this movement in amazement.

The youth dropped to his knees in the snow and with his right forearm hugged one of the straw man's boots to his chest and tried to yank it free. Each time he yanked the straw man's body moved a little in the snow, but the man made no sound. When at last the one boot came free the youth set at the other.

During this time the old samurai said nothing. Looking up, the youth saw that he peered about into the forest.

Soon the youth could bring his hands painfully to his mouth and he sat down in the snow and breathed on his fingers and tried to get them to work. Then he set the boots in the snow and pushed his feet into them and tried to pull them up.

When he had finished, the youth stood and breathed again on his hands and looked at the thatches of straw that lay about the fallen man. The man no longer seemed to know the youth was there.

The youth looked at the old samurai and then leaned over to pull away the thatch, but it was caught on the arrow shaft and the blood was not yet strong enough within the youth's hands to get a good grip. He stood back with his arms bent against himself and his hands to his mouth and looked at the old samurai once more.

The moon cast a bleached light upon them. The shadows of the barren trunks ran down the slope and stretched out at length across the snow.

Stepping forward, the old samurai snapped the arrow shaft at the base and took bundles of the thatch in his hands and yanked at them. They came in rough clumps tied one to another and each bound poorly by twine. Some still lay pinned beneath the straw man's body, as if reluctant yet to part. The old samurai rolled the man over in the snow and pulled the thatch clear. He handed it to the youth.

Face down in the snow, the straw man's dark back rose and fell as he drew breath. The old samurai pushed snow over him and parts of the man seemed to disappear.

Hugging the thatch around himself, the youth found he was shivering. He could not clench his jaw.

The old samurai handed the youth the straw man's short sword. The youth took it between his hands. He found the metal cold and tried to tuck it under his arm against the folds of the thatch.

"Go on," the old samurai said. "To the village. Quietly. There are others about."

The youth took a few steps away, then he stopped. His jaw ached but the chattering of his teeth could be controlled. He looked back at the old samurai. "The box," he said.

The old samurai looked at him in the moonlight. "Go on."

"I hid it in the shrine up the mountainside. Under the platform."

The old samurai drew another arrow from his quiver, notched it to the bow string quickly, and pointed it at the youth.

The youth stepped involuntarily away. He saw his mistake.

The old samurai turned his head slightly to the side without taking his eyes off the youth. "Over here," he said loudly. "I have him."

The youth now saw two men moving toward him through the

trees. One wore a dark vest and one had no hat. The moonlight struck them full in the face, and they were twisting to see the shadowed youth and the old samurai more clearly.

"Hurry," the old samurai said loudly, and the two men moved more quickly through the trees. At thirty yards they saw the bow and slowed.

"Throw the sword away from you," the old samurai said to the youth.

The youth hesitated, but then he took the short sword awkwardly and threw it into the air half a dozen yards away. It caught the moonlight and disappeared with a small sound into the snow.

When the two men were barely twenty yards away their faces could be seen clearly in the moonglow. One of them called out a man's name and he made a visor of his hand to see. The old samurai grunted and lowered his head and stepped to the straw man half-buried beneath clumps of snow and turned him over with his foot. "See if he's alive," he said to the two men.

At ten yards the old samurai turned and shot the closer of the two men through the chest. The youth saw briefly the arrow flash and heard the bow and the dull noise as the arrow struck at almost the same time. The man was suddenly on the ground. His feet moved. When the second man saw what had happened he started to charge, but he had gone only a short distance in the snow when he realized the bow would soon be drawn again. He turned toward the trees and started to run.

The old samurai, holding a notched arrow, ran a few yards after him. Then he pulled up short and raised the bow into the moonlight as if he might shoot into the upper branches of a tree and then he lowered the bow and shot the second man through the back. The man fell face forward into the snow.

The old samurai drew another arrow and notched it and looked around. The youth had run to look for the sword he had thrown away, but to his amazement it could not be found. Now he saw the old samurai and straightened up.

"Go on," the old man said. "Go to the village. I'll follow as far as I can."

The youth edged away, afraid he too would be shot. In a moment he began to run.

"Slowly," the old samurai hissed after him.

When the youth looked back through the trees, he saw the old samurai clearly in the moonglow. He was stooped and scooping up snow in his arms and throwing it over the bodies. The slanted shadows of the trees ran in perfect parallels between them.

❋

The youth squatted in the darkness at the edge of the village and looked about. He had not seen the old samurai again.

Ahead, at the far end of the village, he could hear the theatricals underway. He slipped slowly down into the shadows below the eaves of the houses and crossed toward the noise.

When he emerged again, people and torches were all around. Strong drums beat the air so loudly that he could hear little else. Men were chanting words that had no meaning to him, and their hands waved in the air. Some were half-naked and some dressed in summer wear, and one wore only a cloth about his loins.

A throng of dancers approached the youth beneath a large parasol. Bells and small drums hung from a halberd at the parasol's tip, and strips of colored cord swung and jerked about its edges. A man with a white-powdered face and sleeves bound in scarlet thrust the parasol high and grunted and thrust it high again. In a frenzy around him pressed wide-eyed villagers in brightly colored garments and painted faces and women with bits of mirrors woven in their hair. Some of the dancers held their hands upon one another's shoulders and some held worn flasks of sake that they swung, and in all these dancers there was not one the youth knew, nor any who showed that they knew him.

The youth grabbed at the hem of one in this crowd and shoved in among them to hide. He could smell their sweat even in the cold and in the glow of the torches he could see their sweat. Several pushed back at him roughly.

Soon he was carried with them one and all toward a stage. Hempen torches dipped in wax burned at every corner, and in its center stood a great conifer draped in sacred ropes.

Revelers leaned now so close against the youth that he could not lower his hands. His face was pressed into the sweat-soaked back of a gangly man. A woman beside the youth tottered, and he saw that a man had fallen beneath them. The woman, then the youth, stepped on the man.

Yet suddenly the crowd ahead parted, and from its midst an enormous dancer emerged. He wore a mask much larger than his head, and he was lifted above the others and passed from hand to hand until he bounded onto the stage.

The dancer wore the female mask of *Ame no Uzume no Mikoto*, the goddess who brought laughter to the heavens and coaxed the sun from its cave. Across the shoulders of this false goddess rested a straw broom, and on its end there hung a paper with a drawing of the sexual organs of a woman. The center of the drawing had been smeared with a paste of the deepest red.

Now the dancer in the mask approached the tree and bared large white breasts and thrust her hips back and forth and, as the drumbeat quickened, a second figure leapt out from the back of the stage. He wore a linen hat and a bright purple sash and he carried a long, wooden pestle with the tip painted red in the manner of a phallus. He lunged with the pestle at the blood red drawing on the end of the broom, and he spun about and lunged again. He lunged with the pestle and he lunged with the pestle and each time he drew farther and farther from the tree. Then the female dancer abruptly stopped and raised the drawing high in the air and the crowd cried out to it. The drums beat into a frenzy and the torches dropped and the dancers dropped and fire ran up the ropes and fire bathed the tree and the two masked creatures, crouched and groping before it, spun around and around and around each other, crouched and groping toward the moment to come.

12

In the fifth month of that year, when the snow had largely passed but the air was still cool, the youth walked a narrow path toward the village. The soft leaves of spring were out, and even in the bright sunlight he could not see far ahead. Off in the shadowed woods small patches of snow still lay in places, barely showing white, sullied in the passage of mud and time.

Coming over a rise the youth heard the sounds of horses, uncommon enough in those steep mountain ridges, and soon he saw three saddled and grazing at the edge of the forest. They were strongly muscled and well arrayed. He slowed with caution.

In the grasses at the edge of the trail ahead sat three men. They wore their hair in topknots, and their clothes were of purples and greens and browns and the patterns in the cloth were clearly visible. As the youth drew closer, he saw weapons at their sides.

The nearest of the three men was old, with a forehead cleft and lined, and he nodded to the youth. A second man, much younger, bore the handsome face of an actor. This man nodded, too. The youth had never seen either man before.

The third, the youth realized, was the bearded man.

The youth looked at the third man more carefully and, unknowingly, stopped where he stood. The man wore fine apparel and the beard was clipped and there was now a keenness to the eyes, but the bearded man it was. The man from the night of the storm. The man who had hidden the box.

The bearded man opened his hand and swept it across the top of the grass beside him and asked the youth to come sit by them. He said that they wished to talk with him and that they bore him no ill.

The youth watched them warily. He sat slowly where he was in the dust of the track.

The youth had thought the bearded man dead, and he wondered what his sudden reappearance could mean. The man had killed the hunter in the storm. Others, perhaps, too. And now this bearded man sat in the grass by the edge of the track with the blades rising about him and two men, one on either side, and each of them looked upon the youth. He felt as though he were some creature caught in their path.

The bearded man smiled at the youth. "I have caused you some problems," he said.

The youth looked into the man's face, but he could read nothing there.

The bearded man reached beneath his clothing and drew out a small bundle wrapped in oiled paper. He tossed it on the ground between them. Freed from his hand and clothing, the oiled paper began to unfold on its own. Inside, the youth could see a purse.

"I am grateful for your help," the bearded man said.

The youth did nothing, but only stared at the oiled paper.

The bearded man motioned with his chin for the youth to take it up. "It is for you," he said.

The youth hesitated for a while and then he came forward in a crouch and took up the purse. He took a step back and sat once again in the trail, nearer now to the three men. When he looked into his hands, he saw there a fine silk sack tied with cord. The purse was roughly the size of the rice balls he had brought the bearded man in the storm.

The youth untied the cord. The purse held bent coins of copper and some of tarnished silver and a few thin pieces of gold. For the youth, therein lay a fortune, although beyond the mountains it would not have been of great importance at all.

The youth placed the purse back on the ground.

When he had first looked into the dead hunter's wallet, the youth had marveled at the money there. Over the weeks he had hidden and rehidden it, weighing it, moving it about. But the contents of the dead hunter's wallet were nothing to what lay in the purse before him now.

The youth regarded the bearded man closely. He remembered the strength with which the bearded man had thrown him against the fallen tree on the night of the storm. With small movements of his eyes, he took in once again the weapons the three men bore.

"It is yours," the bearded man said. "Take it up."

The bearded man has returned for the packet, the youth thought, and it is gone. On the morning after the theatricals the youth had told the assistant headman of the village all that had happened, and with others they had climbed to the shrine above the inn and looked under the platform for the packet wrapped in straw. But it was already gone.

The youth wondered what the three men might do.

The bearded man regarded the youth quizzically. "Speak," the man said. "There is some question you would ask."

"Why are you here?"

"To repay you. Nothing more. What other reason might I have?"

The youth hesitated. "When you came to the inn, the night of the storm, and ran back out, some of the guests thought you had 'other reasons' of your own."

The youth meant to suggest that he thought so as well.

The bearded man nodded.

"Some thought you might have something you would not want them to see."

"And they do not? Each of them? They harbor things they do not show themselves."

The youth sat silent. He wondered when the bearded man would ask about the packet.

"I am no thief," the bearded man said in soft tones, and then he smiled and spread his hands wide apart as if to show himself or his clothing, "or if a thief, no more so than any other man."

"Some people were killed that night."

The bearded man nodded and a small breeze blew. The grass moved beside him.

"If you are worried about that," the bearded man gestured toward the purse, "it was not stolen."

"Why would you give it to me?"

"Why did you come to help me in the storm?"

"It was not such a great thing."

"Neither is that," the bearded man nodded toward the purse in the path, and he picked up his weapons and rose to his feet. The actor and the old man, too, took up their weapons and stood. Although the youth was concerned, the three men made no movement toward him. They waited, looking down upon him where he sat in the dust of the track.

They seemed to have done with him.

After a time when the youth neither rose nor spoke but stared into the air between himself and the path, the bearded man asked if there was something else and the youth said there was, but he did not speak further. He sat like that for a time, until at last the youth raised his head and looked into the mouth of the bearded man to avoid his eyes, and asked in an awkward voice about the girl.

The bearded man looked to the others, who shook their heads and shrugged in response. He sat back down in the grass. The other two remained standing.

"The musician," the youth said, "the string player, the girl with the performers," although in his mind's eye he saw the face of the girl as he had seen her in the bath.

"From the inn?" the old man with the cleft forehead asked after a moment, but when the youth said yes, he shook his head in ignorance.

"She has not been found," the youth said.

The three men looked at him blankly, and it became clear to the youth that they had not known she was lost. They seemed indifferent to the fate of the girl, but curious as to why such a question was put to them.

"Did you know her?" the bearded man asked. He had picked a pinecone off the ground, and he jiggled it absently in his hand.

"From the storm. From the time of the storm. She was here for the theatricals. In the village."

"She was from the village?"

"A wayfarer."

"And you knew her?"

"Some."

"Then you would know better than us."

The youth and the three men stared at one another.

"Now you have a purse," the old man said, "enough to live differently, if you wish."

The youth looked instead to the bearded man. "What was it all about?" he said.

The young man with the face of an actor smiled. "It seems it was about a girl."

The youth looked down toward the track once again.

"What great truth would you know?" the actor asked. "What would make a difference for you? At stake were the plans for war with the Russe or the emperor's secret goals in Manchuria. There was a list of conspirators that threatened the lords of the land, or a list of the lords of the land who are conspirators. You helped us keep from others the lay of our defenses. Or our offenses. They are all nothing to you."

"They meant something to you," the youth said.

"Yes, to us. Much."

"I was there," the youth said.

"So were others."

"I helped him," the youth said, nodding toward the bearded man.

"Did you know what you were doing?" the actor said. "Might you just as well have endangered all that he had done?"

There came a silence among them. The needles of a pine behind the three men moved, although the youth felt no breeze.

"Did you love this girl?" the old man said at last.

The youth was not sure how he should respond. It struck him as odd that he had not put this question to himself before. Then, too, in the past he had imagined love differently. He had thought it to be clear and certain, while his feelings now did not seem so easy to define.

"Did she love you? Or use you?" the actor asked after a moment. He seemed amused.

The old man said the two were not always unrelated. He looked more kindly upon the youth. "There was this girl," he said.

"Who is now lost," the actor said.

"But," the old man said, "there was this girl just the same."

The bearded man turned the pinecone about in his hand. "You said this girl was a performer. A string player."

"Yes," the youth said.

"Here for the theatricals."

"Yes."

"So it was natural that she would move on."

The youth nodded.

"But you say she has not been found."

"Yes."

"Where did you expect her to be?"

The youth did not trust his voice. He looked at the needles of the pine above the man's shoulder. They were still. "At the theatricals," he said.

"Maybe she was there, then. There must have been dozens of private parties needing musicians."

"Maybe."

The bearded man stopped and looked at the youth. He drew his eyebrows together. "But you know she might have been playing for a private party. You know performers move on."

The youth said it was not important anymore.

"You thought I might know her," the bearded man said.

The youth said nothing.

"You thought she might have something to do with me."

The youth looked down and shook his head vaguely, so that it might not be clear if he was saying no, or that it was not important, or that the bearded man had simply missed the point.

"Something that she had not told you about."

The youth shook his head vaguely again.

The bearded man looked at the youth for a moment. "I cannot help you on this," he said. "Perhaps no one can."

The youth nodded.

The youth had said it was not important anymore, and in a sense, he thought, it was not.

The girl was gone. He had turned from her at the tree, and she was gone.

She had stood in the moonlight by the edge of the path and called his name, and he had not understood how she could be free. She had turned and run down the path, and he had seen the moonlight upon her back and heard the sound of her running feet in the snow, and in an instant she was gone. He had let her go.

In the days since he had listened for her at the door of the inn and found reasons to go to the village. He had searched along the mountain paths and peered down into the ravines and sometimes he stood and closed his eyes as if by will alone he might conjure her before him. But he could not. He saw only the daylight or the dark and looked at his own flesh and tried to imagine hers, and he asked himself where she was and how she had come to be free.

He had at one point thought that the girl might have freed herself, as he had. Or perhaps that the round-faced man had untied her and touched her and, later, in his haste to recapture the youth, had left her there, thinking her spent.

Or might it still be true, as the youth had feared, that she and the round-faced man had been in league together all along? Perhaps, then, her heart had always lain beyond his reach. Perhaps it was for the box, or to have her contract bought, that she had come to the inn that night—not for him.

The weight of this debate had fallen at times on different sides, and at odd moments each in turn held sway. But in the end all his thoughts and wanderings had come to this: perhaps she had been killed that night by the round-faced man as she ran along the snow path; but, if she were alive, she had never returned to find him.

For it would seem, the youth had come to believe, that the girl was either dead or she had never been interested in him at all. He saw only those choices. In the secret places of his heart he had wondered whether he preferred her dead, knowing that she had cared for him, or living and indifferent to his fate.

It was in this sense then, that he had said it was not important anymore what had happened to her.

Yet, he had asked the bearded man about her.

As he sat in the path at the foot of the bearded man and had asked about the girl, the memory of her face had floated before the youth. It was the image of her that always came to him first.

She was in the bath. Only her head showed above the water. She was looking at him.

He and the tiny dancer had carried Yukiko, unconscious, to the bath and undressed her and placed her in the water for warmth. Later, the tiny dancer had told Yukiko that she owed him no apology or thanks, that he had enjoyed undressing her. And before he could protest, Yukiko had looked up at him, her chin in the water, her eyes wide and bright.

It had seemed to him, even then at the edge of the bath, that he had seen her heart in that look.

And it was, before all else, that look that made him ask about her still.

✻

The bearded man slapped his palms to his thighs and stood once again.

The youth realized with surprise that the men might indeed be going. He bowed low, his head in the dust near the purse so that he could see only their feet.

The bearded man reached his hand down to the youth. "Arise," he said, "you are reborn."

The youth thought the phrase odd, and yet it was familiar. He tilted his head to the side, and it came to him that it was the phrase the old samurai had used the day the youth had been attacked outside the inn.

The old samurai had hooted at the backs of the two men who were fleeing, shaking his empty bow in the air, and he had reached down to help the youth, still splayed in the snow. "'Arise, you are reborn,'" he had said, and now the bearded man said it, too.

The youth looked at the hand of the bearded man as if it were the hand of a spirit.

"'Arise, you are reborn,'" the youth repeated with effort. "An odd phrase."

The bearded man extended his hand again. He said they were

the words of his old fencing teacher, who used to mock his students when they had been knocked to the ground, groaning. "'Arise! You are reborn,' he would say, 'Who stands first?'"

The youth saw now why the bearded man had not asked about the packet; the old samurai had told him all he needed to know. Indeed, the old samurai had most probably recovered it for the youth had told him where to find it.

The youth now understood that the bearded man had come to the inn the night of the storm to meet the old samurai. And something there had frightened him, or someone there had warned him off.

But the hunter had followed the bearded man into the storm, and they had fought. The bearded man had hidden the box rather than be set upon by others while the box was still in his clothes, rather than die in the storm and have it found on him. So he had buried the box instead. But the youth had moved the box before the bearded man could return, and so, unknowingly, disrupted their plans.

The youth saw that it had not been fortune that had placed the old samurai twice at his side, once at dusk by the inn, when the men attacked, and again in the forest that last night. The old samurai had been there to watch him, to find the box. Perhaps to guard its secrets.

The youth remembered, too, the pox-faced hunter who had threatened him and disappeared. Perhaps in this, as well, the old samurai had taken a hand.

All this he now understood as he sat in the path at the foot of the bearded man.

"You have the box once again," the youth said.

The bearded man looked down at the youth, still sitting in the track. He nodded and said that the box was where it should be, and he withdrew his hand. His eyes were flat.

"There was a hunter at the inn. A man with a poxed face."

The bearded man shook his head. He said that he knew nothing of this man, or no more than he knew of any.

Indeed, it was possible, the youth thought, that the bearded man would not know everything the old samurai had done.

The youth sat up straight. He felt the sudden beating of his heart.

If the old samurai had done these things, if he had been by the inn that final night, could he have entered? Could he have stumbled upon the girl Yukiko, tied up by the round-faced man, and freed her?

Could this be the reason she had come to be free and to stand in the moonlight at the foot of the path?

And if she were alive, could there be another reason for her failure to return to the inn in the weeks since?

Could it be, the youth now wondered, that she had never returned to the inn because he had not stayed that night to help her?

Because he had let them threaten her for a box that meant nothing to her? Or to him?

Could she have so misunderstood?

His heart raced.

Surely, he thought, she would have seen that he had no choice but to lie about the box. That he had been forced to flee.

It had never before occurred to the youth that, just as he had come to doubt the girl, perhaps she had come to doubt him. He had never stopped to think that the old samurai might have entered the inn that night and freed her. Now he realized not that these things must be true, but that there was so much he had not considered.

The youth stared into the air between himself and the track and saw nothing, for indeed he looked at nothing.

He realized that one of the men had spoken.

"Was this hunter with the poxed face a friend of yours?" the old man said. He was looking at the youth strangely.

The youth had asked the bearded man about the pox-faced hunter, and the bearded man had said he did not know.

Silent for so long, the youth's thoughts had wandered far from the pox-faced hunter, and the old man had apparently been misled.

"What happened to him?" the old man asked again.

The youth thought to correct him, to say that it was not the fate of the pox-faced hunter that concerned him, but instead he merely shook his head.

"Some things may never be known," the bearded man said. "Maybe that is not how it had to be, but maybe that is how it has to be now."

The youth waited. He thought there might be more, but there was not.

Soon the old man began to rub vigorously at the cleft in his forehead and then to swat at the air before him as if an insect hovered there. The actor, too, looked into the air, and in a moment it seemed they had lost all interest in the youth and the hunter with the poxed face.

The bearded man pointed with his chin to the purse of money that lay still and visionless on the ground. "Don't drink it all up," he said.

As he turned to go, the bearded man took the pinecone he had jiggled and whipped it underhand at the youth.

Without thinking, the youth raised his arm, and the pinecone stung his palm. When he looked in his hand, he saw that the cone rested there. The flanges of the cone were split or bent, and on them there lay the dust of the track. Flecks in the dust caught the spring light.

The youth picked up the purse and hid it in his clothing. He felt the cool air.

In the late morning sky above there hung a crescent moon, and this contended oddly with the full borne sun. On the part of the moon that men might see that day there were sharp edges and gray continents, and these clear as a hand. Yet within that crescent there was nothing but sky, although moon there must be, and moon there would be again.

❀

Within the month the youth headed north across the mountains toward the village of his home. He had left the inn forever, and he carried upon him the dead hunter's wallet and the purse of the bearded man and the little else that he owned. By day he avoided all travelers that he could, hiding in grasses or the trees while they passed. At night before stopping he buried the money in the forest, and the next morning dug it up again. He was on the road three days in this fashion to reach the mountain passes, and in all that time he spoke to others only to ask about the girl.

In the high mountains he passed through small villages, no more than clusters of shacks. The wayside was bleak and rock-strewn, and rocks held down the roofs of the hovels, and the people burned dried moss and manure for lack of any wood. There seemed no reason at all for people to be in such places, save that fate had left them there. Yet, even in these places, he asked about the girl.

He asked although he did not know if she was dead or if she had used him, or, if she were alive, whether she had feelings for him still. In truth he asked long after he had given up hope of receiving answers. He asked because he liked to think of her with him in those high places, far from the inn. In part he asked merely to hear her name.

Atop the last of these passes, he looked out at the barren land and felt anew the strangeness of it, the strangeness within him. He saw among the rocks no clear path, or many paths and none of them easy. Yet this did not disturb him. Indeed, he felt the stronger for it.

He thought of the girl. He thought many times of her face. In the vague aching that he felt, he found some pleasure, too. He sensed a second life within him, one he had not known to be there, and it comforted him.

Where once he had seen love as an allotment, he saw it now

as uncertain and fleeting, revealed only in parts, intertwined with chance and time. He saw it as a changing thing.

But he had tasted of it.

Alone in a wind-swept place, he saw himself as he imagined another might see him there. He narrowed his eyes into a pose and gazed long across the mountaintops. He felt his clothes tug about him and listened to the whistling in his ears. He smiled thinly. He nodded at times to himself.

On the morning of the final day the youth crossed along a north-facing slope where patches of snow remained. In them the hollows of men's footsteps, long buried in the drifts of winter, could once again be seen. These footsteps began where the snow began in places where shadows often lay, and they ran until the sunlight where the snow was no more, and so they seemed to mark journeys of no distance at all that began without import and ended the same and held no meaning whatsoever save what meaning lay in their own passage. And it could happen that a wayfarer, crossing there, could come across these traces of his own way and know them not, or knowing them, have long forgotten what caused them to be; or it could be that he and the ghost of he that traced the empty hollows still might follow and precede and follow one another and look upon the same scene and see two things different altogether, and feel two things altogether different about what they saw.

That noon the youth descended into forest once again. For a time he was followed by a lean, yellow dog with four white forelimbs and cataract-whitened eyes. Its hide was scabbed with age and dust and the youth could count its ribs. He threw a stone at it. The dog stopped and turned its white eyes after the stone. When the youth looked back again it was gone.

Soon the youth entered a village where the smell of wood dust hung in the northern air. From a shack to the side came the beat of a fulling block, and a thin man turning the corner called out the hour as a measure of what had passed and of what remained to come.

He cupped his hands about his mouth and walked a distance and walking called again.

The youth saw ahead a knot of people, and among them a girl in dark blue dress. She wore her hair long and gathered together with a red ribbon halfway down her back. It was in the same mountain fashion as Yukiko had worn.

As he looked more intently, the girl in the dark blue clothing turned slightly to the side. His heart tightened. Although still far from her, he thought she was much like the girl Yukiko, or even that she might be Yukiko, and then it seemed she must be Yukiko and he began to hurry.

Now the girl looked up the street in his direction. He raised his arm, and she looked about to see if there were others nearby to whom he might be signaling. Then she tilted her head to the side to study him and with one hand shielded her eyes from the sun.

The youth walked quickly toward her. The air was cool and the sun shone brightly, and beyond the weathered wood of the village the sky was a deepening blue. He rushed by a battered house that leaned away from the others. As he passed, a workman on its steps suddenly turned and tossed into the street almost at his feet blackened water from a tub. At the last moment the workman cried out, and the youth hopped up quickly into the air above it, laughing at his surprise.

And, on the girl ahead, he saw the beginning of a smile.